Question Number One

"If we were dating and I had been out of town for two weeks, when my plane landed at eight o'clock in the evening, what would you have planned for me?"

"First I would pick you up from the airport in a limousine and then since you're probably tired, I would take you home where dinner would be delivered of some of your favorite foods, timed just right so that it would be nice and hot when you got home. While you were eating, I would run a hot bubble bath for you, filled with luxurious bath salts, with candles lit around the bathroom for a soothing soak. Once you're finished with your bath, I would ask if you wanted a massage. If you did, then I would give you one and afterwards I would tuck you into bed and then say goodnight so that you could recuperate from your trip."

Question Number Two

"If you had to recreate one night or one moment in your life, what would it be?"

"If I had known you in a past life, it would be the Senior Prom. It would have been a magical evening where we would be caught up in the rapture of each other, dancing and holding each other close. I would have the pleasure of holding you in my arms without feeling guilty about our age difference, since I'm slightly older than you. That ceased to matter because I was totally captivated by your astonishing beauty. I knew that you felt it too, because your body trembled as I held you close. We laughed, we talked, we had so much fun that I didn't want the night to end, but of course, you had a curfew. As I kissed you gently on your lips at the door, my future, my destiny, flashed through my mind. That evening will always remain in my mind because you chose to share it with me."

"Did you come to my Prom?" Laughter could be heard around the room.

Books by Adrienne Woods

360°, A JOURNEY AWAITS

Adrienne Woods, an avid reader since the age of three, credits her love of reading to her late grandmother, who would read her parables/stories from the Bible when she was little. A true romantic at heart, she loves to write stories that exemplify strong family relationships, an abiding faith in God and the belief that one can overcome any adversity. With five siblings, it's easy to see why her novels portray such strong family bonds.

Adrienne currently resides in Greensboro, North Carolina where she lives with her husband and her daughter. She is a graduate of North Carolina Agricultural and Technical State University, and holds a Bachelor of Science Degree in Accounting.

FRIENDS FIRST,
JOINED BY LOVE

ADRIENNE WOODS

Pass It On
Publishing

This novel is a work of fiction. The characters and events
portrayed in this novel were created from the author's
imagination and are purely fictitious.

Friends First, Joined by Love

ISBN-13: 978-0-9815849-1-1
ISBN-10: 0-9815849-1-8

Printed in the United States of America

Pass It On Publishing/ July 2008

ACKNOWLEDGEMENTS

Giving all the honor to my Lord and Savior, Jesus Christ, I thank you for all the gifts and blessings that you have bestowed upon me.

To my husband, my hero, and to my daughter, my rock and sounding board; thank you for all of your love, patience and support!

To James and Sheila Meadows, words cannot express my gratitude for all the hard work you've done to help promote my first book. Thank you for the support and encouragement that you have given me. May God continue to bless you!

To my family and friends, thank you for your encouragement, your support and your feedback!

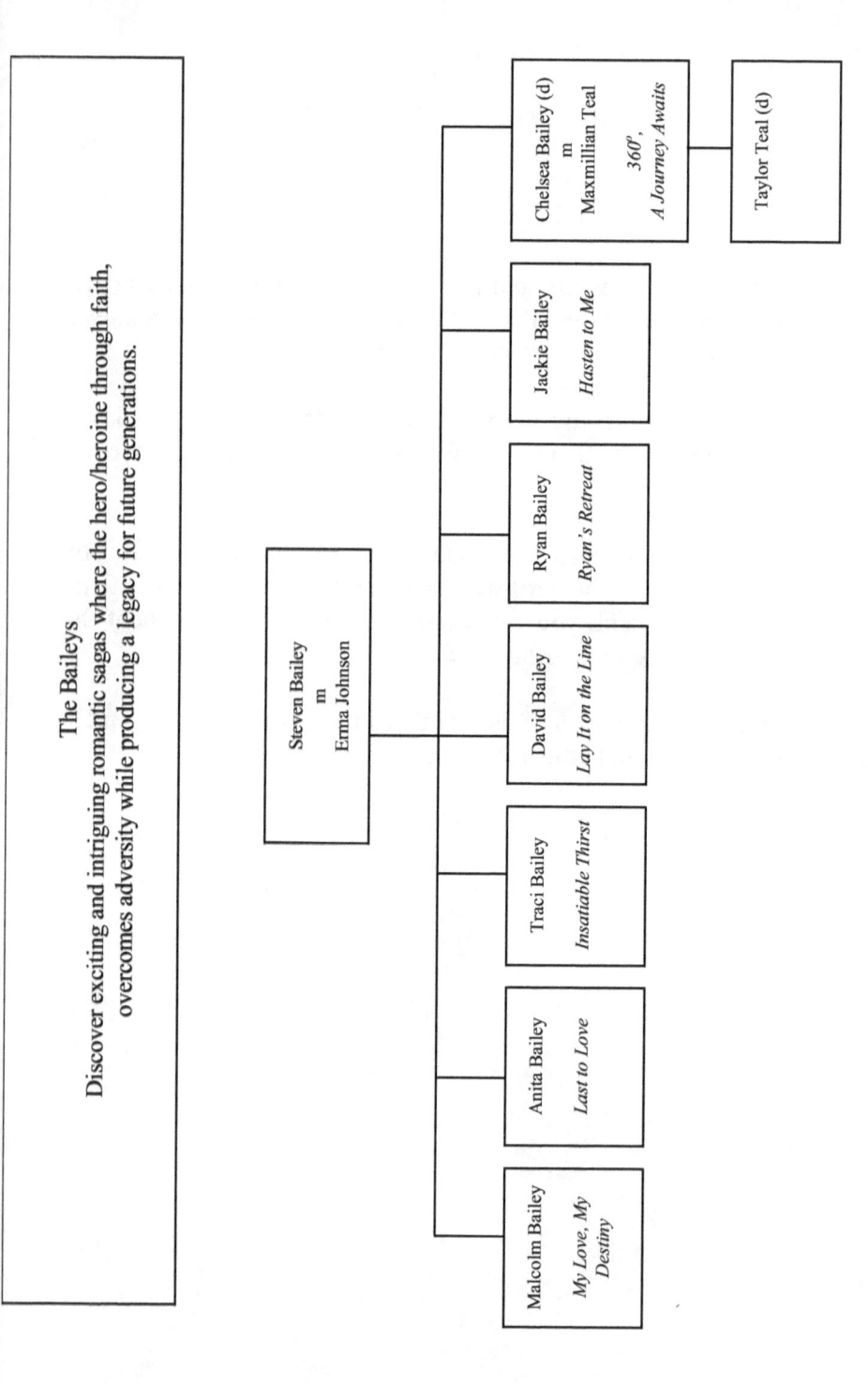

The Baileys

Discover exciting and intriguing romantic sagas where the hero/heroine through faith, overcomes adversity while producing a legacy for future generations.

Steven Bailey
m
Erma Johnson

Malcolm Bailey
My Love, My Destiny

Anita Bailey
Last to Love

Traci Bailey
Insatiable Thirst

David Bailey
Lay It on the Line

Ryan Bailey
Ryan's Retreat

Jackie Bailey
Hasten to Me

Chelsea Bailey (d)
m
Maxmillian Teal
360°,
A Journey Awaits

Taylor Teal (d)

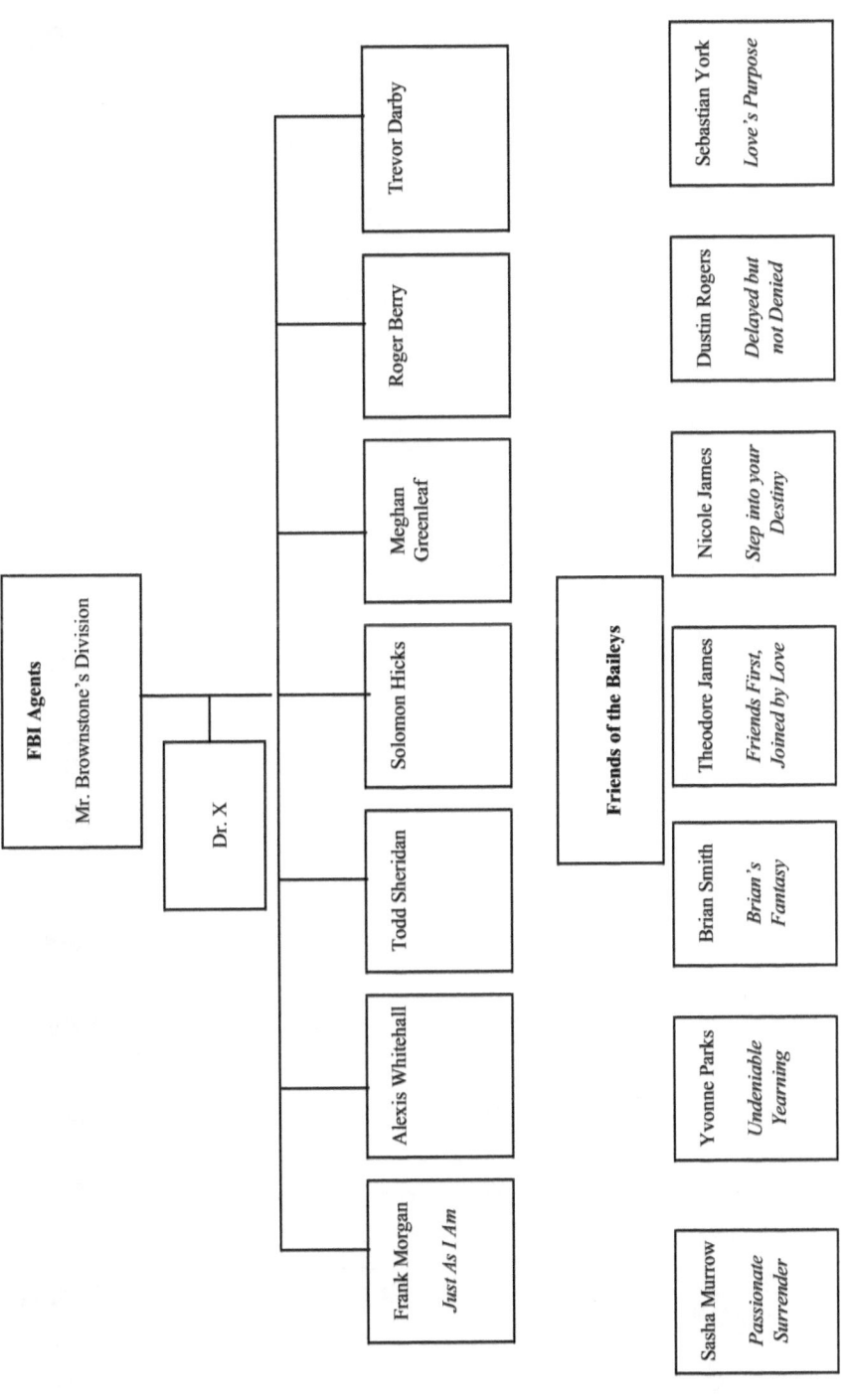

FBI Agents

Mr. Brownstone's Division

Dr. X

Frank Morgan
Just As I Am

Alexis Whitehall

Todd Sheridan

Solomon Hicks

Meghan Greenleaf

Roger Berry

Trevor Darby

Friends of the Baileys

Sasha Murrow
Passionate Surrender

Yvonne Parks
Undeniable Yearning

Brian Smith
Brian's Fantasy

Theodore James
Friends First, Joined by Love

Nicole James
Step into your Destiny

Dustin Rogers
Delayed but not Denied

Sebastian York
Love's Purpose

Chapter One

How does one get the attention of a beautiful specimen of a man, that's so handsome, that even on a good day, he probably would not give you the time of day, as someone worthy of his affections, especially since you've known him since childhood? That's the problem Erica had with Theodore James, or rather TJ as his friends called him. He would never consider her as a potential girlfriend.

She had three strikes against her. One, her brother was his best friend. Two, she was three years younger and had trailed after him and her brother, the majority of their young life and three; she was regulated to the department of being his friend. Everyone knew that once regulated to the "friend" box, you never got out. Oops, make that four strikes. He knew one of her deepest secrets that had occurred during her freshman year of college with a now famous basketball player. Hence her current dilemma.

How was she to compete with the beautiful women that he usually dated, Erica wondered? Ever since TJ was a teenager, he had been besieged by women, throwing themselves at him because of his outward beauty. No one took the time to really get to know TJ.

Believe it or not, he always complained about the attention that his looks drew. Unless you knew him, you perceived him as being aloof and somewhat stuck up. However, after getting to know him, you understood that he was just an extremely shy person that kept to himself. If you started a conversation with him, he would talk to you and keep you entertained for the length of the conversation. He was very smart, witty, and humorous; kept abreast of current events and was a great conversationalist. Additionally, he was an immensely caring individual. He was patient, kind and always treated her with respect. If truth be known, he had all the characteristics of her father and her brother, whom she loved dearly.

What was there not to like? That was just on the inside. The outside was just as pleasing. TJ had a body to die for; rock hard, solid abs, with muscular arms, on a body that was chiseled to perfection and nicely formed muscular thighs that looked as if he could hold a woman standing up and make love to her all night long.

Whew! Just thinking about him always makes me sweat, thought Erica. "Well, I'm all grown up now and I've been living on my own for quite some time. I think that I know my own mind and I'm determined to go after what I want." Erica said to herself, unaware that she had actually spoken her thoughts out loud.

"Easier said than done. You don't even have a plan yet of how you're going to get him to notice you as a woman," said her best friend Sasha. "Un huh, and how are we to overcome that small problem that you still have, missy?"

Sometimes, Erica hated that she had ever took her best friend into her confidence. "My only problem, is how to get TJ to notice me as a woman, not the little girl that he grew up with. Somehow, I'm sure that I will think of a plan to get him to notice me like he did that one evening long ago at my Prom. Unfortunately, whenever I remember that fantastic evening, I also remember the horrific events that followed several months later."

Snapping her fingers in front of Erica's eyes, Sasha shook her head in disbelief. "Don't go there, okay. That's the past. Leave it there."

"Oh well, enough of the trip down memory lane. I have more important things to do than rehash old memories. I've moved forward and put the past behind me. I don't know why that suddenly came up."

"Yes, you do. You're in a quandary about TJ and how to handle your feelings for him. It's not like they've ever gone away. Admit it," replied Sasha, rolling her eyes at her best friend since kindergarten.

"What I want to know is what brought this melancholy spirit on? You've got the job of your dreams, head Chemist at one of the nation's leading personal care companies; a nice house, uh, let me rephrase that, a wonderful house and money in the bank. What's left? Oh, could it be the love of your life, your brother's best friend, that is not only handsome, but smart, funny and treats you like a queen but yet you won't really let him get close to you? Let me know when you come to your senses otherwise, if you don't want him, someone else will."

Rising up from the sofa, Erica walked into the kitchen, to bring back the food that they would eat while they analyzed her dilemma. Earlier that evening, Erica cooked her favorite meal; spaghetti, with yeast rolls fresh from the oven for Sasha and garlic bread, and a salad along with her homemade lemonade. Sasha, pulling the plates and glasses from the cabinet, turned to her friend as she was setting the table.

"I'm waiting for an answer, girlfriend."

"I know." Picking up the lone piece of mail from the black and grey granite countertop, with trepidation, Erica handed the letter to her friend to read.

Scanning the letter, Sasha started laughing. Not just a light shaking of the shoulders, but a deep belly laugh that resonated throughout her body, making her hold her sides, as if she were in pain. Snatching the letter from her hands, Erica angrily stated, "Some friend you are to laugh at what could be catastrophic to my very existence."

Grabbing the letter again from Erica, Sasha turned her back, as she read the letter in its entirety, slowly, from the very beginning. Excitedly Sasha exclaimed, "Oooohh. This is good! I have to hand it to her. She's got some nerve writing this letter. I need to read this out loud, so that you can fully hear and digest the meaning and the importance of this letter!"

"Don't you think that I've read it a thousand times?"

"No. I think that you may have read it and gave up without reading in between the lines. Why else would she write you if something in TJ's actions was keeping them from proceeding to the next level? Listen closely, while I read it."

Dear Erica,

I'm writing this letter just to inform you that the window of opportunity for you to reclaim your lost love is slowly closing. Theodore, or TJ as you call him, with my help, is on the path to recovery, to heal from the hurt and pain that you caused him by rejecting his love.

He has not confided in me but as I've watched the two of you on HangOut Nights, each watching the other when no one is looking, I've picked up on a few things. One, you love him but something in your past that he's aware of, is keeping you apart. Two, it's your doing and not his. Three, it's tearing him apart. Four, he's waiting on you to make the next move, and five, if you don't, then he's moving on. This is where I come in.

Because I want a whole man and I'm confident in my ability to make him happy, I'm extending the opportunity to you, to make one last ditch effort to win his love back. I will temporarily, without drama, step out of the picture for a month, to allow you to either rekindle the love that's simmering just beneath the surface or for you to give up and go on with your life.

Make good use of this time because I'm falling in love with him and will not hesitate to utilize every weapon that's available to me, to win his love, forever.

You have thirty days to either piss or get off the pot.

Otherwise, I'll see you at the wedding in June!

Mia

"Don't you see Erica? Here is your last opportunity to show TJ how you really feel, before he gets caught up in this chick. I know that he still has feelings for you. Anyone with half a brain can see that, except you; one who's supposed to be so smart." Hitting her friend with the letter on her head, Sasha settled down to eat.

"You know, if you've rejected TJ's love once before, he's not going to make the next move. It's going to be up to you to show him that you're interested and are willing to forget the past to embrace the future."

"I think that you're dead wrong Sasha. Haven't you seen them at HangOut Night for the last couple of weeks? Him and what's her face, Cia, Tia, whatever her name is, they seem so into each other, after TJ participated in the dating game."

"Erica, you're so wrong," laughed Sasha. You know perfectly well that her name is Mia. Tell me this then; if TJ is so hooked on Mia, why do his eyes follow you everywhere you go? Why does he watch you with such passion in his eyes that it sends shivers down my spine, and I'm not even the recipient of the look? How did the HangOut Night start anyway? When did TJ decide to participate in the Dating Game? Why weren't you the prize for that game, you nitwit?" Sasha interrogated.

"One question at a time, Sasha. What do you think this is; another one of your sessions?" As a psychologist, it was well known that Sasha would ask a multitude of questions until she was able to ascertain the truth.

"HangOut Night was designed in an effort to make me feel more comfortable about dating, I believe. Max wanted me to feel comfortable in the presence of others if and when I chose to date. He wanted me to feel secure after the debacle with Tim on the night of our Senior Prom and the horrendous sequence of events afterward. Even though Max was in the military at the time and was deployed overseas, he wasn't here when it first happened. I think that deep down inside, he felt guilty that he wasn't here to prevent what occurred; however, he still ended up saving my life. I'll have to tell you about that some other time when Yvonne is present. I'm not so sure that I would be able to get through it without her."

Seeing the remote look in Erica's eyes that foretold of the pain, the suffering and the horror that she had gone through, Sasha reached out to grasp her hand in comfort. "When the time is right, you know that I'm always available to listen."

"I know and I thank you for that. Do you want something else to drink? I'll be right back." Erica quickly disappeared into the bathroom to compose herself.

Upon returning to the room ten minutes later, Erica picked up the conversation where they left off. "HangOut Night is really a private dating service, where the participant's backgrounds are screened heavily, thanks to an idea Max had for starting his own security firm. The participants are a mixture of Christian and non-Christian men and women who are financially solvent, with no baby momma drama, seeking to date similar people in a non-threatening atmosphere. Here's how it works...You get to meet and greet the pool of prospective dates first for five to ten minutes."

"So is it like Speed Dating meets The Love Connection with Chuck Woolery," Sasha questioned?

"Exactly! After the meet and greet is over, the participants are then picked based on randomly chosen numbers each week. They are secluded behind a partition while the questions are asked. The participants are supposed to answer the questions candidly. The chosen one then is selected to go out on a date with the contestant and they are required to come back and tell the group how it went."

"Are the questions the same every week? What happens if the girl or guy gets a jerk?"

"No, the questions vary. Some of them are as simple as asking what would be their favorite date. Others are more complex that requires them to think fast, like what is their favorite fantasy? If the date is a jerk, they press a code in their phone and immediately help arrives to rescue them."

"Why did TJ enter the game? He's gorgeous, he's a gentleman, treats anyone he dates like a queen and is loaded with money. He could date anyone he chooses, of course, except you, since you won't give him the time of day."

"Everyone that comes to HangOut Night eventually has to participate. Most of the time, it's really fun. You get to know the person and in my case, you don't feel as if you're on the date alone. Max or TJ or some other friend, are usually somewhere nearby in case something happens. I really don't trust my judgment anymore considering the mistake I made with Tim, so with HangOut Night, I can mingle, have a good time and then go home without the drama."

"There you go again. TJ is always coming to your rescue. Doesn't that count for something? You didn't answer my other question regarding why you were not the contestant when TJ was a participant."

"I chickened out at the last minute, okay," lamented Erica, with a sheepish expression on her face. "I couldn't help it. What if he didn't choose me? How was I supposed to act after that?"

"You are supposed to do everything in your power to make sure that doesn't happen. I'm so glad I moved back to town. You desperately need my help. When are you going to enter the contest again?"

"I'm not."

"What do you mean?"

"Too much time has passed. He's moved on. I'm not setting myself up for the disappointment."

"What do you have to lose? What about the letter, and the thirty days that TJ will be a free man?

"The best friendship that I've ever had; next to you and Yvonne, of course."

"Would you forgive yourself if you lost out on the love of your life?"

"No."

"Then tell me what happened at HangOut Night when TJ selected his date. After that, I have a plan..."

Chapter Two

Determined to go through with participating in HangOut Night, with the hope that Erica would finally make her move, after repeated attempts to get close to her, TJ decided to lay his cards on the table with Max, her brother and his best friend since childhood.

"Max, do you have a minute?"

Knowing that his friend still carried a torch for his sister, Max was hoping that he would finally do something about winning her love. In his estimation, they both had waited long enough. "Sure, what's up?"

"Max, we've been friends since childhood and I'm pretty sure you know that I love your sister; have loved her for a very long time. She's grown up now and has been living on her own for a couple of years. I promised your Dad that I wouldn't confess my love to her, until she turned twenty-five; however, it's getting harder and harder to control my feelings being around her everyday at work. Something has got to change or I'll go crazy."

"You've got it bad, my brother. What's stopping you from going after her? Does this have anything to do with the series of events that occurred after the Prom fiasco, Tim's subsequent beat down or the unspeakable crime I was unable to prevent?" Max asked harshly, looking directly into TJ's eyes.

Sighing exasperatedly, TJ responded. "Yes, a lot of it has to do with Erica's self esteem after that appalling event. She refuses to let anyone get close to her. Everyone is kept at arms length, even me; the one that would willingly lay down his life in exchange for hers. I thought that I had already proven to her my love but evidently she needs more time."

"I know that she went through numerous counseling sessions. Mom and Dad made sure that the sessions were a priority. We even went together as a family to learn how to deal with what occurred. I thought that she had put the past behind her since she's accomplished so much since then."

"Yeah, well, her professional life is on point. However, her private life is another issue. She's consumed with work, so much that I'm sure she's too tired to think of anything else when she goes home." TJ began to pace back and forth in the room, pondering just how to work out the intricate pieces of this puzzle to bring Erica, his love, back to the vivacious person that she once was.

"So, what do you plan on doing? Continue to date a large number of women to fill the void? Don't you think that it's time to go after what God has for you? Then at least one of us might be happy," he muttered in a despondent voice. Lost in thought he reflected on the issues of his own private life...

Max had gone through his share of pain. He understood fully what it meant to love a woman with every fiber of your being, only to lose her. He didn't want TJ to make the same mistake that he had made with the woman he loved. Waiting too long to declare your love could cost you everything that you valued in life. He knew from first hand experience.

During college, he met a wonderful person by the name of Chelsea Bailey. She had joined the Army Reserve to help pay for her college education. They met at the local Army Reserve Unit one weekend for drills, since the Reserve Unit was also where he received some of his training to be a commissioned officer for his college's ROTC program. Since she was an enlisted personnel, dating her was out of the question because he was an officer. That however, didn't stop his friend Justin from making a bet with him one day while they were in the Unit's office killing time until their paperwork was complete to send them on their next summer assignment.

"Max, have you seen that beautiful honey that just joined the Unit?"

"No, Justin I haven't. Remember you're the one that's always scoping out the women, not me."

"You've got to see her. She beautiful; no, make that exquisite, smart, and intelligent. Everything that you claimed to have ever wanted in a woman, but couldn't find one to match your intellect."

"If that's the case, why don't you try to hook up with her yourself?" Max replied absent-mindedly. He was too busy working on another invention to pay to much attention to Justin. He always had some type of scheme or another he was trying to get Max to participate in. Most were harmless and fun, although quite a few had gotten them into trouble.

"Nah, she's too smart for me. I couldn't get next to her with a ten foot pole. She wouldn't give me the time of day. However, you on the other hand, our very own Rhodes scholar, could probably score easily with her."

"Grow up man. Why does every woman represent a score for you? Women should be cherished, treated with respect, and loved; not degraded nor used solely for your benefit. Sometimes I wonder how we became friends in the first place," said Max as he shook his head in disgust.

Justin, a dependable, hard working officer and someone that you could trust implicitly, was a playa to the extreme. He worked hard and he played hard. His one character flaw was that all women were meant to be enjoyed; in numbers! Dating a woman more than three times during the same month, constituted a relationship to him, which is why he rotated women like he rotated his wardrobe. Although his romantic life was pretty much a revolving door, he was honest to a fault, and went to great extremes for the women he dated to understand Justin's Rules for Dating 101.

"Don't look now because she's coming our way. One hundred dollars says that you can't get her to go out with you on two consecutive dates," whispered Justin, eyeing Max out of the corner of his eyes as his friend was held speechless for the first time since he had known him. Mesmerized, Max followed the woman's walk from across the room until she came abreast of them at the counter in the office.

Saluting them as was the custom when encountering an officer, upon recognition, she proceeded to state her business, in a soft, yet sensual, raspy voice.

Max knew he was hooked as soon as he looked into her hazel eyes that were so transparent, so clear, that one could almost see into the depths of her soul. Shaking his head in disbelief, he cleared his throat to articulate a reasonable answer to her question.

Chelsea, while standing before two very handsome, young, officers seemed to be in control of her emotions. On the inside however, her entire body started to quiver as she glanced up to look into the officer's eyes whose last name read Teal on his uniform.

An unexplainable heat seemed to permeate her body. Never before had a person been able to produce such a response just by looking at her. Eyes wide with shock at the emotions that were coursing through her, she knew that she had to get away before she did something really stupid, like lean in for his kiss.

Grasping the edge of the counter tightly, she blinked her eyes rapidly to quickly hide the indecent and improper thoughts that were running through her head until she was able to get a grip on herself.

He was out of her league. A relationship with him was forbidden, even if he did find her attractive.

Acting like a robot in motion, Max, though completely floored by what had just occurred to his senses, was able to perform the task at hand. After retrieving the requested information for Chelsea from the office filing system, he extended the paperwork to her. In her haste to leave as quickly as possible, her hands accidentally, came into contact with his.

A frisson of heat so fierce coursed down her spine, sending tiny tremors of shock waves throughout her entire body. Eyes downcast, she missed Max's reaction. He was astonished to learn that one simple touch could render such a reaction. What would it feel like if they ever made love? They would spontaneously combust! Unfortunately, he would never know.

A month later, Max ran into Chelsea again at a Wake Forest basketball game. Both avid ACC fans, Chelsea, a Carolina fan and Max, a Wake Forest fan; it had to be fate that kept drawing them towards each other. What would be the odds of them meeting at a Wake Forest game where the attendance was over 26,000 people? Max didn't know but he decided to do something about it. He couldn't get Chelsea out of his mind. Ever since meeting her at the Reserve Unit that day and each subsequent month for drills, he constantly thought about her; during class, at work, at every possible minute throughout the day.

He finally admitted to himself that he had to come to some type of resolution to retain his sanity. Either he was going to go out on a date with her to get her out of his system or he was going to forget about her.

The decision was made for him when he saw her at the Wake Forest game with another man. He wasn't prepared for the rush of emotion that flooded his senses when he saw her with another man. A sentiment he had never experienced before took control. He couldn't believe that it was jealousy that reared its ugly head. Having never been envious of another person or their possessions, this sensation was new to him. Feeling disconcerted, he made a move to retreat. Unfortunately Chelsea, who seemed to be searching the crowd for someone, noticed him.

Seemingly caught up in his infatuation, before he knew what was happening, his feet were moving towards her. As if a magnetic force was holding her in place, Chelsea stood immobilized. Once alongside of each other, Max extended his hand in greeting.

"Hello Ms. Bailey. How have you been?"

Forgetting how to speak for a moment, Chelsea had to clear her throat several times before anything would come out. Feeling a nudge in her side, she turned to look at her companion who seemed to be enjoying her discomfort.

"Mr. Teal, please call me Chelsea when we're away from the Unit. I don't usually stand on formality. Let me introduce my brother, David, who it appears is enjoying himself at my expense."

"Then I insist that you call me Maxmillian or Max." Not understanding her cryptic remark but happy that her date was actually her brother, Max held out his hand to shake David's.

Sizing each other up, David, liking what he saw, did something totally out of character. "Max if you're not here with anyone, do you want to join us? That way you can tell me how you've managed to do what few people have in their entire lives; render Chelsea speechless."

"David, I'm here by myself. My homeboy Justin couldn't make it. I would love to join you, if Chelsea doesn't have any objections." Turning to look into her eyes, Max sought her approval.

Tired of denying herself, Chelsea simply answered, "Yes, please join us."

That basketball game was the beginning of a beautiful, yet clandestine relationship until duty dictated that Max go away…

The day before leaving for active duty…

Laying in bed one night after a completely satisfying, four hour interval of lovemaking, Max regrettably had to break some unpleasant news to Chelsea.

"Sweetheart, you know that being part of the ROTC program involves completing a four year, active military term."

"Yes, Max, but I thought that our relationship was strong and that you would be stationed here in the States; that way we could see if what we have is strong enough for marriage."

"Unfortunately, Chelsea, I've got some bad news for us. Once I graduate, that next day, I will be going to Fort Stewart, Georgia, to undergo intensive training to become a fighter helicopter pilot. I will not be able to contact you or see you until the training is complete, which will take approximately one year."

As he held her close, he told her that it was going to be hard to be away from her, but at every available break, he would come home to see her.

"Okay Max, what you're really trying to say is goodbye right?" Chelsea stated as she sat up fully in the bed. Softly Chelsea started to cry, thinking that this was goodbye.

"Sweetheart, I love you. Nothing can change that but I don't have a choice in going away. It's my duty. When I first signed up, I never expected to meet someone like you and fall in love. It's not going to be easy but I would like for us to still stay together."

"How can we, when you're going to be so far away?"

"I don't know, but we've come too far to lose each other now."

Chelsea started to erotically kiss Max from his head to his feet, trying to loose herself in him, trying not to think about the future. Max lost all train of thought as he also tried to block out reality. He just wanted to feel. He wanted to feel Chelsea's softness. He wanted to stroke her soft back and rain kisses all over her face, her neck, her luscious breasts, legs and hips. He could never seem to get enough of her. Never before had he met a woman whose very presence made him want to instantly become one with her. He loved her as he had no other woman in his life.

Unfortunately reality always has a way of intruding. The sunlight slowly seeped through Max's bedroom window. Each awoke with the one thought that the day came too soon; it was almost time for Max to go.

"Max, you have to take me home. I guess it's time for me to go to class."

"Chelsea, sweetheart, I'm not ready to leave just yet. I have to store up enough memories of you to last until the next time I can break away. Please, come back to bed."

A few hours later, Max dropped Chelsea at her house in the neighboring city, fifteen miles away. As soon as the car stopped, Chelsea immediately jumped out of the car and ran to the door, crying, thinking that this was the last time she would see Max.

Knowing that his leaving was hurting her, Max quickly leapt from the car and ran to the door just in time to put his foot in the door before it closed.

He pulled Chelsea into his arms and whispered, "Please don't cry. You know that I can't take it. Please stop, please stop," he kept murmuring as he kissed her tears away. "I love you. I'm not letting you go. I'll keep in touch and I'll be back at the first opportunity."

True to his word, Max visited Chelsea at first, at every break that he had, which was only a couple of days here and there, once every couple of months. On occasion he had even gotten into trouble for leaving base and driving to North Carolina, which was over five hours away, to see Chelsea. As his training progressed and the intensity of the training increased, his trips became more infrequent and then became nonexistent as he traveled the world performing dangerous missions for the military.

Max reflected on the subsequent events that led him to the various hot spots all over the world, Grenada, Panama, Saudi Arabia and the effect his travels had on his mind, his heart, and his emotions. Not knowing if he would make it out of these countries alive or not, he decided that it would be best if he broke off his relationship with Chelsea. It wasn't fair for him to keep her life dangling for the additional years that he would be in the military. She was young. She should be enjoying her life.

After two years of constantly being in the enemies territory, Max in a telephone conversation, relayed his thoughts to Chelsea. Although he hated to concede defeat, he didn't know when this particular mission would end. It was very dangerous and he wasn't promised to get out of it alive. Therefore, with his heart breaking into a million little pieces, he told Chelsea that he thought it would be best if she started dating other people. After a heated debate where Chelsea attempted to change his mind, Max was resolute in his decision.

He hoped that she would wait for him regardless of what he said.

Unfortunately you often get exactly what you ask for.

Chapter Three

Being away for so long was tearing Max apart. He longed to be with Chelsea; to see her face, to kiss her lips, to caress her skin. However, he had pushed her away. Because of him, instead of waiting for his return, she would by now, belong to another man. He had a few things to settle before he could move forward with his life. There were several job offers that he needed to consider since his active duty term was nearing an end within the next six months.

His first priority though was Chelsea. If she was free, he wanted to prove that his love for her had not diminished in his absence and that he wanted to marry her. He just hoped that he wasn't too late. Max called Chelsea late one evening to ascertain whether or not, he could drop by for a visit since he was in town, so that they could settle the past and move towards the future.

The best laid plans often go awry...

During the years of Max's absence...

It took Chelsea, about two years to begin seeing other men. The first year that Max was gone, he made frequent trips to see her and she in turn, was able to travel to see him. Unfortunately that pattern didn't continue in the second year of his absence. She only saw him once or twice in the early part of that year. Chelsea kept hoping that Max would show up out of the blue to reconcile their relationship. Unfortunately her innermost wish didn't come true that year. Instead she started dating sporadically, looking for men that were the total opposite of Max. She wanted someone that was stable; that wasn't always traveling; someone that was cautious, serene, yet good looking but quiet. Mostly she wanted someone that would stay in place; not be adventurous in life like Max.

She ended up finding a man with those qualities by the name of Alex, and started dating him. They had been dating for approximately a year when Max's call shattered her carefully built, safe existence.

"Good evening Chelsea, did I catch you at a bad time?" Max asked when she spoke breathlessly into the telephone. He tried to put all thoughts out of his head for the reason behind her being out of breath.

After a momentary pause, Chelsea regrouped as she recognized the deep, velvet voice from her dreams. "No Max, I just ran back in to answer the phone. I was on my way out to a basketball game." What she didn't tell him was that she wasn't going to the game alone. She was actually picking Alex up because he was dropping his motorcycle off at his godfather's house. Chelsea didn't particularly like to ride on the motorcycle so she volunteered to pick him up.

"Is this a game you can miss?"

"I guess, why?"

"I'm in town and I wanted to stop by and see you, if that's okay."

In her mind, Chelsea ranted, *Why now, when I'm happy? When I was finally starting to put your memory to rest?"* Aloud she responded from the heart, "Sure, you can stop by. Just call me and let me know what time, okay?"

As soon as she hung up the phone, she grabbed her keys and her handbag and headed toward the door. Just as she was reaching for the doorknob, the doorbell rang. As she opened the door she was startled to find Max on her doorstep with his hand poised to ring the doorbell again. He looked as if he had just stepped out of a GQ magazine. He had on a Versace, pin stripped suit; the perfect image of the top notch businessman.

"I thought you were in Charlotte. Why didn't you say that you were in Greensboro?"

"Probably the element of surprise. I didn't want you to close the door in my face. Even though we've talked, I wasn't sure of my reception."

"Come on in."

For the next thirty minutes they talked about old times and started catching up on everything that was happening in each other lives. Max told her that he had only six more months in the military and then he was calling it quits. He explained that he was on leave for approximately the next thirty days and that he wanted to spend time with her.

"Chelsea, I want you to come away with me."

"What do you mean? Spend the night with you? What about tomorrow?"

"Why is it that all of a sudden you don't trust me? Since when have I had to justify spending time with you?"

"Max, as much as I love you, I want some guarantees. I have to know that you want me with you for more than just sex."

"Sweetheart, do you think that I would come all the way here, driving non stop, ten hours, just to sleep with you? Chelsea, there are no guarantees in life. I want you to come away with me so that we can spend some time together. Tomorrow will take care of itself."

In Max's mind, the ultimate had come true. He was getting out of the military within six months and had started his own company during college, Sole Impressions, which was now doing very well. Now he wanted the coup de grace; his own woman to be with him at his side, as his wife.

When she didn't respond but just stared into his eyes, he tried another tactic. Maybe he was delusional. Okay perhaps his reasoning was a little off. He thought that after he explained why he couldn't call or come by due to his capture; that they could pick up where they left off.

"Darling, I'm sorry for all the pain and hurt that I've caused you during the past ten months. I was on a mission where I was captured and couldn't contact you or my family. My story can be collaborated with my boss if you need proof. You don't know the number of days I wished I could call you and take back my decision to end our relationship. I'm asking for your forgiveness. I'm asking for the chance to start over."

Chelsea considered Max's offer after realizing that the emotional and physical pull was still there, just hidden. Seeing him again made her realize that she had only been fooling herself. She still loved him! In fact, she had never stopped loving him. She had been willing to settle for less because she knew that she could never give her heart to another because it belonged to him. Throwing her arms around his neck she rejoiced in the fact that his capture was the only thing that had kept him from her.

Words couldn't describe the feeling of euphoria that Max felt when Chelsea's body molded to his. Each touch was the caress of a waterfall, falling on supple skin. Each kiss was like water to a thirsty person. They devoured each other. Had they not been at Chelsea's mother's house, they would have taken each other right there in the living room. Since they were, one of them had to call a halt to their raging hormones.

Knowing that she had to tell Max the truth, Chelsea lifted her head. "Max, I took your advice when I didn't hear from you for over ten months and started seeing someone else. If I go with you, I owe it to him to tell him that our relationship is over."

"Chelsea, if you love me, call him on the phone to deliver your news, or better yet, I will gladly tell him," Max said harshly in desperation. He felt that he was losing whatever ground that he had just gained. This man had been by her side for almost a year while he had been away. If she went to explain the circumstances to him, Max felt sure that she wouldn't go with him.

The phone rang repeatedly in the kitchen, until Chelsea finally answered it. Looking at caller id, she felt as if she were in a bad Grade B movie. Picking up the phone she said, "Hello."

"It's Alex. Are you coming to get me?"

"Yes, though it will be in about fifteen minutes." Alex could tell that something wasn't quite right. It sounded as if Chelsea was crying.

"Are you okay? Is something wrong?"

"No, I'm fine but I have company, so go ahead to the game and I'll see you when it's over."

"Who's there?"

"Max."

"Mmmm, I see. Do I need to come over? Are you really coming over once he leaves or will you be leaving with him?"

"I'll explain everything later."

Once Chelsea hung up the phone, Max again pushed Chelsea for a decision.

"Can you pack enough for a two week stay?"

"Only on one condition."

"What condition is that?" Max cautiously asked.

"Let me take fifteen minutes to tell my friend what's going on and that our relationship is over. Then I'll meet you wherever you want."

"No Chelsea. If you're going to be with me, that's not necessary."

Chelsea couldn't believe her ears. Max had never been that inconsiderate. He usually took great pains not to hurt anyone's feelings. She refused to believe that he was jealous.

"If you were in my place, you would do the same. It's a matter of doing what's right."

"Perhaps I was wrong about the extent of our love. Maybe everything was one-sided. Maybe I was imagining that you loved me as much as I loved you; that our love could stand the test of time." Having driven over ten hours to finally see her, in his frustration, Max wasn't handling what he perceived as rejection very well. To him it was simple; her relationship with Alex was over. End of story. He was back. New beginning. Why couldn't she see that?

Too tired to continue to argue, Max gave his ultimatum as he headed towards the door. "I'm giving you one last chance

Chelsea to go with me. Please," he begged, "don't throw this away."

Just as stubborn as Max or perhaps even more so, Chelsea retaliated, "Well then don't leave."

Max walked out of the door straight to his car, a blue 745i BMW, no less. He knew that at any moment, Chelsea would stop him. She had always been able to diffuse his anger with a simple joke or with just a touch of her hand to any portion of his body.

Chelsea, back at the door was saying to herself, "I know he's only kidding. He's just getting something from his car." She changed her way of thinking when Max got into the driver's seat and pulled off.

She started to cry as she realized that both of them were stubborn fools.

Max thought to himself, as his car neared the beginning of the driveway at the top of the townhouse entrance. *I'll just drive to the gas station. I know that she will come and get me.*

Chelsea got into her car and followed Max down the street. When he stopped at the gas station to pump gas, she thought that he didn't notice her or maybe he was intentionally ignoring her, so she drove off.

That one decision changed her life dramatically. She would forever regret that she didn't stop and talk to Max for the next year and a half.

Shaking himself, as if coming out of a trance, Max explained to TJ how crushed he felt when his decision to push Chelsea backfired. How devastated he felt when he delivered his ultimatum and she refused to back down. How both of them were too stubborn to apologize and discuss their disagreement rationally. How his pride was hurt that she would make him wait any longer to culminate his dream of marrying her.

"Max, I hate to break this too you, but from your story, you didn't actually ask her to marry you." TJ said as he digested the information that Max was relaying.

"You're right TJ. That was to come later after we had spent a couple of weeks together. I had everything planned in my mind, that I would come home, that we would rekindle our love and that at the end of the two weeks or however long a time it took me to convince her of my love, that I would propose marriage to her in a lavish setting that she would remember for all time. That's why you shouldn't procrastinate in telling Erica how you feel."

"Yeah, and get your heart crushed in the process. Remember, I did that before and look at the consequences," TJ bitterly retorted.

"You have to seize the moments as they present themselves. Tomorrow isn't promised to anyone. Declare your love and work like hell to attain it and keep it."

Experiencing an epiphany, TJ jumped up from the chaise that he was sitting on. "Max, did you ever see Chelsea to apologize after the ultimatum was given?"

"After awhile. It took me a minute to get over my hurt and anger."

"How much is a minute Max? A week, a month, what?"

"More like four months. Then I accepted that fact that she was right; that the decent thing to do would be to end their relationship face-to-face. That her decision to do so wasn't a rejection of my love. I guess that I was scared that if she went to talk to him, that she wouldn't agree to come away with me. I let fear destroy something precious. That's why I'm telling you that you have to fight for Erica, if you really intend to spend the rest of your life with her TJ."

"Max did you ever try to explain your feelings to Chelsea?"

"Yes, my mother effectively handled that for me. When the incident with Erica went down, she knew how devastated I felt for not being able to prevent it, so while Erica and you were having surgery, she texted Chelsea that I needed her at the hospital and she came."

"What happened after that?"

"That's a story for another day. Right now you need to concentrate on how you are going to get Erica to even go out with you."

"You've given me an idea, Max. Most of the important things in life are really uncomplicated when you come to think of it. We make it more difficult because we tend to stress over the problem and magnify it beyond proportion. I want to become a contestant at the next HangOut Night. I hope that once she sees me as the contestant that will force her to participate in the Dating Game. Then I can begin my campaign of wooing her."

"TJ, I know my sister. I'm not so sure that will work. You need to start wooing her way before you decide to participate in the Dating Game. Spend more one-on-one time with her. Shoot, help her with some of those projects she's working on for the company, of which I might add you are a partner, or did you forget? You could help her formulate some products geared specifically for lovers. Please though, tread slowly. I believe that's she's fully recovered after all the counseling but you might need a backup plan in case she chickens out."

"What do you think I've been trying to do for the last six months? Against my better judgment, when I thought I was dying, before being carted off in the ambulance, I declared my love to her. After recuperating, she acted as if she didn't remember my heart-felt plea. I thought that I would take the high road and not push her due to the cataclysmic events that had occurred. The timing just didn't seem right. I thought that it was best that we continue as friends."

"I see what you mean. That was probably a wise choice. What happened after that though? It's been four years."

"Don't remind me. We're still great friends, but when I try to get close, she pushes me away. "

"Then it's up to you to figure out what went wrong."

"Don't you think that you should be taking your own advice?"

"I wish it were that simple."

Chapter Four

Erica got up to answer the door, when the doorbell rung, breaking her out of her reverie down memory lane with a start. After peaking through the peephole to make sure of the identity of the caller, with a squeal of delight, she threw open the door to hug two of her best friends from high school, Paul and Yvonne.

"When did you guys get back in town?" She laughed as they continued to hug each other in the doorway. "Come on in." Closing the door behind them, she smiled as the two of them sat down on the settee in the living room.

"I'm not going to stay long. Yvonne wants to catch up, while we're in town. We just wanted to give you the news together," said a smiling Paul as he headed towards the door.

Together they exclaimed, "We're getting married!"

Shrieking with joy, Erica and Yvonne, jumped up and down together, all over the living room; to excited to sit down. It had finally happened. Paul and Yvonne were getting married!

"Congratulations!" Giving each of them a hug, Erica shook her head in disbelief. Finally! She was glad that at least one of them was going to get to live their dream.

Knowing that his friends needed to talk, Paul took the liberty of excusing himself so that they could speak candidly to each other. He was almost positive that Yvonne meant it when she said that she would marry him. It had been a long journey, but he wouldn't be satisfied until she said "I do".

"I'll be back in about two hours, no make that three," said Paul as he saw Sasha coming out of a rear room. Pulling his fiancé towards him, he bestowed a long, lingering kiss on her soft lips, whispering in her ear, "Are you sure we can't just elope?"

"No. You're the one that wanted a big wedding. Hurry back soon." With one last quick kiss goodbye, Paul walked out the door.

"What was all that screaming about?" Sasha asked as she advanced further into the living room.

"Yvonne and Paul are getting married!" More screaming and cries of joy could be heard as the three women hugged each other with tears streaming down their cheeks.

"Let me see your ring, girl," Erica demanded as soon as they were able to settle down. Yvonne, with her hands outstretched so that Erica could see the pink canary, two carat, bezel cut diamond on her finger, suddenly burst into tears.

Sitting down on the sofa in the living room, Erica hugged Yvonne until she was finally calm enough to answer the questions that were upper most in her in mind.

"What's wrong Yvonne?" Erica asked worriedly.

"Erica, I'm scared. I can't keep this charade up any longer. I love Paul with all my heart and he's been wonderful to me these last couple of years. However, the more I think about our wedding, the more I keep remembering. It's like I can't blot out what happened anymore."

"Maybe it's time both of you finally told someone the truth about what occurred those nights so long ago." Sasha quietly stated as she pulled up a chair and encompassed both of them with a group hug. Her psychologist training had kicked into gear at the look of utter desolation that was written on both of her friends faces.

Another set of tears started to rain down Yvonne's face, only this time, Erica's tears were with them, as they both were transported back to a painful point in their past that occurred during their high school and freshman year of college...

Senior Prom…

The day before the Senior Prom, Max overheard his sister talking on the telephone with her boyfriend Tim, who was the captain of the basketball team, explaining why she wouldn't meet him at a hotel and why she wasn't like all the other girls "putting out". She said that while she liked him a lot, she wanted to wait until she was married before having sex. She then asked Tim, if there was a problem and if her not "putting out" was contingent upon him taking her to the prom. At that time, he told her no, he loved her and would wait until she was completely sure to have sex and that everything was fine between them. He still wanted to take her to the prom.

Max knocked on his sister's door to see if everything was okay. After she opened the door, she assured him that everything was fine and that she and Tim had a slight disagreement. When asked what the disagreement was about, Erica told Max the truth.

Upon hearing that Tim wanted to have sex, Max sat down on the bed to discuss the situation with Erica. Being three years older, sometimes she would come to him for things that she couldn't talk to their parents about. Max asked her if she was ready for sex and she replied that while she thought that she liked Tim a lot, she wasn't ready for the next step. Something just didn't feel right with him. Max assured her that if she wasn't ready for that step then not to let anyone pressure her into doing something against her will. He even asked if she need a substitute date for the prom. She assured him that Tim said that everything was all right and that he would be there to take her to the prom.

After Max got the assurance that she would be careful, he left to make a phone call. "TJ, this is Max. Where are you man? Are you still on campus or are you at home?"

"Max, I'm still on campus but I'll be there after my last class. You didn't think that I would miss our little sister all dressed up to go to the prom, did you?"

Just like Max, he wanted to impress upon her date that she was to be treated as royalty, like the queen that she was. He always had a fondness for Erica. She was a sweet person, full of life, a human dynamo; full of energy and spirit. In between visits from college, somewhere along the road though, his feelings had taken a decidedly unorthodox turn. He started to feel things for her that was forbidden. TJ noticed that Erica had started filling out in all the right places. He kept telling himself, that he loved her like his little sister and not to confuse that with lust.

Shaking himself to clear his thoughts, he asked, "Max, what time is her date picking her up? I want to be there with you when we talk to her date and to see how she looks."

"That's why I'm calling. It appears that her date, Tim, the head of the basketball team, has a lot more on his mind than the prom. He thinks that by taking her to the prom, it's an automatic score. Erica told him that she wasn't down with that but I have a feeling that either he will stand her up or that he will try to force himself on her. He's the type of person that's never been told no too. I wondered if it would be too much to ask, if you would be on standby to take her to the Prom instead, if this guy doesn't show up? That way I know she's safe with you. If he does show up, we need to make ourselves available to make sure that he doesn't get out of hand afterwards."

"Sure Max. You know I would do anything for Erica. The question is, will she want me to take her?" *That's a laugh. How do you know she'll be safer with me? Sometimes I can't control the feelings that are inside of me when she's around. That's why I was so glad when we went off to college, thought TJ.*

"Of course she would. Next to me, you're her favorite person," said Max. *Literally, he thought. Erica can't love anyone else because she's in love with you. She would jump at the chance for you to take her to the prom or anywhere else. One day, hopefully when she's much older, maybe the two of you will stop beating around the bush with each other. He felt sure that TJ had feelings for her too, even though he seldom let his feelings show. However, during the special moments of Erica's life, he had always been there.*

"What time will you arrive?" TJ went to the University of North Carolina in Chapel Hill, so it was only a short distance to drive, approximately one and a half hours.

"My last class ends at eleven o'clock in the morning. I'll get there around twelve thirty in the afternoon. What's Erica's schedule like tomorrow?"

"She's going to school until eleven o'clock in the morning. Then she's going to get her hair and nails done. After that she'll be here getting ready to go to dinner before the prom."

"Okay, I'll make reservations at the Chop House. Since I have a feeling that the day is not going to turn out like she expected, in order to save her from the ridicule, I am going to do something extra special for her tomorrow. Is she still going to Aunt Samantha's at the salon over on Church Street, or will she be at the new shop?"

"Thanks TJ. I knew that I could count on you. No, she's going to the new salon Mystique, on West Wendover Avenue. They finally completed everything at the shop about a month ago. After you drop her back at home tomorrow night, at a decent hour, I might add, I believe that we have some ass kicking to do." Max smiled to himself. Just maybe, later in life, after they were married with kids, he would get credit for orchestrating this entire charade.

The day of the prom arrived; a bright and clear spring morning. All the girls were excited because they would get to show off their fabulous dresses at the prom and vie for the title of Miss Prom Queen.

Erica went to high school that day, unaware that her life would forever be changed by the events of that day. At eleven o'clock, when her class was over and her early dismissal was granted, she left school to go to Mystique, her aunt's hair salon and pedicure spa.

As soon as she had achieved enough recognition for her work and had paid her dues in the industry, her aunt had opened up her own salon. The hair portion of the salon offered the regular hair services but specialized in color treatments. They were as high-tech as the best Caucasian salons when it came to color. So many times her aunt saw someone with bad color where the hair was breaking that she would often pull out a card and tell them that the first service would be free if they would come to her salon so that she could correct their hair.

The pedicure portion of the salon offered natural nail care. It was usually packed months in advance because the technicians were just that good. The salon offered a sandbox, where the client could walk on fresh sand, which would help exfoliate and minimize the dead skin that became crusty and caked up on one's foot. Erica's favorite part of pedicure service that the salon offered was the petroleum jelly mud mask that was applied to the foot. While in her chemistry lab at school, with the help of her aunt and her brother Max, who was a genius at formulas, Erica was able to manufacture the product and then develop a patent for the mask that later became her aunt's top seller.

Since her Aunt Samantha prided herself on the service at her salon, each client's service was performed on time without anyone having to wait. If a technician was running late, then someone else would start the services to maintain 100% compliance to the no waiting rule. Therefore when Erica arrived, she was immediately seated at the stylist station. Since she needed a relaxer and her long hair was going to be put into spiral curls, it would take a minute before she would get the manicure/pedicure. Approximately one and a half hours later, she was seated in the pedicurist room. In this room, there would be two technicians working on her at the same time. One manicurist would complete her nails while another manicurist would complete her pedicure.

As Erica sat down in the massage chair, she leaned her head back against the head cushion and proceeded to listen to her IPod. She then closed her eyes as she let the music wash over her. Erica was oblivious to the commotion that was caused in the outer portion of the salon when TJ arrived. All the ladies head turned as the fine, dark skinned brother, walked into the salon.

TJ arrived at the salon after Erica was escorted into the pedicure salon. He walked over to "Aunt Samantha" and leaned down to give her a kiss on the cheek. He tried to make it to see her every chance he got when he was in town.

"Good afternoon gorgeous. How's my favorite lady?" TJ asked as he pulled a box of roses from behind his back.

"Ohhhhh, TJ! How are you? I haven't seen you in a minute. Are these for me?" She asked as he handed her the bouquet of roses. Samantha leaned down to smell the beautiful flowers. "You shouldn't have. How do you like the salon? When you were here last, we had just started renovating it. Come, let me take you on a tour. I don't have to ask why you're here, do I?" Samantha smiled as she hugged him around his waist.

"Am I that transparent?" TJ asked in a worried tone. If she could read him that easily then it was possible that everyone else would learn of his secret.

"No TJ. Just to me, only because I would love for my favorite niece to have someone in her life like you. I've known for awhile how you felt. Who else but her family would make it to every important affair in her life other than someone who loves her very much?"

"Ummmm. I do love her but she's not ready for what I have to offer. Once she's finished college, then it's on. I plan to make my move. Until then, I'll look at her life on the peripheral edges as one of her friends."

Samantha reached up to give TJ a hug. She knew that everything would work out in the end. "TJ there will be some tough times ahead that I know are coming but that I can't foresee what they are. Just hang in there and everything will work itself out in the end. Have faith in God that he will direct each of your paths to each other." Samantha was known for seeing into the future or sensing things that were going to happen. Usually the events came true. In this instance, he tended not to believe her. So many years left for Erica to grow up, anything could happen. He would just have to make sure that he stayed close enough to be on her mind but out of harm's way so that she wouldn't get under his skin any more than she already was.

"Miss Sam, where's Erica? I have something to give to her to set the tone for the rest of her Prom Day." TJ smiled.

"Shouldn't her date be doing this? Not that I'm mad that you're right on point," laughed Samantha. "What happens if he shows up?"

"I'll handle that if the moment arrives. Of course I'll revert back to being the other older brother. But if he doesn't, then I plan on being her date for this evening, come hell or high water."

"Go on with your bad self. She's in the Pedicure Salon A. Let me walk with you to the salon so that you can surprise her. I know that she'll be ecstatic to see you. Take care and I'll see you tomorrow, to hear about your wonderful night!"

"Okay, thanks Miss Sam," TJ replied as he pulled the other box of roses from behind his back. Taking a deep breath, he proceeded to Salon A.

As he opened the door, Samantha gestured to the manicurist that they be quiet so as not to disturb Erica. She also motioned for them to leave the room for a moment. The rest was left up to TJ. When the manicurists left the room, TJ sat the roses in the vase that was located on the side table and proceeded to sit down on the pedicurist stool. He then grasped Erica's foot and started to massage it with some of the scented lotion that was available.

Erica meanwhile, was enjoying the foot massage. She thought that it was strange, that she would get this type of pleasure from a simple foot massage. She could tell that the massage was being given by a man. His hands were slightly callused with caused a unique, rather pleasing sensation. Her Aunt Samantha did say that one of her employees, a man, had taken the Reflexology course so that he could perform the foot massages. Maybe they had a man to come into the room for the foot massage portion of the pedicure. Since she trusted her aunt there was no reason to worry, therefore she didn't open her eyes to confirm or dispute her theory.

Working his way from her foot to her thigh, TJ gloried in the feel of Erica's skin in his hands. He massaged her ankles, her calves and with no thought to what he was doing, his hand inched upwards to the bend in her knee. If she didn't wake up soon, TJ thought, thinks could get pretty interesting. As he leaned over her knee his breath caressed Erica's skin, like the sweet whisper of an erotic dream that one wanted to capture and retain. His only thought was that he was very tempted to let his lips follow the path that his hands were traveling but he knew that he would not take advantage of her like that. He had to regain his control.

Erica immediately jumped at the scorching heat that seemed to race up her body at the inappropriate touch to the bend in her knees. Her eyes popped open and she squealed with joy at seeing TJ. "When did you get back in town TJ?"

"Hi sweetheart. I thought that I would come and surprise you on your special day." TJ got up from the stool and walked around the pedicure basin to the front of the chair and leaned over to give Erica a kiss on her cheek.

Erica, at that point had leaned forward to remove her IPod from her waist to put it to the side so that she could stand up and give TJ a hug. Instead of TJ's kiss reaching her cheek, because of the angle that she was leaning, his kiss actually touched her mouth. Shocked and surprised at his miscalculation, TJ froze for a moment.

Erica however, took advantage of that moment, thinking that this was probably the closest that TJ would ever be for her to kiss. Instead of pulling away, she actually deepened the kiss. As their lips moved in one accord, a sigh escaped her lips. Molten lava felt like it was racing through her veins. TJ took that time to delve deeper into the kiss in an attempt to taste every crevice possible. His tongue moved with a swiftness to capture hers in a sensual mating that was as old as time. With an overwhelming passion that he couldn't seem to control, he gathered Erica into his arms to prolong the kiss. As their tongues continued their duel, TJ's sanity returned. He shouldn't be doing this. It was too soon. The timing was all wrong. In a superhuman effort to regain some of the control that seemed to have deserted him, TJ broke off the kiss.

Leaning his head on hers, TJ took a deep breath of air into his lungs. He didn't think that a mere first kiss could make him feel this intense. His body was craving hers. Luckily he came to his senses in time before things really got out of hand; like locking the door and exploring the pleasure that he knew was just under the surface.

Lurking to explode with a touch or one more kiss.

She was not his. He had to remember his promise to himself. That she needed to live a little before being subjected to his wants and desires, his love. "Sweetheart, I'm sorry. I didn't mean for that to happen. A man could get into trouble kissing you like that."

Not knowing exactly what he meant, whether he was sorry for kissing her so heatedly or whether he was sorry for the kiss at all, Erica began to gnaw on her lower lip, thinking that she had embarrassed him by initiating the kiss.

TJ cupped her face into his hands, as he read the confusion in her eyes. Always honest to a fault, TJ replied, "Erica, I never do anything that I don't want to do. I loved kissing you, however wrong it was. You belong to someone else. You're young and you have your whole life ahead of you. Can we chalk this down to an aberration on my part? Will you forgive me?"

"There's nothing to forgive. I always wanted to know what you tasted like. The question is, will you forgive me?" Erica smiled at TJ. She had shaken his cool resolve. He felt something. She could tell by the response in his body. Although he might not do anything about it, he did feel something. The kiss was wonderful. To lighten the situation, Erica stated with enough sass in her voice to give TJ notice that she was indeed a mature young woman, "You know, I couldn't let the opportunity pass by without indulging in one of my fantasies. But just so you know, I belong to myself and yes I'm young, but that doesn't mean that I don't know my own mind."

Smiling, that the moment of passion induced tension had passed, TJ hugged Erica again as he stepped away from her and walked around the table to present her with the dozen roses.

"Sweetheart, these are for you. May this day be everything that you have ever hoped it would be and much more."

"It's definitely off to an auspicious start. These roses are beautiful and they smell heavenly. I can't wait for the day to continue. Can I take you home with me?" Erica asked as she settled her nose in the beautiful bouquet.

"Have you forgotten that your date will be by your house shortly to pick you up for dinner?"

"Oh. What a way to bring me back down to earth with a thud. Unless that date is with you, everything else at this point will be exactly that, pointless. Well, I guess I had better call the technicians back in so that they can polish my toes then I'm off to the house to dress." Erica grudgingly admitted, not caring that she had just exposed her true feelings to TJ. "Will I see you after I'm dressed, before I head out to dinner?" She asked as he opened the door and walked with him to the front of the salon.

TJ, decided that not commenting on what she had just revealed would be best for both of them. He couldn't take much more. It was going to be hard enough later, to see her dressed and then to know that someone other than him would be enjoying this special day with her. "You can count on it." Quickly, without giving it any thought, almost as a reflex action, he pulled Erica to him as he planted a hard kiss on her lips as he said goodbye and stepped outside the salon and walked to his car. *Don't look back, he kept telling himself.* Instead, he pulled out his cellular phone and called Max to let him know that he was in town and that he had just left Erica at the hair salon with a dozen roses, his gift for her special day.

Erica stood right where TJ had left her with her fingers touching her lips that he had just singed with his parting kiss.

Samantha, fanning herself at the heat she had just witnessed, that was generated from Erica and TJ, looked very pleased with the progress that the two were making. With her next question, she jolted Erica out of her daydreams and brought her back to reality, with a playful swat on her buttocks.

"Honey, let's get a move on. I believe that there's still work to be done before you're ready to leave and have dinner with that fine young man."

"Darn it Auntie, why did you have to remind me? Can't a girl have her dreams? He's not my date for this evening. Tim is taking me to the prom, or so he said yesterday before our disagreement.

"Erica, what do you mean?"

"Auntie, I'll tell you all about it while they are polishing my toes."

Chapter Five

Erica made it home in record time to take a nap for two hours then to get up and dress for her evening. Not hearing from Tim, gave her pause to wonder. Was he really okay with her decision not to have sex? She didn't ponder on this question for long. She was used to taking people at their word. If he said that he would take her, then that's what she believed. A person's word was their bond, her father always taught her. If they didn't stand by their word, then they could not be trusted.

"Honey, come on down. We need to take pictures before Tim arrives," called her mother from the bottom of the stairway.

Looking in the mirror to check her appearance, Erica smiled to herself. *This dress is perfect. I can't wait until TJ sees this on me.*

"Whatever happened to Tim?" Her conscience questioned. "See you've forgotten about him already. What's the use of going with him to the prom? It's obvious that he's a substitute, plus the fact that he's a jerk, if sex is the main thing that's on his mind."

"Oh shut up, Conscience. We were doing good forgetting about TJ until he showed up today, remember? We made a deal that we would put our infatuation for him in a little box, never to be opened again, unless of course he initiated the first move. Then all bets are off. That kiss today qualifies as the first move in my

book." I must be going crazy, talking to myself like this, thought Erica as she slowly descended the stairs.

Erica's father, Josh, had the videotape out, recording her every move. Her parents always did this for every special occasion in her and her brother's lives. After he was satisfied that he had captured the essence of the dress and his baby girl, Josh shut the recorder off.

"Okay princess, what time is Tim supposed to pick you up?"

"Six o'clock Daddy."

The clock already read six fifteen. *He's just running a little late, thought Erica.* They were supposed to have reservations at Lucky 32 at six o'clock. Never in her wildest dreams did she think that he would stand her up.

Josh looked at his watch then looked at his daughter and asked in a gruff tone of voice, "Would anyone like to tell me what's going on? How can your date be late to pick you up for the Prom? Have you called him yet?"

"No, Daddy. I was going to give him a few more minutes. You know how Tim's always running a little late." Erica hedged. Just then Erica's cell phone went off. "Maybe that's him now. Hello." It was her friend Sasha.

"Hello Sasha. What's up? Are you at the restaurant yet?"

"Ummm, that's why I'm calling, Erica. I don't know how to tell you this, but…….."

"Just tell me Sasha." A shiver of apprehension raced down Erica's spine.

"I hate to be the bearer of bad news, but Tim is here with Yvonne. I took a picture with my camera phone, since I wasn't sure if you would believe me. Did ya'll breakup? I thought that he was supposed to be bringing you. What happened? It should be coming through to you now", she whispered because they were sitting two tables over from Erica's "boyfriend".

Erica turned pale as a ghost as she stared at the picture that was coming across the telephone. The picture that was taken and then emailed to her was a picture of Tim, her boyfriend, and Yvonne, her best friend, feeding each other at the restaurant;

seeming to be having the time of their lives. She felt betrayed. *No wonder he didn't seem to care that I wasn't putting out*, she thought. *He already had a standby.*

Max, looking at the horror on his sister's face, snatched the phone from her to see what would cause her to turn so pale. Erica took that moment to quickly runs upstairs and flop on her bed, trying to stop the flow of tears that were springing forth. Erica's mother Chandra, ran upstairs to see if she could comfort her daughter.

"He's a dead man after I finish with him," said Max angrily as he stomped out of the house, with his father running after him. Josh wanted to make sure that Max didn't do anything stupid that would jeopardize his military position as a Captain in the ROTC program at his college.

"Max, wait up. Hold on son," said Josh as he tapped on the window of the car that Max had gotten into.

Max rolled down the window and asked very calmly, "Yes Dad?"

Josh looked at his son as if Dr. Jekyll and Mr. Hyde had inhabited his body. "What gives? Just a minute ago, you were very upset. Now you seem so calm. What's going on?"

Because of their open and honest relationship, Max told his Dad the truth; everything concerning the telephone conversation Erica had with Tim that he overheard and his suspicions about what would happen tonight.

"How do you plan to take care of Tim?" Josh asked idly as he too was formulating a plan that would teach that boy some manners.

"Dad, we've got this. TJ will be here in a few minutes to escort Erica to the Prom. After the conversation I had with Erica, I asked if he would be on standby in case things went down like this. Haven't you noticed that for every special occasion for Erica, he's always around? He was planning on stopping by anyway to see what she looked like in her attire before sadly watching her go off to the Prom with someone else. Dad, he has feelings for Erica but he is resolute in his position that she needs to go to college, graduate and experience life first. He doesn't know that quite a few of us are on to his feelings for Erica. Usually, he hides them pretty well."

"I just hope that he doesn't wait too long to let her know how he feels. After the Prom though, TJ and I, are going to teach Tim a lesson in manners. He could at least have had the decency to call and cancel along with inviting someone else other than Erica's best friend to the Prom. Too bad the joke is going to be on him. I daresay, that when TJ takes Erica to the Prom tonight, she won't be thinking of anything else. Now tomorrow, things might be different."

"Okay, it seems as if you have things covered. That makes me feel better. I'm glad that you love your sister so much that you would go to all this trouble to make sure that her name and reputation remains in tact. I taught you well. It sounds like I need to have a talk with TJ." Josh smiled in delight at the talk that he would have with the man that had secretly loved his baby girl for a very long time.

Suddenly a limousine pulled up alongside the curb in front of the house. The chauffeur got out of the driver's seat to hurriedly open the back door before his passenger got out. As anxious as he was, he probably would open the door himself, thought the driver. *Oh, to be young and in love.*

Once the door was opened, TJ slowly emerged with a grin on his face, once he saw Max and Josh's startled expressions. He looked resplendent in a four button Armani charcoal grey suit that emphasized his muscular body. Being a college student with a part time job, they knew that this evening would cost TJ a pretty penny. It warmed Josh's heart to know that TJ would go to this length for a date that he hadn't even known would occur.

"Good evening Mr. Teal. Max. Sir, it would be my pleasure if you would allow me to take Erica to her Senior Prom, if she'll go with me, based on what's happened here tonight. I have reservations for her at The Chop House on Pisgah Church Road Sir, and from there we'll go straight to the Prom. I promise to have her back in time for her curfew," TJ stated as he shook the hand that Mr. Teal had extended once he approached them.

"TJ, I think that its shows just how much character you have, to step in at the last minute and take my daughter to her Senior Prom because her so-called boyfriend chose to stand her up. To do it with such style, shows that you not only have class but that you've developed into a great young man. My wife and I thank you from the bottom of our hearts for helping her to gracefully save face during this difficult situation. Please accept this as a token of our gratitude." Josh reached into his wallet to retrieve five hundred dollars and gave it to TJ.

Not even looking at the money that was extended, TJ replied, "Mr. Teal, I'm sorry but I can't accept your money. I would do anything to help alleviate the pain and suffering she must be experiencing because I love Erica, Sir, and one day I would like to ask you for her hand in marriage; once she's ready. I realize that this conversation is very premature but those are my feelings, Sir. I wanted to do this for her. I'm just glad that you're giving me the opportunity to spend time with her on such a special occasion."

"Mmmmmm. That certainly was enlightening. Will you allow her the opportunity to continue to evolve as a person, go to college and graduate? Will you allow her to follow her dreams and support her in any endeavor that she deems necessary? That means no marriage proposals until she's at least twenty five." Josh emphasized, looking deeply into TJ's eyes, trying to ascertain his sincerity.

"Yes, Sir. It's my desire to support her in every endeavor that she undertakes, especially graduating from college. I feel that college is an important step as part of the maturation process. I plan to be on the peripheral of her life until I feel she's ready for things to go further."

"Good. Then you have my blessing. Let's go in and see how much damage has been done and what we can do to repair it. You boys go on inside. I'll be with you shortly." Josh then walked over to the limousine and paid the driver for the evening along with a handsome tip. The driver in turn, handed him the money that TJ had already paid.

Not knowing what Erica wanted her to do, since she refused to answer the phone after the picture mail, Sasha decided to take matters into her own hands to diffuse the situation and find out what the hell was going on. She looked over at her boyfriend Todd, and together they said, "How are we going to handle this?"

Laughing, she quickly kissed him on the lips. "You know me so well. Let's put a stop to this. No one treats my friend like that. I can't figure out what's up with Yvonne though. She's supposed to be deeply in love with Paul who left last year, to go into the military. I've known her as long as I've known Erica. She wouldn't do this to her." Together they got up to go over to the table where Tim and Yvonne were sitting.

Taking a seat, Sasha asked, "How's everything going, Tim and Yvonne? Aren't you missing someone? Where's Erica?" she asked, looking pointedly at Tim.

Before he could answer, Yvonne giggled as she replied, "Hi Sasha. Oooh girl, these drinks are to die for. I don't usually drink but Tim suggested that I try one of their Virgin Daiquiris. This sure tastes pretty good, not to have any liquor in it. I wonder how they make it. If I didn't know any better, I would swear that I tasted something funny."

Taking one more sip and swallowing, she hiccupped. Cupping her mouth, she murmured, "Excuse me but I think this is coming up." Hastily she rushed from the table.

"Funny how she didn't answer my question," said Sasha as she rushed after Yvonne with the hope that someone would tell her what was going on.

"Tim, what's going on? Why are you here with Yvonne and not Erica?"

"Oh, well, you know how it is," he replied, grinning unashamedly. "Can't a person change their mind about who they take to the Prom? A man wants to spend time with someone who's willing, if you know what I mean."

Ever so quickly, Sasha's boyfriend Todd, leaned forward and grabbed Tim by the lapels of his tuxedo so that their faces were mere inches apart. He then quietly relayed his intentions, that if he didn't answer some pertinent questions real fast, his body parts would be sore and stiff after the butt kicking he was about to receive. "Let's start by telling me, where Erica is and let's move on to why you are here with her best friend acting as if you are about to have sex right here in the restaurant?"

Not wanting his face to be disfigured or any limbs to be broken for fear that his college basketball scholarship would be in jeopardy, he hurriedly tried to bluff his way through an explanation. "Uh, uh, there's nothing really to explain. Erica dropped me and Yvonne agreed to go out with me since her boyfriend could not get any leave from the military. It's not my fault she can't hold her liquor."

Realizing his mistake, Todd quickly punched Tim in the stomach. "You know that Yvonne doesn't drink. She just mentioned that you ordered her a Virgin Daiquiri. Did you pay someone to put something in it?"

"I don't know what you're talking about," said Tim as his eyes darted back and forth across the restaurant, wondering where the waitress was that had helped him place the drug in Yvonne's drink. Good, he didn't see her. Now if only he could figure out how to bluff his way out of this.

"Oh you don't? Let's just see how long it will take to question every waitress here to see if your story pans out? Or better yet, what if I pull out my trusty set of tools that I wouldn't go anywhere without, to see if you're telling the truth." Todd released his hold on Tim as he proceeded to reach into the vest pocket of his tuxedo to pull out what looked to be a small leather case.

"Don't even think about leaving. I assure you that I can cut your legs out from under you faster than you can stand and take one step." After extracting a small vial and setting it on the table, he looked at Tim. "Now would be the time to tell me what I want to know before the police arrives, or in your case, before trouble arrives."

Picking up his phone, he sent a text message to Max, Erica's brother, who also happened to be one of his best friends. The text message that read, "Tim had been handled", was a technique to diffuse the situation. He knew that Max was probably already on his way to the restaurant to do some bodily damage to Tim's face and other body parts. He couldn't let Max jeopardize his commission in the military over a stupid fight.

"What are you, an amateur scientist? I don't have to tell you anything," blustered Tim. So the guy could throw a good punch. Well, on the field he was known as being able to accept a good hit. He would have to do more than that if he wanted to get the truth out of him.

Todd proceeded to pour a portion of Yvonne's drink into the vial. Just as he suspected, after swirling the contents of the vial in a circular pattern for several minutes, the color of the liquid in the vial started to change colors. The change in color denoted that some type of drug was present in the drink as well as some form of liquor.

"Well, well, well. What do we have here?" Todd leaned forward to deliver another blow to Tim for giving drugs to one of his friends. This time the blow was to one of his legs; hard enough to feel, but not hard enough to break. He wasn't a thug but he wanted to let Tim know that his behavior would not be tolerated.

With a loud exclamation from Tim, several heads turned towards their area in an attempt to see what the commotion was about. Most people assumed it was a fight over the woman that had rushed to the restroom. Their waiter returned to see what the commotion was all about.

"Sir is there anything wrong?" The waiter asked anxiously as he came abreast of the table.

"Yes, as a matter of fact there is." Gently laying a fifty dollar bill on the table and pushing it towards the waiter, Todd asked, "Could you send the bartender over that prepared the drinks for this table? It appears that liquor along with an unidentified drug was mistakenly put in the Virgin Daiquiri that my friend, who is a minor, requested. She is currently experiencing some sickness as we speak in your restroom. Additionally, could you alert the waitress for that table near the window where we were previously sitting that we are going to join this lovely couple for the remainder of our meal? Please assure her that she will get the gratuity for our meal."

"Sure sir.

Yvonne barely made it to the bathroom before she threw up the contents of her stomach in the sink closest to the door. "Ugh. What was in that drink?" She wondered. After turning on the faucet, she cupped her hands underneath the water spout to rinse her mouth out. As she lifted her head, she felt lightheaded and sank to the floor, moaning as she wrapped her arms around her mid section. It was in that position that Sasha found her as she burst through the door.

"What's wrong Yvonne?" She asked as she attempted to help her friend to her feet.

"I don't know but I feel sick to my stomach". Grasping her stomach, she headed straight to the nearest toilet. Sinking down on her knees she emptied what she assumed was the remaining contents of her stomach into the bowl.

"Could you please explain what you're doing here with Tim?" Sasha asked as she wiped her friend's face with a damp paper towel.

"Since Paul could not get any leave, I decided that I would go to the Prom by myself and just hang out with you guys there. I came to the restaurant to get a to-go order and that's when I ran into Tim. He suggested that I hang out with him and Erica and go to the Prom with them. I became a little uneasy when I saw Tim but didn't see Erica. He explained that Erica had made a pit stop in the bathroom and that she saw some friends of hers and would be right over after she said hello." Immediately Yvonne, started moaning again as another fierce cramp assailed her body. Moving quickly, Sasha was able to help Yvonne into a semi upright position, with her face barely reaching the top of the bowl before her stomach overflowed again.

"Just stay right there a second and breathe in deep even breaths. Do you think that your stomach will be settled enough until we can get you home? My purse is back at the table. I should have some Pepto in it that you can take." With one hand moving in small circles, Sasha gently massaged Yvonne's back.

"No. I mean yes. I don't feel very well. My stomach is churning and all I want to do is go home and lie down. I don't want to spoil the rest of your evening though. Just let me grab my purse and I'll drive myself home. Thanks."

"There is no way that I'm letting you drive in this condition. I'll drive you and Todd can follow us in your car. Then when you're feeling better, we can all go to the Prom together. Grasping her phone that she had sat down on the floor when she was helping Yvonne, Sasha, pressed the speed dial button for Todd.

"Baby, how is Yvonne doing?"

"Not good. Her stomach is cramping something fierce and she's been sick ever since she came into the bathroom. Do you know what's wrong with her?"

"I have a fair idea. I believe that Tim tried to give her a date rape drug so that she would be more pliable to sleep with him. I'm getting ready to talk to the bartender right now to see what she was actually given so that we know what the consequences will be. Do you think that her stomach is settled enough for her to make it home?"

"If we leave right now, she might be able to make it. Can you follow us in her car? I don't want to leave her alone."

"Sure sweetheart. Hold on a minute. There's a phone ringing at the table. It sounds like it's coming from Yvonne's purse. Do you want me to answer it?"

"Please answer it Todd; maybe it's Paul. He was supposed to take me to the Prom. He's probably just calling to chat since he couldn't make it." Yvonne advised softly. "We'll be right out. If it's Paul, tell him to hold on."

Yvonne and Sasha slowly made their way from the bathroom to the table. Before they could take ten steps, a waitress stopped them in the hallway.

Touching Yvonne's arm, the waitress spoke hesitantly. "Miss, I wanted to apologize to you. The man that you are with gave me $50 to put a date rape drug in your drink. I couldn't bring myself to do it but I did give you a strong laxative that would make you to sick to be taken advantage of tonight. Other than some diarrhea you will be okay. Just take some Imodium to plug it up and you will be just fine to continue to enjoy what's left of your Prom. If I were you I wouldn't go out with him anymore. I started to pull you to the side but experience has taught me that some women won't believe you even if the truth is staring them in the face."

"Bless you even if my stomach doesn't feel up to par right now. You probably saved me from getting raped." The waitress then disappeared through a back door, never to be seen for the rest of the evening.

Hugging each other close, they said a silent prayer, because the grace of God who was watching over them had provided an escape route even when the Devil meant them harm. They walked back to their table. While he was waiting for the women to come from the bathroom, Todd found out that Paul was waiting for Yvonne at her house to take her to the Prom. After having briefed Paul what went down at the restaurant, it was agreed that he would stay there to wait on them to drop Yvonne off. That under no circumstances was he to come to the restaurant to settle the situation and end up getting sent to Ft. Leavenworth for a crime of passion.

"Yvonne, let's get you home so that you can clean up nicely and then we're all going to the Prom to enjoy ourselves. Sasha, call Erica back and let her know that we are going to stop by and pick her up too. She will not sit at home tonight and let this scumbag win."

To Tim he leaned forward with his face only inches away to say, "Mess with one of these girls again and the police will not be able to find enough body parts to identify who you are. This is a warning and a promise. I don't make idle threats." Todd pushed Tim back in his seat and hooked his arms through the girl's arms and proceeded to walk out of the restaurant.

Chapter Six

Things were going quite well for Erica and Yvonne at North Carolina State University. Erica received a full scholarship to attend the university with a double major in Engineering and Biology, while Yvonne's concentration was in Architectural Engineering. Both of their academic lives were progressing nicely and their social calendars were limited due to their caseload, but still time was made for fun.

Life was good with the exception of the situation with Erica's roommate, Naomi, a girl from her hometown. Even though Erica and Yvonne were not roommates as they had originally planned, due to the Housing Department's mistake, Erica thought that everything would still be cool, because they knew each other in high school and were friends.

When classes first began, everything was fine until Silas, one of the guys that Naomi was interested in dating, ignored her overtures to expand their friendship further. Silas politely rebuffed Naomi when the overtures became increasingly sexual in nature, with excessive hugs and the stroking of his arms or chest (if he didn't see her coming first), whenever they encountered each other during their breaks or at social events.

After he realized that Naomi wouldn't leave him alone, a confrontation occurred in public at the Union, the meeting place or food court in the middle of campus. One day, she went too far with her "innocent caresses", when he was conversing with Erica about one of their biology class assignments. Mad at Erica for witnessing the ridicule that she brought on herself, Naomi found out the reason why she was rebuffed. Silas had feelings for Erica. It was written all over his face; the longing in his eyes, the rapt expression on his face whenever she talked. That was all that was needed to turn a good friendship between roommates sour.

Anger began to fester within Naomi's mind, making her hard to live with, disagreeable and spiteful. The situation became compounded when Silas asked Erica out on a date several weeks later, after a group study session, and Naomi happened to be eavesdropping on their conversation.

Hearing a noise outside the open door to her room, when Naomi accidentally bumped into the hall table, Erica closed the door to retain some semblance of privacy. Since she wasn't remotely interested in Silas as a boyfriend, Erica let him down gently, stating that she had someone back home. Although Silas didn't like her answer, he was thankful that she didn't take advantage of him by playing him and leading him on as others would have tried to do. Erica expressed to him that friendship was all she was willing to offer because her heart belonged to someone else.

Instead of talking to Erica about her feelings, Naomi continued to harbor ill feelings towards her for "taking her man", even though the man had no interest. Events spiraled out of control from that day forward. It was becoming increasingly hard for Erica to abide the rudeness and snide comments that seemed to increase every day, along with her items being ransacked but not stolen. She asked the Resident Adviser if she could switch rooms but was put on a waiting list since they both shared a quad with two other people. They deemed it wasn't necessary since they could close their individual doors.

Since the second semester was almost over, with spring break occurring the following week, Erica thought if she could just tough it out for two more months; she would be rid of the craziness for good. For her sophomore year she would get an house to avoid the headache and hassle of a roommate. Thinking she could handle this minor crisis, she didn't even tell her parents or her brother about the latest altercation with her roommate. Sometimes the best laid plans often go awry

Unstable, insecure people do evil things. That was the conclusion that Erica came to when she walked into her dorm room to find that the suitcase that she was taking on her spring break vacation had been pried open and the contents had been cut up and destroyed into tiny little pieces. More angry than afraid, she went storming into the rooms of her suitemates to see if they were in the suite when the vandalism occurred. Of course they appeared to be just as shook up as she was that someone could break into her room and vandalize her property to that extreme.

Getting up from the chair in her suitemate Amy's room, Naomi, sarcastically retorted, "To bad I didn't think of that myself," as she brushed past Erica to go back into her room.

Before she could get beyond the threshold, Erica had grabbed Naomi by her weave and swung her around so that they were standing face to face. "Are you the one that vandalized my property? If there's some problem that you have with me, let's get it out in the open and deal with it. I've had enough of your bad attitude and I'm tired of dealing with your issues. Get a life."

Leaning forward in Erica's face, Naomi stated, "Yeah, I did it. So what? It's not like you're going to hit me. You're miss goody too shoes. Even back in high school I couldn't stand you. You always thought that you were better than everyone else. You took my boyfriend, Tim in high school. Noooooooooo. That wasn't enough. You took Silas away from me too. I ought to beat your behind for all the pain that you've caused me." Naomi then took a step toward Erica with true menace in her eyes.

"I wouldn't advise it if I were you," said Erica as she got into her fighting stance. "You don't stand a chance. Furthermore, I never knew you and Tim had a thing going on. If you had a problem with us dating, you should have mentioned it then when we first started dating. I wouldn't have gone out with the jerk in the first place."

"We didn't have anything going on until after you started dating. Since you wouldn't put out, he came on to me and since I liked him I gave him what he wanted. I was his, but that wasn't enough. He wanted you because he couldn't have you, but he always came back to me."

Looking with disgust at Naomi, Erica demanded, "You mean to tell me that you don't have any more respect for yourself than to be second best in some man's eyes? That the best you can get, is someone else's leftovers? Get real. Where's your self esteem? Stop going after other women's men. Find someone who really cares about you. Do you know how many other women Tim was sleeping with while you "professed your love" for him? Plenty, I later found out. As for Silas, he was never yours to begin with. You only wanted him because he showed an interest in me. It's all becoming clear now. You wanted to take him away from me like your convoluted mind thinks I took Tim away. You need help. I pity you. Get out of my way. You aren't even worth the butt kicking I was going to give you."

That last statement was all it took to incite Naomi into acting irrationally. She lunged towards Erica who had turned her back to go into her room to clean up the mess that was made. She caught a glancing blow to the middle of her back, which made her hit her mouth slightly on the iron bed as she fell. A piece of her tooth came out. All hell broke loose then.   Staggering up from the bed, Erica regrouped. Her brother Max had taught her how to defend herself. Spinning around, she caught Naomi off guard, because her recovery was so quick. Jabbing with her right hand, she punched Naomi in the nose. Not enough to break it but enough for her opponent to know that she could. Of course blood, starting to spew forth.

With disbelief written on her face, that Erica actually connected, Naomi attempted to kick Erica in the mid section. Missing Erica's mid section by a mile, the ineffective blow caught her on the thigh. Erica delivered two sharp kicks to Naomi's middle with the swiftness of a panther along with a round house kick that sent her sprawling to the floor, writhing in pain.

Amy, then stepped between them with raised hands. She didn't want to see Erica get expelled. Naomi, on the other hand, had to go. Too much drama. The bickering she could take, but vandalizing someone's property was the last straw. "Get up Naomi. Unless you want to get expelled from school, I would advise you to get yourself together and get something to stop that bleeding! There will be someone knocking on the door shortly to find out what the commotion is all about. There are witnesses to your drama so I would suggest that you come up with a plausible excuse for everything or kiss your college scholarship goodbye. You know that State has a no tolerance fighting policy."

Immediately, the RA and the campus police came knocking on the door to investigate the problem. "Ladies, what seems to be the problem?" The chief of the Campus Police Department questioned, looking from one girl to the other as he glanced around the common area of their living space.

"Erica, how's your father? I haven't seen Mr. Teal since Christmas. Be sure to tell him I said hello. Now, tell me what happened."

"Hello, Mr. Peterson. I'll let my Dad know that you asked about him. Naomi and I just had a slight altercation, that's all. It's been resolved now," Erica replied, looking straight into Naomi's eyes.

"Naomi? Care to tell me your version of what happened?"

"Nothing happened, sir. We just had a slight disagreement, which ended up with us pushing the furniture to the side to settle it with a good old fashioned wrestling match."

"Is that how your nose came to bleed?"

"Yes sir. Erica had me pent pretty good, but I refused to give up and ended up hitting my nose in the process. It's all good now, and I would greatly appreciate it if you wouldn't write us up.

"Since I know both of your parents, I'll let this go after I have a talk with them. Naomi, I believe that you are still on scholarship, correct?" At her nod of assent, the chief, continued, "I will not write ya'll up this time but make sure that you don't repeat this behavior or you will get expelled from school." With that said, the chief took his exit without attempting to look around further in the suite.

"See what I mean? Even the chief takes pity on poor, little Erica." Refusing to understand that the chief just did her favor, Erica could only shake her head at Naomi's attitude.

"You just don't get it do you? He just saved both of us from getting expelled. If you stay out of my way, I'll stay out of yours for the remainder of the semester. Don't start nothing, won't be nothing."

"Erica, you may have beaten me this time but I *will* get the last laugh. You had better watch your back. Retribution will be fast, swift and incomprehensible."

Chapter Seven

Three weeks went by without an incident therefore Erica assumed that Naomi had come to her senses, since things were getting back to normal and she was trying to be friendly. Being so focused on her studies, Erica didn't pay too much attention to Naomi's behavior. Lulled into a false sense of security by her suitemates deception, Naomi decided to make her move.

By telephoning Tim, who was at a neighboring college, that Erica was alone for the weekend, since her suitemates and her girlfriends had gone away for the weekend; she offered Tim the opportunity to pay Erica back for the beating that he received after the Prom. Max, TJ and Paul, had roughed him up pretty badly after the Prom for mistreating Yvonne by spiking her drink and for dumping Erica because she wouldn't have sex with him.

Tim, who was a coward, had vowed to make the girls pay for his transgressions. He thought; what better way to make them pay than to carry out his original plans for the Prom. Instead of one person, he would make sure that both Erica and Yvonne paid the price. The only thing that was needed was the place and an opportune time.

Naomi, came through yet again for him. He enjoyed using her. She was the only woman who didn't mind that he was unfaithful; that he was sleeping around with various women. She was sprung for life. She was gullible, yet cooperative and didn't belittle him because of his problem.

At last! He would finally get what he wanted; Erica in his bed! She was the reason that he had this fixation and couldn't perform. Little Johnny wouldn't cooperate with other women except for Naomi, who took the time to treat him right and coax him out, even if only for a little while. There was no way that he would miss this opportunity to prove to everyone that he was capable of bedding anyone that he wanted, once he got over this obsession. Time to put his plan into action.

"Erica, do you and Yvonne want to go to the café to eat? I don't want to go by myself," said Naomi the following morning.

"Sure. Let me call Yvonne to see if she's ready."

The three of them left the dorm room to walk to the cafeteria to eat. Since both Erica and Yvonne liked to eat a hot breakfast, Naomi was the first one to sit down at the table. All of her equipment was ready to put Tim's plan of action into place. If habit were true to form, Erica and Yvonne, would forget something and would have to get back up, leaving their food unattended, to retrieve the forgotten items, giving Naomi the perfect opportunity to pour a clear, odorless drug onto their food.

Sure enough, both forgot something. As they got up to get their utensils and condiments, Naomi went to work. When Erica and Yvonne sat back down, they were none the wiser. It would take about two hours before the drug took effect, according to Tim. Naomi couldn't wait to see what happened next. Finally! Retribution was about to take place.

Two and a half hours later, Erica started to feel stomach pains. Initially they weren't so bad, but after about an hour, the pains increased in their intensity. She called Yvonne, to see if she was experiencing the same symptoms.

Crumbled over with pain, Erica was barely able to dial her friend's number. After attempting to dial the number three times she was finally able to get it right.

Concerned because it took her friend so long to answer, Erica was about to hang up. When Yvonne finally came on the line, she sounded very weak and very sick.

She whispered, "Hello, help me," before the phone went crashing to the floor. Erica knew that something was wrong.

Crying brokenly, she attempted to yell into the phone, "Yvonne. Yvonne. What happened? Are you okay? Are you sick?" The exhausted cry that was supposed to come out sounding strong instead came out sounding miserably faint. With the last ounce of strength left in her, Erica, placed the phone in her pocket, just in case TJ called since he was coming to pick her up to take her home for the weekend after her last class. She then crawled to her dorm door in an effort to get Naomi's attention for help.

Standing in her room, waiting on the call that was sure to come, Naomi rushed to Erica's rescue. "What's wrong? Are you in pain? Why are you grabbing your stomach? Why are you on the floor? Was it something you ate this morning?"

Very feebly, Erica asked, "Can you take us to the infirmary? Yvonne is sick also. We have to go and get her from her room."

Helping Erica sit-up on the couch in the common area, Naomi declared, "You wait right here. I'll go get her and together, I'll take you both to the hospital. That way you'll get seen faster. I can borrow my boyfriend's car. Just wait right here."

Picking up her cell phone as she ran out the door, she called Tim. "Everything is going according to schedule. They are both in so much pain. I really think that they should go to the hospital. You said that they would only be in mild discomfort. I'm starting to get worried."

"Naomi, everything will be all right. I have it all under control. If you give them the pills I gave you, once you're on your way, they'll calm down. Once we get to the cabin, I'll give them something that will settle their stomachs. Just meet me there."

Clicking over to another call, Tim didn't give Naomi the opportunity to question him further. Little did she know that the pills she would give them would knock them out for several hours; enough time for them to arrive at the cabin and for him to put the next phase of his plan into action.

Rushing to Yvonne's room, she was able to get in without any problems. Yvonne had used her last bit of strength to unlock the door. Stepping into the room, Naomi announced, "Yvonne, Erica sent me to help you to the infirmary. Where are you?"

"In here. In the bathroom. I'll be out in a...." Retching could be heard from the slight crack in the doorway.

Wiping her mouth and helping her stand to her feet, Naomi soothingly proclaimed, "Everything will be all right in a couple of hours. I'm here to take you to the hospital. Let's go. If you'll hold on to me, I'll walk you down to the car."

At last, with two more trips to the room and to the car, Erica and Yvonne were situated and all set to go to the cabin. Leaning over the back seat, Naomi gave them two pills to help "ease the pain" that was beginning to overwhelm them. Thinking that the pills were Tylenol or some Excedrin capsules to stop the pain, they gratefully took it and swallowed. Minutes later, they were unconscious. An hour's drive to the cabin and the weekend was starting to look very good.

It wasn't like Erica not to be punctual, thought TJ. She knew that he was coming to take her and Yvonne home for the weekend. *What could have happened? Were they at the library? Did they lose track of time?* TJ wondered as he continued to knock on the dormitory door. *Why wasn't she answering her telephone*, TJ pondered as he dialed her cellular number? No answer. He then tried Yvonne's number. Again, no answer. That was strange. *Their voice mail should have picked up*, thought TJ. If their phone was turned off, that meant something drastic had happened. As college students, their phone was their life. If you took that away, they would be lost. They only turned it off when they went to church.

That feeling of unease that had been with him earlier started to return. He had already contacted his parents and his sister to see if anything was wrong, but they were all fine. The only other people that was as close to him as his family was his best friend, Max's family. After hanging up with his mother, then his sister, he contacted Max and Erica's parents, who were vacationing in Hawaii. They were doing quite well. Unfortunately Max was overseas so he wasn't readily available for TJ to talk too. That left only Erica for the reason for his concern; which is why he decided to come to her dormitory two hours earlier than previously planned.

Trying not to panic, TJ gave himself a pep talk. *Okay, they are not late, I'm just early. They will be here shortly. I'll just have to wait.* Ten minutes passed. No one appeared.

He decided to go up to Yvonne's room to see if perhaps they were there. Walking swiftly towards the elevator, TJ impatiently paced back and forth, waiting on the elevator to return to Erica's floor. Since it was taking too long for the elevator to return to the floor that he was on, TJ decided to take the stairs. Dashing out the door, he took the stairs two at a time. With his heart thumping rapidly, he slowed down only when he came abreast of Yvonne's room.

Knocking several times produced the same results. Not knowing what else to do, he headed back to Erica's floor. He intended to knock on every door available to find out if anyone had seen her.

Twenty minutes had passed. Still missing. Where were they? He couldn't shake the feeling of unease that seemed to resonate within him.

Tired of waiting passively while his heart continued to feel queasy, he decided to go and talk to the Chief of Police, a personal friend of the family.

Rushing towards the elevator to head to the campus police, TJ demanded, "Hold the elevator, please."

"Hi, are you looking for Erica?" The woman inquired as the signal sounded that the doors were about to close, just as TJ crossed the threshold.

Smiling at the woman who appeared to know his friends, TJ asked, "Have you seen Erica or her friend, Yvonne today? I was supposed to take them home for the weekend."

Too bad this good looking brother seemed to be taken, thought the woman as she sized him up and down, literally drinking in the essence of him. Breathing deeply of his Hugo Boss cologne that gently wafted across the expanse of the elevator, the young lady replied, "Yes, I saw her about several hours ago headed out with Naomi. Erica and Yvonne appeared to have eaten something that disagreed with their stomachs. They were in terrible pain, so Naomi volunteered to take them to the infirmary." Glancing at her watch, the woman added, "They should have been back by now."

"Do you remember what time it was that you last saw them?" Hearing that Naomi, Erica's nemesis had taken her somewhere didn't bode well for his peace of mind. Erica would not willingly go anywhere with her due to the trouble she had caused since the start of their freshman year in college.

"Yes, it was around twelve o'clock. Can I do anything to help," she asked worriedly?

"Yes, can you show me where the infirmary is?" Grabbing the woman by the arm, they swiftly left the building and headed across campus to the infirmary.

At the cabin, Tim walked to the car, to help extricate the ladies from the back seat. They were still drugged; still asleep. Good. Now the only thing that was left, he thought to himself, was to tie them up and he could have his way with both of them, without anyone stopping him. Maybe he could do a threesome if Naomi was interested. She had come too far to turn back so she would have to stay at the cabin, either willingly or by force. It didn't matter to him.

Picking Erica up in his arms, Tim walked through the door, and down the narrow hallway to the master suite to gently place her on the king sized bed. Bending over the woman lying lifeless on the bed, he suddenly kissed her lips. He couldn't help himself. She was so beautiful, and she was his! Finally!

Naomi, walking silently into the room, witnessed his adoration of the woman she had come to hate. Clearing her throat, she asked, "Is that all you're going to do? Just kiss her? I have something better in mind." Walking further into the room, she sat down on his lap, rubbing her hand across his chest, his back; down to his navel and beyond. Already in a semi aroused state from kissing his fantasy, his nature rose with her touch.

Turning his head to kiss Naomi fully in the mouth he uttered sweetly, "This is the prelude to my private fantasy, of which you play an essential role. I want to take you right here and now, but I need to take care of Yvonne first. Why don't you freshen up and then we can get started?"

With one last kiss, he departed the room to return to the car to hoist Yvonne over his shoulder, as he grabbed their remaining bags before heading back into the house.

Naomi, feeling pretty keyed up, decided to take a shower to relax. She was excited at what they were able to pull off. Anyone left on campus would only remember that she was taking her friends to the infirmary because of an upset stomach. Smiling in the mirror as she dried off, Naomi put on the sexy lingerie that she had recently purchased; ready for whatever Tim had in mind. *Tim was aroused just from a single touch of her hand! Imagine the possibilities that lay in store for them for the remainder of the night, she thought excitedly,* totally blocking out the fact that two other women were at the cabin against their will.

Chapter Eight

Upon arriving at the infirmary, TJ discovered that Erica and Yvonne had never made it to the infirmary. There wasn't a record of them ever checking in. Something suspicious was going on. Pulling his cellular phone from his waist clip, TJ contacted the Chief of Police. Mr. Peterson, this is Theodore James, sir. How are you? How's the family"

"Everyone is doing well TJ. What brings you to our campus or should I say who?" Mr. Peterson laughed.

"Everyone has jokes these days. Am I that transparent or is the hometown grapevine working overtime," TJ inquired?

"Only to someone, who's been in love with the same woman, for a very long time. What's up?"

"Sir, Erica and Yvonne are missing. Naomi took them somewhere, supposedly to the infirmary but they never showed up."

TJ went on to explain to the Chief, all the problems that Erica had gone through that the Chief was unaware of. The Chief then explained the altercation that he had been called to breakup that Erica had failed to mention to TJ or to her family.

"TJ, I'm headed your way. Meet me at Erica's room and we'll start from there. Do you want me to contact Erica's parents? Where is Max?"

"Erica's parents are in Hawaii on vacation and Max is overseas doing training. I'll contact them sir."

TJ questioned the young lady that helped him find the infirmary. "Ma'am, excuse my manners. I was so worried about Erica that I didn't get your name. I'm TJ, a close friend of Erica and Yvonne."

"So you're the one. Ummmm... My name is Mackenzie. Is there anything that I can do to help? I can ask the students on our floor if they recall anything out of the ordinary. Erica has been a good friend to me, so I want to do everything that I can to help."

"Do you happen to know the style, make and description of the car that they went off in?"

"Sure. She was driving her boyfriend's car. It's a tricked out, black, older model Mercedes with the license tag, NBA bound. Naomi's boyfriend is from your hometown if I'm not mistaken. She's always bragging about how the scouts are encouraging him to go pro at the end of this year."

Very softly, with danger evident in his voice, TJ asked, "Do you happen to know her boyfriend's name?" In the back of his mind, TJ already knew the answer; Tim, Erica's boyfriend from high school, who had ditched her the night of the Prom. How did he figure into the picture? It had to be him. He was the only one arrogant enough to put something like that on his license plate before he was actually drafted.

"Sure, it's Tim Mannes, the starting center for Duke."

"Mackenzie, thanks so much for all your help. I'm going to go back to her dorm room to wait on the Chief. If you remember anything else, let the Chief know. I would also appreciate your cooperation in keeping this quiet, at least until a press release has been issued. We don't know for sure what occurred and we don't want to falsely accuse someone of a crime," TJ cautioned. "Can I ask one last question before you leave? Why did you refer to me as "The One"?"

Breaking into a captivating smile, Mackenzie replied, "Her heart, her hero. You're the reason the guys here don't stand a chance. It's been nice meeting you."

Shaking his head in disbelief, TJ could only hope that he could play the hero once again to save his beloved. With despair in his heart he dreaded making the next set of calls.

"Hello, Mrs. Teal, this is TJ. I hate to bother you again but I have something very important to discuss with you and Mr. Teal. Can you conference in Mr. Teal?" Knowing Max's love of invention and gadgets, the cellular phones that his family had, were top of the line with features that were not yet available on the open market. He was just thankful that Max had installed video conferencing capabilities on their phones so that he could communicate with Erica's family all at one time. Max's original intention was that when his baby sister went off to college, she could talk to him or their parents, anytime, anywhere and feel like they were just in the other room.

"TJ, what's wrong? Does this have something to do with Princess?" Mr. Teal demanded in an agonized voice.

"Yes sir. I'm afraid that she's been taken somewhere by her roommate, Naomi. We have confirmed that Erica and Yvonne got into the car with Naomi, thinking that she was taking them to the infirmary for acute stomach pain, only they never made it. Due to the problems that existed between them, some known to you and some that the Chief just divulged, I know that Erica would not have willingly gone with her unless she was under duress or drugged."

A loud moan, more like a wail, could be heard from Mrs. Teal as she dropped the phone and began weeping. With an abrupt, "We'll be on the next flight out. Keep us informed!" from Mr. Teal, the call was disconnected as he sought to console his wife, who had sank onto her knees, sobbing uncontrollably only to grasp her husband's hand as he knelt with her, to lead them in prayer, asking God for his grace and mercy to keep their precious daughter safe, until she could be found. He knew that time was of the essence.

Shaken, upon hearing Mrs. Teal's sobs, TJ was determined to finish the next call without falling apart. He hated to hear a woman crying. To know that the woman in question was crying because of his beloved, it tore him apart. The next call wouldn't be any easier.

Picking up on the tenth ring, Maxmillian, or Max, as he was known to his friends, answered his phone.

"What's wrong TJ?" Max questioned foregoing the preliminaries, knowing that TJ would only call and put the urgent code in, if it was an utter emergency.

"Max, I'm afraid that Erica's been taken somewhere by her roommate, Naomi. We have confirmed that Erica and Yvonne got into the car with Naomi, thinking that she was taking them to the infirmary for acute stomach pain, only they never made it. Due to the problems that existed between them, some known to you and some that the Chief just divulged, I know that Erica would not have willingly gone with her unless she was under duress or drugged."

"How did this happen? I thought everything was under control, and Naomi had finally come to her senses. What happened? Was there any witnesses? Have you tried to call her on her cellular phone? Did it ring and go to voicemail or did it not pickup at all?" All of these questions Max fired at TJ after his initial gasp of disbelief.

TJ rushed to bring him up-to-date on all that he knew. "Max, please tell me that you have some sort of gadget that you've built that will help us find her; I mean them," spoke TJ in an agitated, weary voice. "I don't know what I would do if I lost her."

Knowing the strain that TJ must be in, loving his sister from afar, being her best friend, but not claiming her as he had wanted to do for so many years, Max relented with some of his questions.

"TJ, I do have some gadgets but they won't function from here. She has a tracking device in her phone that I installed before she went off to college. Also she has voice activated commands in her phone in the event she can't use her hands. Unfortunately, it will only work if her phone is turned on. I'll still in the process of developing the mechanism that will track her based solely on the power left in the battery. Just keep trying to contact her. That's our only hope right now. After you get finished with the Chief, I'll need you to go to my house to initiate the tracking signal. I'll have to pull some strings but I'll be on the next flight out. It's going to take me about six hours to get back to the states."

Walking back into the other bedroom, Naomi was shocked to see all that had transpired while she was taking a shower. Seeing the two women tied to the bed was appalling! In her absence, Tim had taken their escapade to a whole new level. What started out as an innocent joke now had turned deadly serious with dangerous repercussions.

Backing quietly from the room, without disturbing Tim, who had started to strip the women of their clothes, Naomi turned upon clearing the doorway, and ran swiftly to the other bedroom to contemplate her next course of action.

Upon entering the bedroom, Naomi, who was slightly out of breath, from having raced up the stairs, leaned on the door as she quickly locked it. This was more than she had bargained for. What should she do? Leave or help them escape?

Now that she saw what Tim was planning, Naomi didn't want anything to do with this charade. The original plan was just to scare them out of their wits by bringing them to the cabin and then leaving them to find their way back. Since they were knocked out from the drugs when they were brought to the cabin, it would be days before they were rescued. This little adventure was payback for Tim getting beat up after the Prom.

She had to think of a plan. Pacing back and forth in the bathroom, Naomi finally sat on the edge of the bathtub to think. What should she do? Leave by herself or help Erica and Yvonne escape? Considering the state that Tim was in, how enlarged he was, maybe she could use that as leverage. After all, that is why she came to the cabin, to use her feminine wares to get him to propose. It had been a minute since their last encounter.

Yes, that's what I'll do, thought Naomi. Tim was always more agreeable after a good night of sex. He would give her anything that she wanted. With him possibly going to the draft, she wanted to hang on to him as long as possible. No sense in messing up a good thing. Now that her decision was made, Naomi felt better. She would encourage Tim to let Erica and Yvonne go before he messed up his chances of going to the draft.

Kidnapping or rape wouldn't look good on his record prior to him being drafted. After he had been drafted, then all bets were off. He would have the money then to afford the best attorney if he got caught. If he wanted to replay this little scenario, then fine, let him, as long as she was an NBA wife with all the fame and wealth that went along with the title. She was good at staging things, having learned as a child from her mother. In her mind, Naomi was free from guilt. They were just playing a joke on a friend.

Even though Naomi thought that she had escaped without being noticed, her feminine scent gave her away. Tim detected her scent in the air when she entered the room as well as when she quickly departed the room. Looking at his clever handiwork, he checked everything to make sure he wouldn't be presented with any surprises. Smiling to himself, he pondered what her next move would be.

She couldn't escape; he had the keys to the car.

Leaving the house was impossible because he had fixed the locks on each door to only open once without a key. By returning to her room, she was now also imprisoned. Deciding that his goal here had been accomplished, he sauntered out of the room to deal with Naomi.

With a heavy tread, Tim walked nonchalantly upstairs to Naomi's bedroom door. Twisting the knob, he released a demonic laugh, after confirming his suspicions that the door was indeed locked.

"Naomi, are we about to play another game? There's no use hiding from me. I have the only key that will let you out of the room. See, this door has a two way lock. You can lock it from the inside but as the master keyholder, I can unlock it from the outside." Tim explained as he opened the door to find Naomi sitting on the bed pulling up the thigh-high stockings.

Deciding to bluff her way out of the perilous situation, until she could find a way to escape, Naomi finished pulling the stocking up her leg and attached it to the garter, showing as much leg as possible. "The door was locked for a reason Tim. I wanted to surprise you." Naomi said as she rose from the bed and walked over to the dresser.

Picking up her brush, she began to stroke her shoulder length hair with the brush, while showing her body to its best advantage in her skimpy negligee. In the past, this gesture seemed to stimulate Tim's sexual appetite. If she could just lull him into a false sense of security, she might be able to get away, thought Naomi, who was watching Tim with narrowed eyes, ready to defend herself with the lamp from the dresser if the need arose.

Seeing the glossy look in his eyes, Naomi began walking towards Tim with the intent of giving him exactly what he wanted so that when he went to sleep, she could escape. What was the use of letting all that adrenaline go to waste?

Wanting to see how far she would go or what she intended to do, Tim stood rooted to the spot; ever watchful of her hands and eyes.

Driven by her lust, midway to the point where Tim stood just outside of her reach, she pulled the top bow loose on her peignoir. One side fell open, to expose a two piece negligee of the sheerest fabric that he had ever seen.

It concealed yet taunted him.

As if in a striptease act, she released the other two ties that were holding the peignoir together. As the fabric slithered down her arms, to lay pooled at her feet, Tim pulled her to him and delivered a bruising kiss that was meant to teach her a lesson about tempting him. Knowing that her sexual appetite was very high, and when aroused, she had tunnel vision, Tim used that knowledge shrewdly. What she thought would be a fifteen minute interlude turned into something she was unprepared for...

Three hours later...

Upon awakening from their drug induced sleep, Erica and Yvonne immediately became conscious of three things. One, they were not at the infirmary; two, they were in a very precarious situation in an unfamiliar room, and three, danger was imminent.

Unless something drastic happened, a horrific ending was planned for their lives. Someone had gone to a lot of trouble to make sure that they were vulnerable, defenseless and powerless to stop the inevitable. Their horizontal, side by side positions on the king sized, four poster bed, which dominated the otherwise empty room, left little room for misinterpretation.

Somebody planned to accost them.

Lying in the middle of the bed, their outer limbs were tied with a heavy, thick rope, to the bed's headboard and footboard. Their other limbs which formed an X pattern on the bed, being bound together at the wrists and at the ankles, made it difficult to move.

Escaping was impossible.

With their hands and feet tied, their assailant had free reign over them.

Any upper body movement was unbearable because the ropes were tied extremely tight, however that didn't stop them from attempting to break free.

The person they thought was their friend now held them captive.

Hearing a sound that indicated that someone was coming, Erica motioned for Yvonne to stop squirming and to be still. With a nod of her head she pretended to still be asleep with her eyes closed and her head dropped over to the side. Yvonne followed suit, both praying that God would spare them and that the person responsible would not enter.

Tim, after having satisfied Naomi fully, probably for the first time since they had been sleeping together, in his haste to find something that would quench his thirst, left the door key on the nightstand. Going downstairs into the kitchen to get several beers, he decided to take a hot shower, before he made Erica and Yvonne suffer mentally and physically for the pain, the suffering and the embarrassment he received the night of their Prom.

Just before he went into the bathroom for his shower, he had to make sure that Naomi was still asleep. After walking into the room to make sure that she was still slumbering after his energetic and physical, almost brutal workout, with satisfaction, he retreated to the shower.

As soon as the shower could be heard running and enough time had elapsed for Tim to be standing under the soothing spray, Naomi jumped up from the bed and raced downstairs as fast as her bruises would allow...

Chapter Nine

Rushing into the room, Naomi tried to unloosen the ropes that bound Erica and Yvonne. Tim had tied the ropes too securely! Where was a knife when you needed one? Realizing that the kitchen was just a few feet away, she rushed through the doorway to see if any knives were on the countertop.

Yes! A butcher's block was located on the countertop, next to the refrigerator. Grabbing two knives, one which she held in her hand and the other which she hid in her socks, she raced back into the room.

Leaning over the footboard where the women's feet were securely tied together, Naomi worked feverishly with the knife to cut some of the knots free. She was only able to get one of the knots free on the rope that connected their legs. Racing against time, she then moved to the headboard where she untied the gag that covered their mouths and cut two of the knots on the rope that secured their joined hands, before Tim reentered the room.

"What are you doing Naomi?" Tim yelled, advancing towards his girlfriend, shaking her fiercely for five minutes before slapping her and knocking her to the ground. Tim, beside himself with rage, thought that she was attempting to kill Erica with the knife. No one would hurt her before he had a chance to sample her wares!

In the midst of shaking Naomi, the knife fell and hit Erica on the thigh, inadvertently hitting the cellular phone that was in her thigh pocket. The slight jar to her thigh was enough to turn the phone on. Thank God for a brother that loved gadgets, thought Erica. Max had modified her phone to include a video conferencing mechanism so that she could converse with him and her parents visually. He also had equipped the phone with voice activated controls; meaning the phone responded to voice commands to dial a number or send a text message.

With narrowed eyes, Tim stood over Naomi questioning her motives. "I asked you a question, Naomi. What were you doing?"

Standing to her feet, she tried reasoning with Tim, while Erica and Yvonne kept working on unloosening the ropes that bound their hands. "I was untying their hands and legs. They've been in that position long enough. You said that you only wanted them to be stranded here at the cabin on Lake Norman directly across from the pier. Besides, they need to go to the bathroom. Think of your career, Tim. If you rape them, your chances for going into the NBA are over."

"No one will know what happened here, because no one will be alive to tell the story. Naomi, hand me those pills on the table. After they take these pills, they will be clamoring for me to make love to them. I might suggest that you take one for yourself. I've taken a Viagra pill and I'm ready to sample what they denied me on Prom Night."

Picking up the knife, Tim moved to the footboard and tugged on the ropes, to make sure that they were still sufficiently tight enough to prevent movement. Next he moved to the headboard to check the ropes that bound their hands but he was sidetracked as he gazed at Erica's lush lips. Bending forward, he brushed his lips against Erica's only to be bitten as his lips connected with hers. An attempt to head butt Tim, only succeeded in providing a glancing blow to the side of his head.

With a slight grimace of pain, he then held her head still as he placed a bruising kiss on her closed mouth as he brushed the knife against Erica's skin. Up and down her leg the knife traveled until it came to rest at the bend of her knee. With one swipe of the blade, a tiny prick of blood appeared on the knife.

At her wince of pain, he laughed. "That's for not cooperating. You are finally mine! No one knows where you are. I WILL have my way with you before the night is over!" Licking the knife with his tongue, he walked towards the kitchen to retrieve some ice to apply to his busted lip as well as a towel to eliminate any blood that could be used as evidence.

"Naomi, give them the pills. My patience is running out. You have exactly five minutes to do as I ask or you will face the same result as them."

Seeing that Tim had lost all reason, and seemed to be quite capable of committing murder, Naomi, who wanted to live, did as she was told.

When Max arrived back in the States eight hours later, due to a delayed flight, TJ met him at the airport. Max's parents arrived from Hawaii, within twenty minutes of Max's flight. After brief hugs from everyone, TJ brought them up to speed on their progress as they were driving to Max's house.

"TJ, I want to thank you for everything that you've done thus far in trying to locate my princess. I'm glad that your uneasiness caused you to leave Chapel Hill earlier than planned. Without you acting on your instinct, your feeling of apprehension, we would not have known for several days that Erica was missing."

"Sir, how did you know that's what had happened?"

"Erica had informed us that you would take her and Yvonne home this weekend. For you to contact me just to confirm that everything was all right was out of the ordinary. We began initiating plans then to return. That's about the time that you called back to notify us that Erica was abducted."

"Max, what about the video conferencing mechanism in Erica's phone. Can we use that to try to contact her?" Mrs. Teal asked.

"Yes Momma we can, as long as she has her phone on. When TJ tried to contact her earlier, it wasn't on. That in itself alerted him that something wasn't right."

As soon as the car pulled into the parking space, Max jumped out and hurried up the steps to his luxurious house, followed closely by his parents and TJ. Once inside, he went to one of the spare bedrooms that was actually his command central. It was filled with a lot of his gadgets and inventions, some of which he had received patents for and had sold to various companies for huge sums of money.

Flipping several switches and typing commands into others, the entire wall that housed a theater like movie screen, came to life. To keep herself busy, Mrs. Teal went into the kitchen to fix everyone something to eat.

Looking at a light beeping on his instrument panel, Max was able to detect that Erica's Blackberry phone was now on. Because the phone was turned on, by running a series of commands, Max was able to start tracking Erica's cellular phone signal using GPS receivers. The GPS receivers would measure the distance of her phone's signal to the nearest mobile tower or masts, the length of time it takes to reach the tower and the signal strength. Subsequently after receiving that calculation the position would then be plotted on a map. This would then give them a basis point for the beginning of their search.

After gathering all the data, Max was able to pinpoint the location of the tracking signal just outside of Charlotte, North Carolina, near Lake Norman. To reach Lake Norman, it would take approximately three to four hours of driving time from their current location, depending on who was driving.

Mrs. Teal, after receiving the signal location telephoned the airlines for flight information. She confirmed that a commercial flight, first class, non-stop would take only fifty-two minutes to Charlotte from RDU (Raleigh/Durham Airport). Unfortunately none were available for that evening. A non commercial flight with layovers would take approximately five hours. They didn't have that kind of time to wait for a commercial flight. Mr. Teal, while Max was working on the signal, called in a few favors to get a private jet to immediately take them to Charlotte. Luckily, Max's information could be downloaded to a laptop computer.

While flying to Charlotte from Raleigh, Max and TJ thought it best to use the telephone's microphone in order to "hear" the conversation between Erica and Yvonne and her captors, Naomi and Tim. Simultaneously, TJ typed in a series of commands at Max's instruction to use the video conferencing tool to project the interior image of the room onto the screen, where Erica was being kept.

Everything was black. Either she had the phone covered with some type of cloth or the phone was in her pocket. Mr. Teal then asked his son if he had finished developing the program whereby the phone could replay past conversations that the microphone would have taped since the unit had been turned on.

"Yes Dad. I installed the program the last time Erica was home but I haven't tested it yet."

"Right now son, this may be our only opportunity."

Listening to the replay of their captors previous conversations, confirmed their worst fears. Erica had been hurt and could potentially be bleeding. Mrs. Teal didn't want to think of the other atrocities that could occur if they didn't get to them in time. Their rescue was more important now than ever. Erica was a bleeder. The tiniest little cut could bleed just as much as if a major artery was cut. Most of the time, she would have to be rushed to a hospital to receive a shot in order to stop the bleeding.

With a sense of rage, TJ angrily paced back and forth on the jet while Max muttered to himself all of the terror tactics that he would use on Tim once he found him.

Cooler heads needed to prevail.

"Max, TJ, calm down. We need to devise a plan to locate the cabin that they are in. Tim isn't too smart. He thinks that he is above the law. I'm sure that he used his credit cards to plan all of this."

"Dad, I've already spoken to Trevor. He's tracing any credit card usage from Naomi and Tim in the past two weeks. I'm sure we'll hear something from him soon." Trevor was Max's computer hacker friend that had infiltrated the US Government's computers at an early age and had subsequently landed a job in computer security to build better safeguards against future hackers.

As soon as Max finished speaking, his cellular phone rang. Trevor had isolated the credit card usage to a gas station in Lake Norman which was just eighteen miles northwest of Charlotte. Unfortunately this luxurious community of over five hundred and twenty miles was spread across four counties. Pointing to a map on his computer, Max, thinking like a criminal, deduced that Tim would have taken them to an isolated cabin in the most populous community, which was Huntersville. He probably had use of the cabin from one of the boosters that was plying him with money in return for representing him after he became an NBA player.

Max had Trevor then trace all known property holders in that area for prominent boosters or people affiliated with the NBA. Mrs. Teal, who had been quiet up until that point, questioned whether or not they wanted to get the police involved. Both Mr. Teal and Max assured her that the police and the FBI were already working behind the scenes. A special consideration had been given to Max to work with the FBI during the summer months after he graduated from college and was serving his mandatory four year military term. His unique inventions and his knack for locating missing persons during his reconnaissance missions had previously served him well. He just hoped that those same skills would come into play now to help save his sister and her best friend...

Chapter Ten

Taking the pill of Ecstasy that Tim had given her, Naomi walked over to Erica to place the pill in her mouth. With her back to Tim, Naomi held her hand in front of Erica's mouth to keep the pill from being spit out. Silently she mouthed for her to pretend to swallow and she would catch the pill in between her two fingers. It was a trick she learned when she was little when her mother used to give her pills. She had a selfish intent for not giving them the pills. She didn't want them to enjoy their time with Tim. If he had to hurt them then so be it.

"You won't get away with this Tim!" was all that Erica could say before Naomi acted like she was crushing the pill in her mouth. Repeating the same procedure with Yvonne, Naomi then turned towards Tim for his approval.

"What do you want me to do now?" she asked.

"I want you to sit and watch," he replied. Never in his wildest dreams would he suspect that Naomi would betray him, thought Tim. However, just in case she had any ideas, he decided to throw a caveat into the mix.

"Naomi, you know that this is my last fling before we get married, don't you. I realize that I can't live without you. I wanted to prove to you that I'm over this obsession for good.

That's why you're here. Once this is over, we'll be married and enjoy the good life."

"Are you serious," she exclaimed?

"Yes, and I even brought you a ring. Come here."

Reaching inside of his pants pocket, he produced a one carat white gold, diamond solitaire. "When I make it to the pros, I'll get you a bigger ring; one that you can pick out."

Jumping up and down, she couldn't contain herself. She threw her arms around Tim's neck. Yes! They were going to get married after this was over! "You can do what you want with them this last time." Naomi replied as she gave Tim a long lingering kiss. She didn't care as long as she could live the lifestyle that she wanted.

Grimacing with the pain that she no longer could hide, as she tried to free herself, Yvonne, cried, "Naomi, have you lost your mind? Don't you see that he's playing you? That he's just using you to get your cooperation? What about Erica? How can you stand there and watch her bleeding? Please help us escape! Do you honestly believe that he will let you live after being a witness to everything that's he done here at this Lake Norman cabin straight across from the pier? Or better yet, what makes you think that he won't try to pin all of this on you? Technically, you were the one that brought us here. Think about that as you wear his ring." With a vicious slap, Tim snapped Yvonne's head to the side.

"Ooooh. I love it when you get physical!" Grasping the hand that he used to mistreat Yvonne, Naomi kissed it tenderly. Naomi then turned to Tim. "I need to go to the store to get some champagne and some other items. You don't want to create any babies here. We're going to celebrate." Dashing towards the door and grabbing her handbag off the kitchen countertop, Naomi was halfway through the door before Tim stopped her.

"Make sure that you are not followed and that you use cash for your purchases. If you are not back in twenty minutes then the movie that I created showing your part in this and your part in killing these women will be played on every news station in the South within thirty minutes. At that point, every cop and FBI agent will be swarming this part of the country to find you. Now as my wife, you won't be able to testify against me. Your choice. Make the right one."

Tim then turned around dismissing Naomi to get back to the business at hand. In his twisted mind, he wanted them to fight back to heighten his sense of arousal. Holding the knife in one hand, he bent towards their feet that was connected, and cut the ropes. Next he cut the ropes that secured their feet to the bedposts.

Afraid to move for fear that he would cut them with the knife, Erica and Yvonne remained motionless until they could judge what his next move would be. It didn't take them long to ascertain his next move. Tim stripped right before their eyes without any sense of shame. They couldn't believe his actions! Whatever drug he had taken had stimulated him to a degree that looked painful.

With the knife poised in an extremely precarious position, against Erica's navel, Tim began to cut the buttons from her pants, knicking her here and there as the buttons popped loose. He had only removed the top portion of their clothes previously.

Erica and Yvonne fervently cried aloud their prayers to God to rescue them and to diminish Tim's manhood before he had a chance to accost them. On one accord, with their feet free, they put their legs around him in a bear hold, squeezing with all their might, until he was forced to drop the butcher knife. Then with a swift knee by Yvonne to the groin, and an upper cut by Erica, Tim fell to the side, gasping in pain.

Using a cheerleader move, they jack-knifed into a headstand, and twisted off the bed, like a round-off cartwheel, into a standing position. Thereby forcing the ropes to pull apart and break that previously held their hands together in the middle of the bed. Suffering broken arms were a small price to pay for breaking free.

The consequences would have been worse, by far.

With no time to spare, they ran out of the bedroom, down the stairs to the front door. It was locked from the outside. They couldn't open it no matter how hard they tried. Frantically searching for another way out, they ran to the kitchen to try the back door. It wouldn't budge. Something was blocking the door from the outside.

Since Tim was advancing on them, they grabbed the tablecloth from the dining room table and tore it in half. Wrapping the piece of tablecloth around their heads, they ran straight through the Palladium style window that spanned the entire dining room of the cabin and broke it. Landing in a heap on the ground, they were slow to get up after being cut in several places by the shards of glass that lay on the ground beneath them. Looking back towards the cabin, they could see that Tim was hurriedly attempting to pull on his shirt and pants.

Yvonne and Erica then helped each other up and proceeded to run towards the densely populated woods that were located at the rear of the backyard. Erica's blood, however, left a pathway for him to follow. Since nightfall was fast approaching, Tim stopped at the garage to grab a flashlight and a gun. With the blood drops as his guide, finding them wouldn't be a problem. There were several small sheds about a half a mile away that they could find shelter in. They would have to take shelter in one of them in order for Erica to rest, based on the amount of blood that she was losing.

Ten minutes later, the police picked up Naomi at the local gas station and she led them back to the house. She was caught because she had attempted to use her credit cards to purchase the items that she needed since in her rush, she left all of her cash back at the cabin and the store's teller machine was down. Sensing that she was about to be arrested, Naomi decided that her best acting ability would come into play as she concocted a story about the weekend rendezvous that her boyfriend had planned at a nearby cabin. She demanded to know why they were detaining her.

The police burst into the house, only to discover that no one was there. Upon inspecting all the bedrooms in the house, it was discovered that someone was injured and had been bleeding for quite some time; judging by the pool of blood on the bed and the drops of blood that led to the backyard.

After finding the blood on the bed, Max examined the pattern of the blood and concluded that the blood was from a topical wound. With little time to spare, Max and TJ immediately struck out into the woods that they noticed when they surveyed the house, to find Erica and Yvonne. Both simmering with rage, they hunted the culprit with deadly intent.

Running swiftly as their legs would carry them, resting every ten minutes, Erica and Yvonne ran deeper into the woods only stopping to staunch the flow of blood from Erica's navel and legs. Hearing footsteps behind them, they ran harder than ever before. Looking behind them to judge the distance between their attacker, they didn't see the shift in the terrain. Just as a bullet whizzed by Yvonne's ear, from the gun that Tim fired, the shift in the terrain caused them to go tumbling hard, down the hill, snagging their limbs on trees and rocks, as they eventually landed at the bottom of a ravine.

Injured, battered and bruised, with broken arms, and unforeseen internal problems, both women were too disoriented to move right away. After getting their bearings, and realizing that danger was still imminent, they crawled to their knees in an effort to stand upright. Getting up was extremely painful and complicated. Erica, unable to continue as pain threatened to engulf her, asked Yvonne to continue without her.

"Yvonne, go find help. I can't continue. The pain is too great. I've got to find something out here to stop the flow of blood. This tourniquet isn't working. The loss of blood is making me nauseous and the pain is intolerable," Erica panted as she leaned against a tree for support.

"We're in this together, friend. If I go, you go. If you stay, I stay and we'll face this together. Do you think that Tim will give up now that we're down here and he has no way of getting to us unless he falls down this ravine too?" Yvonne moaned as she grabbed her abdomen in pain.

Lunging forward, she forgot about her pain as Erica slumped in a heap to the ground. Eyes glazed with pain, she whispered again for Yvonne to go get help. Not willing to leave her friend at the mercy of a lunatic, Yvonne began the arduous task of pulling Erica to her feet.

Frantically searching around them for an escape route, they half shuffled, half staggered, slowly toward the small bush of trees to their immediate left that would provide some cover, when a rustle in the bushes was heard. Frightened, they froze. Gazing upward toward the top of the ravine, they were startled to find that Tim was looking down at them with a gun in his hands.

Just as Tim took aim and pressed the gun's trigger two successive times, TJ dived from the bushes and soared through the air, to position himself in front of Erica and Yvonne. The bullet that was intended to kill Erica instead hit TJ in the shoulder. The other bullet aimed a bit lower to Yvonne who had staggered backwards hit a snake that was several feet away.

Erica's moan of despair could be heard for miles around. Fearing the worst, she crawled to the spot where TJ landed and cradled his head in her lap. Crying profusely, she apologized over and over to him for leading him into danger.

"TJ, I'm sorry, so sorry for what happened to you. Can you forgive me?" Bending over his body in a weak attempt to staunch the flow of blow that was spilling forth from his shoulder and giving no thought to her own injuries, she kissed his lips ardently.

The pain was so great that responding to her kiss was difficult but TJ tried with all his might to kiss her with the pent up emotion that he had stored away for what seemed like years. Exhausted, he fell back to her lap, trying desperately to talk, as he drew his last breath. Erica leaned closer to understand his whispered declaration.

"Erica, although this isn't the best time to tell you this, I have to before I leave this earth. I love you with every fiber of my being, with my heart, mind, body and soul. I want to marry you, if you'll have me."

In the next instant, TJ collapsed.

Simultaneously as the shots were fired, Max, at the top of the ravine, who had advanced on Tim from his weak side, placed a roundhouse kick to Tim's arm to send his gun to the ground, far into the thicket, out of reach.

Recovering quickly, Tim turned in his fury to the person that made him miss his target. "What the.....?" Realizing that the person that stopped him was Max, Erica's brother, he adopted his second plan of action. "Max, what are you doing? You could have made me kill them! I was trying to save their lives. That snake was about to strike. Thankfully I had my gun with me," Tim responded innocently. "How did you find me? I was so worried that Naomi would harm them. Luckily I was able to get her to leave and then I was able to rescue them."

"Save it for someone who will believe you." With disbelief, Max commenced to delivering a beat-down that was worse than the one Tim had suffered the night of the Prom. The only thing that saved Tim from being beaten to death was the arrival of the police who instantly pulled Max away.

Chapter Eleven

Erica and Yvonne were taken to the hospital for an extensive examination, while TJ was immediately taken into surgery to remove the bullet from his chest. Yvonne's immediate prognosis from the ER doctor was that she had suffered some internal injuries to her stomach. She would have to undergo a series of X-Ray's to determine the extent of the damage that was done when she fell down the ravine.

Because Erica had lost so much blood during the ordeal and continued to lose blood once she was admitted to the hospital, the doctor feared that she would need a blood transfusion. Knowing that their God answered prayers and that by his stripes, we are healed; the family huddled together to pray for their daughter, Yvonne and TJ. Their prayer was for their mind and bodies to be healed and restored.

Just as soon as they had completed their prayers, the doctor hurried into the waiting room to announce that they would have to operate immediately on Erica in order to stop the internal bleeding. Turning her head into her husband's shoulder, Mrs. Teal softly cried as she tried to gather some of his strength to deal with this new series of events. Mr. Teal hugged his wife as he led her to a seat, murmuring soft words of encouragement that the Lord would not have brought her through one ordeal without making a way for her to survive the next one. He admonished her that their faith was just being tested but that they would not give up on God.

At that moment the waiting room's doors opened to reveal TJ's parents, his sister Nicole and Yvonne's mother. They had been contacted as TJ was being carted off to the hospital. To soothe their fears, Mr. Teal brought TJ's parents up to speed on his condition. Luckily the bullet that struck him didn't hit any major arteries so his prognosis was good, barring any infections. Since Yvonne was in another examination room and not in surgery, Mrs. Parks quickly left to attend to her daughter, with a promise that she would check back with them for Erica and TJ's status.

Shortly thereafter, Max's former girlfriend Chelsea, quickly strode through the doors into the waiting room. She immediately walked to where Max was standing over by the window, seemingly lost to all that was around him. Just as she neared him, he turned towards her, as if sensing her presence. Words were unnecessary as she walked into his open arms. Even though she wasn't supposed to be there, he was glad that she was. He needed to draw on her strength, to loose himself in her comfort.

Max felt as if the world stood still as he embraced Chelsea. It had been too long since he had seen her. Cupping her face in his hands, he whispered brokenly his desire for her as he lowered his lips to kiss her luscious mouth. The kiss was so searing, so provocative, that Chelsea had to grab a hold of Max's shoulders for support as she melted against his body. Only the sound of the hospital's intercom system, brought Max back to his senses.

Releasing her mouth, he rested his forehead upon hers. It took all of his control to remember where he was and why he had brought the kiss to a stop. His sister was having surgery and whatever was going to happen between him and Chelsea had to wait, at least until he was sure Erica and TJ would survive. Taking her hand, he led her to the couch where his mother and father waited along with his godparents.

Before they approached the couch, Max asked, "How did you know what happened and that I would be here?"

Looking a little apprehensive, Chelsea answered, "Your mother texted me that you needed me so I came right away."

Looking over Chelsea's head, Max stared at the woman who had given birth to him. She was amazing! Even though she was just as distraught, she was always thinking of others.

His parents welcomed Chelsea with open arms. Knowing that the decision to end the relationship had been Max's idea, because of his line of work, they understood that there was still some unfinished business between their son and the love of his life. Chelsea's arrival proved that along with the scorching kiss that they witnessed. Mrs. Teal fanned herself, as a brief smile rested upon her mouth. She knew what it felt like to be branded. Her husband's kisses and touch were still so sensual, so erotic, even after twenty five years of marriage, that she oftentimes wondered how they survived when they came together.

Sending another prayer to God for Max to realize all that he had lost, Mrs. Teal arose from the couch to hug Chelsea tightly. Chelsea returned the hug fiercely while mouthing "thank you" silently. It wasn't a secret that they hoped Max and Chelsea would get back together. Until then, they would continue to treat her as a beloved member of the family.

With a pat to her son's face, Max's mother spoke candidly, "This operation is Erica's second chance at life. Max, please take this opportunity for your second chance." She then moved back to her resting position beside her husband.

His mother knew him so well, thought Max. She knew that he had thrown himself into his work in an effort to forget about Chelsea. To forget about his decision to end their relationship because of the nature of his job. During their active duty service, Max and his childhood friend Frank, who were pilots as well as members of the Special Forces Unit, were called to various hot spots all over the world; Panama, Grenada, Kuwait and Iraq for Operation Desert Storm. Their superior training caused them to participate in many reconnaissance missions.

It was during these missions that Max and Frank honed their investigative skills. If anyone could find military personnel missing in action, it was them. When their active duty term was nearing an end, they were recommended for a job with the Bureau because of their outstanding service record. Frank immediately accepted the position. Max however did not accept the position until Chelsea's rejection devastated him so completely that he needed to get as far away as possible from the life that he had known. The Bureau provided him an opportunity to do just that. Both men pushed themselves into their jobs and became the Bureau's leading detective task team for international affairs.

Maybe it was time to help heal some wounds from the past.

Several hours later the doctor came into the waiting room with good news. They were able to stop Erica's internal bleeding and she was recuperating in the Recovery Room. She was still in intensive care but stable. Barring any other complications she should be moved out of intensive care in a couple of days. A loud Halleluiah was heard throughout the waiting room while several family members were dancing with joy for God's miracle.

The doctor that performed the surgery for TJ made his entrance while everyone was celebrating. Smiling, he advised the group that more celebrating could be done because TJ was also out of surgery and expected to make a full recovery. He was moved to a private room where he was stabilized.

Yvonne was the only person from the ordeal that didn't need surgery. She did however have to get a cast put on her arm from the fall down the ravine. However, after attempting to get up from the examining room table to go home, she collapsed from acute stomach pain. Panic seized the examining room. Doctors rushed in trying to figure out what could be wrong that the X-Ray's didn't reveal. Was it her appendix? Was she too suffering from internal bleeding? Was she hemorrhaging? Was irreparable damage done to her uterus? Only time would tell. She had to spend several days in the hospital before they were able to figure out the cause of the pain.

Suffering from jet lag and after retrieving dinner from the cafeteria for his parents and godparents, Max decided to go home to straighten things out with Chelsea and to get some rest. Kissing his mother goodbye with instructions to call if Erica or TJ took a turn for the worse, he quietly left the hospital, walking hand in hand with Chelsea, who drove them to his house.

Pulling into the parking lot at his house, Chelsea parked her car in the driveway. Unfastening his seatbelt, Max leaned over to give Chelsea a quick kiss on her succulent lips. "Thanks for bringing me home. Do you have a minute for us to talk?"

"Are you sure that's what you want to do after everything that you've been through? Why not wait until things have settled down a little bit?" Chelsea asked trying to prolong the moment when she would have to confess that while she had never stopped loving him during the years of his absence; she was carrying another man's child.

"Yes, I'm positive. Although the question I should be asking is do you have someone else in your life right now even though you came to be with me in my time of need?"

"Not anymore."

"Please come in so that we can talk."

Knowing that a future or closure would not be impossible without the truth, Chelsea relented and stepped out of the car.

As they walked up the driveway to Max's house, Chelsea said a prayer that God would give her the strength to tell Max the truth and that eventually he would forgive her. Once inside, Max led Chelsea to the living room to sit down on the couch.

Now that they were both in the same room, things seemed a little awkward at first. Taking the initiative, Max reached out to hold Chelsea's hands in his.

"First, I want to apologize for the way I acted the last time I saw you when I demanded that you forget about the person in your life and go away with me. That was selfish of me and I hope that you can forgive me. I saw your actions as a denial of my love and I was hurt. Consequently I reacted to that hurt with anger. I wanted to hurt you just as you had hurt me; so I left thinking that you would stop me. When you didn't I figured you had made your choice."

Getting up from the couch, Chelsea exclaimed as she paced back and forth, "Max, it was never my intention to hurt you. I was simply trying to do what I felt was right about telling the person I was currently seeing that everything was over. When you left I assumed that you were playing; that you would turn around. That night I thought that I had lost you forever. When you didn't call back to apologize or to discuss what happened, I tried to put the past behind me and move forward with my life."

Coming to his feet to stand behind her, Max gently placed his hands on Chelsea's shoulders as he turned her around to face him.

"Believe me, I've had several months to understand how you may have felt. It's been replaying over and over in my mind. I just didn't know how to repair the damage that I had done. I wasn't even sure if you would speak to me so subsequently I put off calling trying to find the right way to approach you. Thank God my mother saw fit to help me."

Feeling the need to touch him, unconsciously Chelsea ran her fingers up and down Max's chest. She had to be completely honest with him. Chelsea pondered for a moment how to tell him all that had transpired after he left. "Max, I'm afraid you don't understand all that occurred when you left."

"Then baby help me to understand."

"That night and the subsequent days, weeks and months were rough. I had lost you and damaged a good relationship with someone that I felt I could be happy, content with. I just wanted someone that was safe, stable and that was good to me."

"All the things you felt that I wasn't, correct? What about love Chelsea? Were you willing to live without that?" Max questioned bleakly.

"In a way yes. You were gone for four years, well three and a half years in the military. After you chose to end our relationship that awful night, I went to visit Alex to explain what happened. Our relationship continued. I guess he thought that he could make me forget you. But it never happened and consequently our relationship was stormy at best, because he felt that he could never live up to your standards."

"Are you still seeing him?"

"No, we had a major disagreement that caused our relationship to end."

"What type of disagreement, if I may ask?"

Deciding to plunge right in, Chelsea confessed, "I'm pregnant and the doctor confirmed that I'm six weeks pregnant. Before you say anything, let me explain. Before Erica had her surgery, you knew that I had been involved with someone, after you ended our relationship. Well it seems that I became pregnant a month or so before you came back. When I told you that I wasn't seeing that person anymore it was the truth. We're not together because he asked was I still in love with you and I couldn't lie any longer and I told tell him that yes I was. He then said that he was tired of competing with a ghost and that if I still loved you then that I should do something about it."

At the swollen silence that was in the room, Chelsea rambled on, "If I had any idea that I was pregnant, I wouldn't have slept with you. That would have been unfair to do that and know what I know now, without telling you first. I'm sorry. If you want me to leave, I understand."

Max just looked at Chelsea like he was hearing impaired or was in a state of shock. He couldn't believe what she had just told him. If that was the case, then that meant that the guy that she chose to go to after his ultimatum, was the same person that was the father of her child. To clarify his thoughts, he choked out, "Who is the father and why isn't he here with you?"

She looked away for a brief moment as if to gain some courage, she turned back and whispered, "Alex."

"Don't tell me that's the same guy that you chose over me."

"Unfortunately it is."

"I hate you for this. No, I could never hate you but I am hurt even though we were not officially back together then. It seems that we are victims of bad timing. What are you going to do?"

"Well the father doesn't want to have the child, so I guess I'll raise the child by myself."

"Chelsea, you should take him to court to make sure that he supports you because you didn't make the baby alone. If he's any kind of man, he'll do it without having to go through the courts.

"I'd rather he just drop off the face of the earth. I won't force him to acknowledge his child.

"Given that you're just getting out of a relationship, how did you come to be here?"

"I received the text from your mother that you needed me and felt like God was intervening in my life, so I came. What do we do now?" Chelsea asked as she looked into Max's eyes momentarily before casting her eyes downward in an attempt to hide the tears that seemed to always be present.

"That's up to you. It's obvious to both of us that we still have very strong feelings for each other. Do you want to explore those feelings or do you want to leave the past in the past?" Max asked hoping that she would see that a relationship with him was now possible.

"I want to explore the feelings that are still in my heart."

"Let's discuss this further. What I would like to do, you know, in your current position you can't."

"Why not?"

"Because it wouldn't be right, not if you and the father are getting back together."

"Rest assured that once he told me to have an abortion, there wasn't anything left."

"Well I am tired. I just drove from Georgia. Can we lay down and rest?" Max asked as he started to yawn.

"Sure," Chelsea said as she went to get some blankets and a pillow for Max to share the guest bedroom.

"Chelsea, wait. Stay here with me for awhile," Max said as he rested on the duvet. Grasping her hand, he pulled her down beside of him. "I can't say that I'm pleased that you're pregnant with another man's child. I would be lying if I said that I wasn't.. However you did that while I was gone. I'm the one that's accountable for you seeing someone else in the first place. Now if the child was mine, it would be a different story. By the way, how many months are you?"

"Six weeks."

"Are you sure that the baby isn't mine?" Max asked calculating the last time that they had made love.

"What do you mean?"

"If I remember correctly, I was here two months ago on leave for the last time before my final six months left in military."

"You're right, but I was, according to the doctor already pregnant then.

"Are you positive that it's not mine?"

"Yes, I'm sure even though I wish that it was yours."

As they stretched out on the bed, Max started to run his hand over her abdomen. Gently caressing her belly, he told Chelsea how sorry he was that he had stayed away all those months. How he wished that the life that was growing inside of her was his.

"Chelsea, even though you are carrying another man's child, I'm here for you. You only started another relationship after ours ended. It was unreasonable for me to expect you to remain celibate and not move forward with your life. As much as I wanted to forget you, I couldn't. I still love you. Nothing has changed that. I don't resent you or your unborn child. Because your child is apart of you, I will love it also. Don't shut me out. Let me be apart of your life.

"Max just hold me. Make me feel loved and cherished like you used too. I just want to feel right now. Since you left, it's been hard in more ways than one. I just want to start over. Is that possible?"

"Yes Chelsea. Let me show you how life can be. But promise me that you will make him support his child."

"I promise."

"Now come here and let me love you from head to toe."

Sweeping Chelsea into his arms, he walked towards his bedroom, kissing her passionately with an ever increasing ardor as he gloried in the fact that all was not lost and the love they felt for each other would be given a second chance.

    Since Max had gotten special permission to leave to help rescue Erica, he had to leave within two days to return overseas to continue his top secret mission. With a kiss and a prayer he was off again to serve his country. Max and Chelsea conversed at every opportunity since his sister's recovery even though he had six more months left before his military career would end. Chelsea and Erica became good friends while Erica recovered from her wounds. It was almost like having a little sister around. Max's parents were elated that their son seemed to have restored his relationship with Chelsea.

    Several days after Max left, Chelsea began experiencing problems with the baby. Coming out of the bathroom that evening, Chelsea slowly walked to the kitchen to get a drink of ginger ale. It was the only thing that seemed to help with the nausea. She couldn't understand what was wrong with her. When she was first pregnant, she never had morning sickness; now all of a sudden it was every day for every meal. Plus she was spotting. *"I'm going to have to go to the doctor to see if there's anything wrong,"* she thought. *"I'm in way to much pain for to this to be normal."*

    After closing the refrigerator door, Chelsea turned around to head to the bedroom when she felt a fierce, sharp pain in her abdomen that doubled her over in pain. As she tried to get up, another sharp pain stabbed her, sending her to the floor in agony. Clutching her stomach in misery, crying profusely, fearful that she was losing her baby, Chelsea laid on the floor, in too much pain to move. One of God's angels must have been watching over her, because the telephone started ringing. Praying for strength, she crawled to the kitchen to pick up the telephone. Holding her head near the receiver, she could only cry out, "Help" before she collapsed.

    Luckily, her sister Ryan was the one that was calling. She rushed over to her house and opened the door with her house key.

On the way she took precautionary measures to call 911 for an ambulance. Chelsea was barely conscious when they arrived.

At the hospital, when asked if several tests could be run, Ryan admitted that Chelsea was pregnant so the tests would be limited to prevent undue radiation from harming the baby. After a medical examination was completed it was ruled that Chelsea had a severe case of indigestion. Giving her something mild to soothe the indigestion, she was able to go home after several hours. When inquiring about the spotting, the doctor told her to check with her regular physician as soon as possible. Sometimes it was normal in the beginning stages of pregnancy for that to occur.

When Chelsea visited her doctor the following week, she told them about her experience the previous week at the Emergency Room. To make sure that the baby was alright, her doctor wanted to perform a complete checkup. After the examination, she inquired whether or not, Chelsea had experienced any pain or spotting during that weekend.

Surprised, Chelsea admitted that she had. The doctor then informed her that it was possible that she was going through a miscarriage. She wanted to take another pregnancy test just to make sure. After submitting to a urine test, the doctor came back with a negative reading which confirmed her suspicions that in fact a miscarriage had occurred. Not trusting the urine test, the doctor wanted to perform a blood test just to be on the safe side. The blood test came back positive.

When asked how they could get different readings from two different tests, the doctor replied, "I trust the blood tests over any urine test. Honey you are still pregnant. However your due date has been pushed back. You're not as far along as I had estimated."

Going home, Chelsea didn't think anything about what had occurred. The baby was fine and she felt better having visited her doctor.

Chapter Twelve

Erica and Yvonne, after their recovery tried to put their life back together. With counseling and the grace of God, they managed to complete the semester with good grades. Luckily with parents as educators, and uncles as well known attorneys and the NBA not wanting any negative publicity, they were able to keep their nightmare out of the papers. After a brief recovery in the hospital, they were able to return to school and not miss a beat.

TJ decided not to pressure Erica about his feelings considering that her emotional state of mind was very fragile. She needed time to heal. He made a vow while recuperating in the hospital that he would become an integral part of her healing process. As long as he had air to breathe, he would help her heal and in time he prayed that he would be able to declare his feelings again. In due time, he felt that she would be able to reciprocate them.

On the other hand, Erica was at first confused as to why TJ was back to acting like the brotherly TJ instead of the man that professed his love. Jumping to the wrong conclusion, she felt as if TJ didn't want her anymore because he thought that she had actually gotten raped. She just didn't know how to confront him with her suspicions or even if her suspicions were right. He still spent time with her, made her feel loved and secure but none of the sexual overtones were there that she had become used too.

"Missy, did you ever think that he's waiting on you to let him know that you want to move beyond the barrier that you've created?" Her conscience often asked.

Sure she had been the victim of a set of unfortunate events but through counseling, she had come to terms with it. She was ready to move past being the victim to being a survivor and taking back control over her life and living victoriously through Christ Jesus. Therefore she would complete her degree early and start working in her field. Maybe by then she would figure out how to live without TJ if that was possible.

Back to the present several years later...

"Wow, what an incredible story," spoke Sasha as she held Erica and Yvonne's hands in hers, giving them extra support to continue and hopefully complete their journey towards healing. Sniffles could still be heard, as they made an effort to control their emotions.

"What happened after TJ was shot and Max beat Tim up for attempted rape and murder?"

Angry all over again at the injustice of the court system, Erica replied, "Tim managed to get off on a technicality. Since he didn't actually rape us, he was just charged with a misdemeanor for aiding Naomi in pulling off a prank."

Yvonne then added, "He had the entire scenario well planned and arranged. There was a video that he created that showed us willingly getting into a car with Naomi, even though we were doubled over in pain. He even had sound footage where Naomi was recorded as offering to take us to the infirmary and the clips of where we went inside but decided not to stay because the infirmary was full. We then decided to go to an Urgent Care facility. After leaving that facility with sample prescriptions for the pain, which was food poisoning, the video showed us taking some pills after which we fell asleep."

Picking up the story as Yvonne became emotional again, Erica relayed, "So they couldn't get them for kidnapping. The video then shows Tim carrying us into the house to recuperate. There was a voice over on the tape where Naomi indicated that we wanted to recuperate at the cabin by the lake."

Gesturing wildly, Sasha exclaimed, "Wait a minute, this doesn't add up. What about the rope burns on your wrists and ankles along with the cuts on your bodies? How did they explain how you ended up in the woods after busting through the dining room window, much less running through the woods and falling down a ravine?"

"That's where things get interesting. The tape shows Naomi tied to the bed during their lovemaking session. It doesn't show us. Tim made it look like we got the marks from our journey through the woods when we fell down the ravine and our foot got caught up in a thicket of bushes."

"You've got to be kidding me. How come this never made it to the media?"

"Let's just say that money talks. They viewed the evidence on the tape as irrefutable proof that we were the brunt of a joke, and not accosted nor kidnapped. You know how it is with future NBA or NFL players that are expected to go high in the draft. If they stand to bring millions to a team's organization, they are willing to overlook minor infractions with the law. They have the wherewithal to spend however much money it takes to make the matter go away. Plus, I don't think our parents wanted us to be subjected to the ridicule that this would cause so I'm sure they played a hand in keeping this out of the local papers."

"How did you feel when he wasn't charged?"

"I think that I can speak for both us. We felt ashamed, degraded and abused. Because of that incident we still have scars that may not show on the outside but they are still prevalent within us."

"I'm so sorry that both of you had to endure this. How has this changed your relationship with your significant other?

Yvonne, I see that you trying to move ahead with your life by getting married to Paul, who has stood by you throughout this entire ordeal. What leftover feelings are causing you to doubt his love?"

"Sasha, don't think that we don't know what you're doing. You're playing the psychologist and caring friend all in one. Well, since I need all the help that I can get, I'll be honest and play along with you. I love Paul with all of my heart. He's been wonderful and hasn't tried to pressure me into having sex. We agreed early on in our relationship that we would wait until we were married to make love. However, just the very thought of being in that position, lying prone on the bed, with someone hovering over me, makes me physically ill. All I keep imagining is Tim, when he tried to accost us."

"I understand completely what you're saying Yvonne, but it doesn't have to be that way. If you trust in God, he can take away your fears and make you whole again. He can restore you! All you have to do is seek his face by praying, believe that he can restore you and it will happen. Please know that it's up to you when that will occur. Plus, there are other ways that you can make love without feeling vulnerable in that position."

"What do you mean?"

"Perhaps you had better call Paul to let him know that you're going to be here awhile," laughed Sasha.

"Dr. Sasha-Ruth, do you have some goodies to give to me?" Yvonne giggled, jumping into the spirit of things, willing to let go and let God handle her situation.

"Yvonne, the key is to find a position where you won't feel threatened. You might start of by lying side by side on the bed facing each other. Another position would be to try sitting in a chair, where you control the movement. If the chair proves to be too hard, you can always simulate the same thing in the bed, just by leaning against the headboard. If Paul is flexible, you could always try the hug position, where you make love standing up with your legs wrapped around his waist. This position should be relatively easy to accomplish since you barely weigh one hundred and ten pounds.

"Is it really that simple?"

"It can be with the one that you love and who loves you with his mind, body and soul. But you have to take a chance on love and trust Paul to do what's right for your comfort. Believe me, if he's waited this long, he'll treasure the love that you're giving him forever."

In a quiet voice, Erica chimed in, "Von, it also might be a good idea to warm up to the task. Try taking little steps at first, like setting aside an entire afternoon of kissing; letting him caress you with only his lips. The benefit is that you're being intimate with your mate even if you don't go all the way."

Warming up to her subject, Erica continued. "Next, let him use his hands to reacquaint himself with your body, caressing you from head to toe, from the tip of your breasts, down to the soles of your feet. If you can't take his actual hands on you for an extended period of time, try using an object such as a feather."

"Hold up E. Have you been holding out on us?" Yvonne questioned with a grin on her face. It sounded as if someone had gotten busy recently.

"I wish! My knowledge only comes from fantasizing about what I would do to TJ if given the chance." Slapping a hand over her mouth, Erica realized that she had said too much.

"Now that's what I'm talking about!" Yvonne and Sasha screamed in unison as they high-fived each other and danced around the room. Slowly Erica was starting to feel again if she was thinking of TJ.

"What's wrong with ya'll?" Erica asked in bewilderment.

"There's hope for you yet. Tell me, how are things going with you and TJ?"

"They're not as you are well aware. We had this conservation earlier, remember? I don't know what to do. When we went to the Prom, we had this connection; it was beautiful. Then the incident occurred, as they referred to Naomi and Tim's cabin of cruelty. "When he was shot, with his last breath before he passed out, he declared his undying love to me. Now he's back to acting like I'm just his best friend." With hands thrown up in the air, she started to pace back and forth. "I give up! I just don't know which TJ will show up at any given moment."

Chucking to themselves, Yvonne was the first to ask, "Erica how do you want him to act?"

"All I've ever wanted with TJ is forever; marriage, kids, the whole nine yards. Now that might not be possible." Going to the kitchen countertop, Erica picked up the note that Mia had sent and handed it to Yvonne.

After perusing the letter Yvonne asked, "Okay, what exactly is stopping you from going after TJ?"

"For some reason, you and Sasha can't read today. Hello, he's already involved with someone."

"For a scientist, you are remarkably a blond at times. The letter indicates that Mia is willing to step aside so that you can attempt to set ablaze the fire that's unexplored between you and TJ. I say that you take her up on it and let the chips fall where they may."

"Even if I was inclined to try, what should I do?"

The next day, Erica decided to start Campaign Restore, the action plan her friends helped her to formulate to win TJ's heart again. Her first sortie would occur at Sole Impressions, the personal care company that Max and TJ created with the help of their parents, during their junior year of college. The opening of the hair salon and day spa by Max and Erica's Aunt Samantha, was the catalyst to Max and TJ creating their own personal care company.

In order to succeed at any endeavor, Max and Erica were taught by their parents, who were Professors at the local University that one had to formulate a plan or goal, identify the objectives of the goal, outline the steps needed to accomplish the objectives, and then work the action items to reach the desired outcome. Both had used this method constantly throughout their lives to achieve great success.

Now was not the time to deviate from the plan.

This reasoning led Max to meet with his aunt one day to discuss a business venture that he felt would increase her business at the salon and make the salon unique among African Americans. First the service alone would set her apart from most salons. It was often customary for African Americans to wait for hours upon hours to get their hair completed in some salons. The next service that would set her salon apart, were the top notch professionals, that she had working with her, who specialized in a specific field. She only employed the best professionals and paid them as a commissioned salon, the industries highest salaries.

To further set the salon apart, Max proposed that his aunt sell her own products, that were customized and tailored to her clientele; the urban community. These products would be created and manufactured by the company that he was forming with TJ. With the advent of these products she would be creating her own brand to use and retail these products in her salon.

Aunt Samantha quickly agreed to Max's proposal. She wanted to further expand her salon and this was just the way to do it! When Erica had created the petroleum jelly mud mask in high school, she wasn't sure of the reception she would get when she started using the products on her customers. She felt that the product was very good and had done wonders on the soles of the customers that participated in the test market. Never in her wildest dreams did she think that her niece and nephew would create an entire line of products geared for the urban community that she would get the privilege of selling.

That was just the beginning. TJ, Max's closest friend since childhood, who might as well have been a member of the family, since he spent just as much time at their house as he did his own, added another dimension to the company. In addition to the personal care products, like body butters, body wash, body sprays lotions, mud masks, and bubble bath; he also wanted to have a separate division for just perfume. He loved the way a woman smelled, especially his mother and sister.

Seeing the way his father responded to his mother when she wore certain perfumes, sparked an interest in TJ to research and learn all that was possible about the perfume industry.   His ultimate goal was to become one of the primary leaders in the industry by creating a complete line of sensual, exotic perfumes.

Thinking back on that time, Erica smiled to herself. What started out as a small business by two young entrepreneurs had developed into a multi-million dollar business. Staring out of her office window, at the beautiful expanse of grounds, Erica marveled at what they had accomplished simply with a desire growing up to create a global company owned by African Americans that would relax, restore and replenish one's soul. From their research they learned that the urban community, (African American, Asians and Hispanics) was the leading ethnic group to spend billions of dollars in the personal care industry. Thus, they created, designed, and manufactured bath and body products, perfume, cosmetics and candles, specifically for the urban community. Their products were sold globally which enabled her to travel extensively during the summers from college.

The building was a contemporary design, four stories high, that looked more like a four star hotel than a place of business. The grounds consisted of lush, beautiful grass with waterfalls strategically located around the entire building. It had four wings, one for each group of products that were manufactured. Each wing was very secure and tightly guarded and access into the wing was only possible by a security badge. There was an atrium garden where all the wings intersected at the middle of the main building.

The company provided an atmosphere where the employees worked with little or no stress and were rewarded whenever the company surpassed their quarterly goals. Consequently, all the employees that had been with the company from the very start were extremely loyal. To reduce the stress associated with most jobs, Sole Impressions had an on-site daycare, a cafeteria and a gym.

Working in the company had actually saved her sanity after the cabin incident. After working herself to near exhaustion for the last couple of years, in a foreign city after graduating from college, she had reached the point where she was tired of running to escape the memories from her past.

She was glad that she had finally relented and became a partner in the business. It was past time to come home. *"Watch out TJ, here I come,"* Erica said aloud, as her spirit agreed with her vocal declaration that she was taking back everything that the devil had stolen from her. Walking out of her office in the Research and Development Wing on the ground floor, she headed towards TJ's office in the Executive Wing, which was located on the fourth floor, to begin the next phase of her life.

Stopping at the Executive secretary's desk, who was a middle aged, stylishly dressed, mother of three, that ran the entire Executive Wing like a drill sergeant, Erica asked, "Hello Mrs. Maness. How are you today? Is Mr. James busy?"

With a smile, a humph and a roll of her eyes, she declared, "For you, Mr. James is never too busy. Hold on a second, and I'll let him know you're here." Mrs. Maness had known TJ and Erica since they were born, having lived in their neighborhood all of her life. She was also Erica's mother's best friend. When her husband had been killed in a car accident the first year that the company started, she needed something to occupy her time while she went through the grieving process, since her children were grown and had lives of their own. She decided to reenter the work force and had never looked back. Grateful didn't begin to express the way she felt for what she considered her extended family.

With a knowing smile, ever the matchmaker, after receiving confirmation from Mr. James to send Erica in, she decided to offer a piece of advice, "Erica, I've known you all of your life. When are the two of you going to realize that you are made for each other? Time is too precious to waste!"

Before turning the doorknob to enter the suite of offices, Erica turned back towards Mrs. Maness, with a shocked expression on her face. "What do you mean? How do you know..." she sputtered before Mrs. Maness interrupted her.

"Child, I know what's its like to be content to love someone from afar lest you get your feelings hurt. Too afraid to trust your heart to lead you in the right direction after so many disappointments. Too leary of messing up a great friendship. Did I ever tell you the story about how Mr. Maness and I became a couple?"

To bewildered to speak, Erica shook her head no just as TJ came to the door to see why Erica hadn't entered his office yet. Ever conscious of Erica's welfare, he wanted to make sure that nothing was wrong.

Silhouetted in the doorway, TJ in a five button, Versace grey, pin-stripped suit, smiled as he rested his frame against the door. Smiling at the woman who held his heart, TJ spoke. "Erica, I see you've been detained."

"I won't be but a minute. Mrs. Maness and I were just catching up," said Erica as she faced TJ with a vibrant smile.

Knowing that the moment had passed to disclose information to a receptive ear, Mrs. Maness smiled as she turned back to her computer. At least she had planted a seed in her mind. "Erica, whenever you want to know the full story, just call me or stop by." Mrs. Maness was just as determined as Erica's mother to do whatever it took, to bring the two of them together since it seemed they were not making any headway by themselves.

Leading Erica back into his office, TJ closed the door and stopped briefly as she advanced into the room. What a view! He loved the way her hips swayed ever so slightly from side to side as she walked. As a petite person with such a small waist, one wouldn't think what rested beneath it would be so round, so curvy! How he loved this voluptuous woman! It was high time for him to put his plan into action to regain her trust so that he could declare his love once again.

"To what do I owe the pleasure, Erica?" TJ asked as he sat down behind his desk. He felt that it would be in his best interest to sit down because just looking at her brought an arousal that he was helpless to control. Never before in his life had he had issues with controlling his hormones; only around Erica. Determined not to frighten her off, he eased his chair forward to hide the excitement in his lower body.

"Is it a pleasure TJ?" Erica asked as she perched on the corner of his desk, with her bottom positioned fully on the desk thereby giving him little choice but to either back up and let her see the effect she had on him or to sit there and appear indifferent to their forced closeness. Since they had been friends for so long it wasn't unusual for them to rest on the corner of each other's desks.

It was all TJ could do, not to reach out and caress Erica's thighs as he swung them to the middle of his desk, so that she was positioned at the apex of his legs; then lean her backwards as he dropped featherlike kisses along every inch of her beautiful face that his lips could reach.

Entranced by the leg that Erica was swinging back and forth, which pulled slightly ajar the sarong skirt that she was wearing, TJ shook himself and proceeded to gather some papers that were lying on his desk. Erica discreetly, pulled the folds of the fly-away skirt together with her hands by laying the right end on top of the other.

Laughingly Erica muttered an excuse. "Forgive me TJ. I love these skirts but they are not too practical when you want to swing your legs. It's a habit I've had since I was a child."

"Perhaps not, but they accomplish exactly what they are meant to do." TJ replied as he placed his hand on the leg that was moving back and forth.

"Why do you say that? What do you mean?" Erica queried breathlessly when his caress caused a sweet sensation to ripple throughout her body. She was fascinated and held immobile by the play of emotions that were expressed in TJ's eyes as his face leaned closer towards hers, seemingly suspended in mid-air.

"I can show you better than any words that could come out of my mouth." Unerringly his lips found hers and his mouth seared her lips with a scorching kiss while his hands were fastened beneath her hips in an effort to bring her closer. Flicking the sarong sideways, TJ moved his hands to encompass Erica's hips as he pulled her towards him to the edge of the desk. Whispering that the purpose of the sarong was to tempt and to tantalize, he bent his head to deepen their kiss.

Deep within the recesses of his mind, he knew that he should slow down; that he was going to fast, but unfortunately his body was out of control. His body hungered for more of her touch, more of her essence. Thankfully, the need to breathe brought him to his senses.

Raising his head, he started to apologize but was interrupted as Erica, who was unwilling for the kiss to end, brought his head back to her lips, plunging her tongue into his mouth, carried away by the ecstasy that his kiss invoked.

Flicking back and forth, bending and moving, rotating in a circular motion, touching every crevice possible, their tongues danced a tango, as Erica moaned in ecstasy. When his hands came up to grasp each side of her head, to send the kiss to another level if that were possible, Erica flinched. At that moment, TJ chastised himself, knowing that he had gone too far, too soon.

Erica, unable to believe the depths to which she had responded and then subsequently rejected TJ when he grasped her head, chose that moment, to jump from his lap and race out of the room, sobbing as if the devil himself were chasing after her.

Stunned, TJ demanded, "Erica, wait!" as he attempted to stop her mad dash out of the room. Rushing to the door behind her, he ran straight into Mrs. Maness.

"I'm sorry Mrs. Maness. I didn't mean to hurt you," said TJ as he grasped her shoulders to keep her from falling while looking in despair at Erica as she ran down the corridor.

"TJ, what happened?" Mrs. Maness asked, blocking the path when he made a move to step around her.

Slamming a fist into his other hand, TJ muttered an expletive. "I kissed her and when she responded, I lost it. I took her too far too soon. Excuse me but I need to go after her to apologize." Attempting to step around her, Mrs. Maness laid a hand on TJ's arm.

"TJ, let her go. Right now she needs to be alone. She's dealing with emotions that she doesn't quite know how to handle. She has to come to terms with the way she feels for you, while at the same time putting the past behind her. You have to let her come the rest of the way by herself."

"What guarantee do I have that she will? That she won't shut me out like before? I want to help her but she creates a barrier and every time I believe we're making headway she takes two steps back," he furiously declared.

Turning around, he went back into his office and slammed the door. Too frustrated to work any more, he grabbed his suit coat from his office chair that had come off in the midst of their making out, and headed out the door.

Passing Mrs. Maness' desk, he stated, "I'll be out of the office the rest of the afternoon."

Closing her eyes, Mrs. Maness said a silent prayer for the young couple asking God to help heal their hearts and to give them peace about the past, while moving them in the right direction towards their destiny.

Chapter Thirteen

Back in her office, Erica rushed right past her secretary into her office and collapsed onto the chaise that was located in the corner of her office. *Oh my God, what have I done?* She kept asking herself over and over again.

"The very moment he simply wants to kiss you, you decide to take it to a whole new level," said her conscience. "Yet when that level is reached, you regress and start having flashbacks. You project Tim's crazy behind over TJ's. What's wrong with you? Didn't that man take a bullet for you," her conscience reminded her?

Her secretary, Pauletta, blinked as Erica swept by her in a flurry of activity. She was astonished that Erica was so flustered and seemed to be crying. Getting up from her desk, she fixed Erica a cup of tea, hoping that whatever was wrong, that she would feel better with something hot inside of her. Knocking gently on the door, she proceeded to enter Erica's office after the muffled "Go away" was heard.

"Ms. Teal, here's some tea for you to drink. I hope that everything is all right. If there is anything that I can do for you, please let me know." Ready to leave the room, Pauletta began walking towards the door.

"Pauletta, please stay.   Maybe you can help me."

At that moment, the telephone rang. Seeking permission, Pauletta answered the phone on Erica's desk.

"Sole Impressions, Erica Teal's office, how may I help you?"

"Pauletta, this is TJ. Can I speak to Erica?"

Looking at Erica who was frantically shaking her head no, and had started to cry again, Pauletta frowned as she answered, "No, Mr. James, she's here but she's on another call. Can I take a message?"

After taking a message, Pauletta hung up the phone and sat beside Erica on the couch to comfort her.

"Did you and TJ have a fight?" Anyone that knew them, knew it was only a matter of time before they became a couple. If you were in the same room with them, you could feel the chemistry and the love that radiated from their eyes. Their friends at the office just couldn't figure out what was keeping them apart. There were several pools in the office as to the date when they would officially become a couple.

"No, but this time I think I've pushed him away for good. He probably thinks I'm certifiable."

"That can't be true Erica, because he just called. What happened?" Pauletta, who was actually Chelsea's cousin, had come to work at Sole Impressions during the summer of her freshman year of college and had been working there ever since. As an aspiring designer, the job gave her the freedom to be creative while providing her an excellent income. Even Max had indicated that when she had created her complete line, he would sponsor her and help her manufacture and distribute her clothing line.

"TJ kissed me."

"And the problem with that would be what? Everyone thinks that ya'll are a couple anyway. Surely, you've kissed before."

"No, you don't understand Pauletta. He really kissed me this time in his office. The kiss that says I want to devour you. A kiss straight from your deepest fantasy. The kind of kiss, where you're at his desk, standing between his legs and he leans you back on the desk to consume your lips."

"Again Erica, what's wrong with that? It sounds pretty hot to me. What did you do then?"

"I flinched when he grasped my head." At Pauletta's quick gasp of surprise, she continued, "Yeah. Unfortunately it reminded me of when Tim had Yvonne and I tied up at the cabin."

"Surely, he understood when you explained to him, how his imprisoning your head made you feel."

"Umm, that sounds good in theory but it didn't quite happen that way. Once I flinched, I started crying because I knew that I had hurt him; then I panicked and ran out of the room without stopping until I came in here."

"Oh, Erica. Did he try to stop you from running?"

"Yes but Mrs. Maness ran into him and blocked him from coming after me."

"Why then didn't you want to speak to him? It's obvious that he's checking to make sure that you're okay."

"I don't know what to say to him after the way I reacted. How about, oh TJ, I love you and I love it when you kiss me but sometimes you make my skin crawl? I don't think that would go over very well."

"Erica, snap out of it. That's not funny. Did you ever think that it's only certain things that remind you of your appalling experience? Could it possibly have been the way his hands held your head? Especially if you're in the throes of passion and he grabs your head to either angle it another way or just to run his fingers through your hair, you might mistake that for holding you as a prisoner."

"Ohhhh, you're good. I didn't think of that. All I saw was Tim leaning over me with the knife. Will I ever be rid of this horrible nightmare? Can TJ deal with this as my future boyfriend? I used to think that he didn't care after the incident since he hadn't tried anything since then, but today proved just how wrong I was. He still has feelings for me."

"Anyone can see that. It's up to you to get past the nightmare and embrace your destiny. I think that you should apologize to him as soon as possible and explain to him how that kiss made you feel; the good and the bad."

"How did you get to be so smart?"

"I had a good teacher."

Giving Pauletta a hug, Erica grabbed her pocketbook and headed from her office back to the Executive Wing. Taking the elevator to the top floor, she hurried down the corridor to TJ's office. Seeing Mrs. Maness, Erica apologized for her earlier behavior and inquired if TJ was available to see her for a few minutes.

"Erica, I'm sorry, TJ has already left for the day."

At her crestfallen look, Mrs. Maness hastened to explain. "After you left, he kept chastising himself for rushing you. He wanted to come and make sure that you were okay but I asked him not too. I told him that you needed some time to come to terms with how you felt about him along with putting the past to rest. Are you ready to move forward?"

Hugging the lady who was like a second mom to her, Erica shook her head as she answered, "Yes. With God's help and TJ's, I can get through this."

"One last word of warning though, Erica. Don't shut him out. Let him know what works for you and what brings back painful memories. He loves you enough to take it slow at the speed that will work best for you but you've got to meet him halfway."

"Thanks Auntie. Do you know where I can find him?"

"No he left right after you did."

"I'll just have to find him and make it up to him."

Leaving the parking lot, with his tires spinning, TJ headed towards the gym across town that offered a boxing ring instead of working out in the gym at Sole Impressions. He needed to work off some stress for an extended amount of time and sparring with a worthy opponent for about an hour would help him to relieve some of his anger. If he ever saw Tim again he probably would kill him. He had really messed up Erica's mind. He had taken away her trust in men. She couldn't even enjoy a normal relationship with a man due to his callous behavior. Slamming the door to his car, he went to his trunk to retrieve his work out clothes.

Walking inside the gym, Tony, the manager took one look at TJ and knew his fighters were in for one hellavu fight. It would probably be best if he took this one, otherwise someone was liable to end up getting hurt.

"TJ, wanna go a couple of rounds? It's been awhile since I beat you," Tony jokingly called out.

"Bring your A game, Tony. I'm spoiling for a fight."

Looking at Tony's size was deceiving. He was small in statue, only about five feet, eleven inches, weighed approximately one hundred and ninety pounds, and packed one hellavu punch. TJ and Max had learned the hard way that it took a great boxer to out-box Tony. He had cut them down to size on many occasions. Today though would be different, TJ thought as he changed into his workout gear and donned the gloves. He had to let go of his anger before he saw Erica again.

After sparring for about an hour, TJ had finally been able to pound the anger out of his system. He had given Tony a very physical fight. Sitting down on the side of the ring, Tony breathing very hard, asked, "What's wrong TJ? I haven't seen you this mad since your junior year of college when Erica was hurt. What happened?"

"It's because of that same mess that I'm here. I thought that she was over the past and had healed from Tim's craziness, but today I did the unthinkable and let my hormones run out of control. She came into my office today wearing this sarong skirt that swayed and billowed every step she took. It was very sexy and seductive. Then she sat on the corner of my desk leaving her legs exposed. That's the only way I can rationalize why I initiated a kiss and was on the verge of acting out one of my Erica fantasies. The kiss was powerful and passionate; then I stopped, thinking that I was going to fast. She then cupped my face and pulled it back to her lips. I reached up to grasp her head to deepen the kiss and that's when all hell broke loose. She flinched and then started crying and ran out of the room before I knew what had happened."

"TJ, you know what she went through. It's going to take some time."

Holding up his hand, he stopped Tony before he could continue. "Before you go any further, I'm not mad at Erica. I'm mad at myself and at Tim. Sometimes I wonder if she will ever be able to forget what happened and enjoy a normal relationship with me. I've waited for the last four years for this woman to heal. I'm not about to give up now but honestly I don't know how much more I can take. Every time I'm around her and we're back to being "just friends", it's like I'm reduced to being a teenager again. All I want to do is whisk her off to a deserted island for a couple of weeks to prove to her that I love her and that with time I can make her forget all the pain and suffering that she went through."

"TJ, perhaps you need to go to counseling with her when the time comes and she's ready to commit to being in a relationship with you. Until then, just take it one day at a time."

"I know. I'm trying. When I leave here, I'm going to try to see her tonight to apologize for letting my hormones run wild and for rushing her. Hopefully, she'll forgive me."

TJ's phone rang at that moment. Quickly picking up the phone, thinking that it was Erica, he eagerly answered, "TJ".

"Cuz, what's up? Mia and I are in town. Where are you man?"

"Carl? When did ya'll get here and how long are you staying?"

"Man, the family is relocating back down here. Mia and I wanted to come and scoop you up and take you over to our new place."

"I'm at the gym over on Wendover Avenue. If you come over then I can follow you."

"Okay, we'll see you in about ten to fifteen minutes."

"Good, that will give me time to shower before you arrive."

Carl and Shauna Miaonette, or Mia as she was known to the family, were fraternal twins. Growing up, the three of them were inseparable before their parents, TJ's aunt and uncle, moved up north due to a job promotion. The twins would then spend two weeks of their summer break in the South before returning home to New Jersey then just before school started, he and his sister Nicole, would go to New Jersey for two weeks. It was cool growing up.

They pulled up within seconds of each other, outside the gym, with Mia driving a sporty Chrysler Crossfire. To say that someone was making bank was putting it mildly. Mia arrived first at the gym, since she was only a few minutes away at the restaurant picking up dinner, when they called. She was just getting out of the car when TJ came outside to put his things into his trunk. Walking over to her car, he held the door for her as she exited the Crossfire. Leave it to Mia to drive something sporty and fast. He was surprised that she didn't drive a Porsche, since she was a Funny Car race driver for NHRA. She was the African American counterpart to Danica Patrick.

Reaching up on her tiptoes, she embraced her favorite cousin as he swung her around in his arms like they used to do when she was a child. Since she was so petite, it had always been a running joke and became their favorite greeting. Setting her back on her feet, they both laughed.

They didn't see the Silver S430 Mercedes that slowed down as it turned the corner. Erica, who was driving to TJ's house couldn't believe her eyes. There was TJ at the other gym that he sometimes used when he was sparring, with the woman from HangOut Night in his arms! The embrace only lasted a few seconds but was indelibly ingrained in Erica's mind. Slowing down, just to make sure that she wasn't hallucinating, Erica's eyes confirmed that yes, the man was TJ and a woman that resembled someone that she knew. Could it be his date, Mia? She wasn't sure.

What were they doing together? Her letter indicated that she was going to step aside for thirty days. *Had she changed her mind, she thought?* With tears streaming down her face, she drove on for about three additional blocks before she was consumed with too much pain and tears to drive. It was unfortunate that she jumped to the wrong conclusion. Had she watched them for another five minutes, she would have seen TJ embrace Carl who had pulled into the parking lot on a Harley Davidson motorcycle just minutes behind his sister. Consequently, Erica decided that if TJ could replace her that quickly, then she didn't need to explain what caused her to freak out at the office when they kissed.

"Hey man, this gym is nice! I need to check this out!"

TJ took both Carl and Mia inside the gym to show off its amenities. None the wiser to what had just occurred, after they were finished, TJ and Mia walked outside, leaving Carl at the receptionist's desk, in his erstwhile attempt to obtain her telephone number.

Chapter Fourteen

TJ called Erica several times that evening while he was visiting his aunt and uncle and again when he returned home, but didn't get an answer. Feeling worried, he decided to drive by her house to make sure that she was alright. Parking his car along side the curb of her house, he dialed her number again. Seeing a light on in the bedroom, TJ knew that Erica was home but she still didn't answer the telephone. He felt sure that she was avoiding him. That left little then to the imagination. He had totally freaked her out with his desires by moving too fast and by kissing her too passionately.

With a feeling of defeat, TJ tried to convey into the telephone, his remorse for the way that he had acted. "Erica, I know that you're probably at home by now. I wanted to apologize in person but since you're not taking my calls, I guess you don't want to see me. I offer you my sincerest apologies for taking things too fast. I had planned to go slow with you, to be there for you; but every time I touch you, I can't seem to control myself anymore. I simply crave your touch, your kiss. It's crazy. What started off as a simple kiss turned into so much more. I can't apologize for kissing you because I've wanted that to happen for quite some time now. I do however humbly apologize for taking you to a place you would rather not remember. Please forgive me." Any additional words were cut off as the answering machine clicked off.

Dialing the number again, TJ left another message. "Erica, if you're there, please pick up. We need to talk. After I left you today, my cousins, the twins, Carl and Miaonette, came to town and met me at the gym. You remember them from our younger years, don't you? Well, they wanted to meet you. Let me know if you're willing to do that. If I scared you today and you don't want to further a relationship with me, just tell me. Your friendship means a lot to me, and if that's all I'll ever have, then I'll accept that. Just talk to me."

Click. The answering machine hung up again.

TJ decided that he might as well go home because he had done all that he could do. The next move was Erica's.

Erica, who was in the bathroom soaking her sorrows away in the tub, awoke to she sound of the ringing telephone. She hastened out of the tub and ran into the bedroom to answer the phone only to be greeted with silence since the caller had hung up. "Oh well, whoever it was will call back," she thought as finished drying off. Donning a pink, silk, transparent, barely there bathrobe, she went downstairs to the kitchen to grab a late night snack. Even though she didn't have a significant other to wear the bathrobe for, she enjoyed sexy lingerie and the way the material felt against her skin.

Feeling restless after eating some fruit, she walked into her home office, deciding that she might as well work on some of her projects since she wasn't sleepy. Sitting at her desk she reached over the phone to grab her formulation notebook, and noticed that light flashing on the answering machine. Deciding that now was as good a time as any, she pressed the playback key to listen to the message. Several calls were from family members and friends but the one that captured her attention was the message left by TJ's sexy, deep voice.

Hearing TJ's voice sent mixed emotions through her. He sounded as if he had lost his best friend, which is how she felt. She could identify with the pain and the confusion that she heard in his voice. What she didn't understand was if he truly felt the way that he sounded in his message, then why would he turn to someone else. Furthermore, how dare he call her after he had his arms around another woman!

"Is that what really happened? Was it a simple hug? What took place after the hug," her conscience asked? On a roll, her conscience kept picking away at the barriers that she had formed in her mind to protect herself from getting hurt. *"Did you stop and speak, giving him a chance to clarify the situation? Do you suppose that TJ could have other friends that happen to be female? Is it possible that you misinterpreted what happened? What did you do? What you do best; run. When has running ever solved anything?"*

All of these thoughts were running through her mind as she leaned over to delete the message before listening to the rest of it. Feeling out of sorts, she decided to hear him out, listening to the inflections in his voice, his tone, and to what he was actually saying. Placing her hand over her heart, tears started to run down her face. He sounded hurt, frustrated and mad at himself. The machine then clicked off leaving Erica to wonder if TJ was going to say anything else.

The answering machine then played another message. Listening with bated breath, TJ's voice sounded husky and mellow as he continued his plea for Erica to call and talk to him no matter what time of night when she finally listened to his message.

To ease his burden, she picked up the telephone to dial his number. She couldn't stand to know that someone else was in pain because of something that she did. As quickly as she picked up the telephone, she hung up after noticing the time. It was eleven o'clock. She needed to get some sleep.

Upstairs in her bedroom, she went to sleep thinking about what she should do; talk to him or wait for him to approach her.

"He did," muttered her conscience. "He called you. The ball is now in your court."

Praying to God for answers she drifted off to sleep. After tossing and turning she finally conceded to God and got up an hour later. She had asked for guidance and she assumed he was answering her prayer. Her spirit demanded that she get up and call TJ.

Dialing TJ's number, she waited for him to answer. Sitting up in bed, she glanced at the clock on her nightstand. It was only twelve o'clock. Should she call him? Maybe he was still up. Knowing TJ and the night owl that he was, Erica was sure that he was still up. What if he wasn't in? About to hang up, after four rings, TJ's answering machine clicked on.

"Hello, I'm sorry I'm unable…"

"Hello, hello, hold on a moment while I turn this machine off," said TJ in a husky voice that sent shivers down Erica's spine.

"TJ, this is Erica. I'm sorry for calling so late but I got your message while I was in the bathtub and then I drifted off to sleep. I didn't actually listen to it until just now."

TJ closed his eyes as he imagined her curvaceous body, with water glistening off of her, lying supine in the tub with tiny tendrils of hair curling around her face.

"Erica, I drove by your house earlier to apologize after I left the gym where my two cousins from New Jersey met me to take me to my aunt and uncle's new house. Only one light was on so that must have been when you were soaking in the tub. That's when I left the message. I had hoped that you would at least give me the opportunity to apologize in person and then if you didn't want to see me, I could gracefully leave." It was common knowledge that Erica did her best thinking and inventing new formulations for new products in the tub.

Yes! She thought; *his cousin. He's not seeing anyone else.*

"Why didn't you answer any of my earlier calls after you ran out of my office? Were you avoiding me? What happened to change your mind?"

"To be completely honest, I drove by the gym and caught a glimpse of you hugging another woman and it upset me since not just an hour earlier you were kissing me so ardently."

"Erica, this is not a conversation that we need to have over the telephone. Can I come over so that you can look into my eyes and I can look into yours, so that there will not be any more misunderstandings between us?"

"Yes," she whispered. Quickly she said a prayer that at least they were going to try to resolve whatever it was between them. Knowing that it would take him at least twenty minutes to reach her house, Erica tried to formulate the details of the plan to win the man that she had loved for as long as she could remember. Turning another page in her formulation notebook, she decided to treat TJ as a project in terms of writing a list of goals that she would have to accomplish in order to achieve her objective: a successful relationship with TJ that would eventually lead to marriage.

She listed the goals she wanted to accomplish on the paper for Campaign Restore:

- Objective 1: Peace concerning the past
- Objective 2: Better communication with TJ
- Objective 3: Relationship with TJ
- Objective 4: Marriage to TJ

Then she listed the steps she thought would be needed to accomplish her objectives.

- Action Items #1:
  - Pray to God for peace to help reduce the flashbacks that she continued to have.
  - Let go and let God heal her heart.
- Action Items #2:
  - Apologize to TJ for running away.
  - Talk to TJ about how she felt when he kissed her.
  - Explain her fears and her concerns.
  - Inquire about his relationship with Mia → was it still in progress, was it on hiatus or was it over?
- Action Items #3:

- o   Work up to getting closer to TJ. This she would have to do in stages.
- o   Ask for his assistance in completing some projects at work that would require her to touch, taste, and feel specific body part of TJ's.
- o   Start to go out on dates with TJ and then let nature take its course.
- o   Arrange a HangOut Night and become a contestant.
- ▪ Action Item #4:
  - o   This would take care of itself if one through three were successful.

At the ring of the doorbell, Erica hurriedly put her Campaign Restore plan in her desk drawer and went to the door to let TJ in. She checked the peephole to make sure that TJ was the one at her door before opening it.

Looking at her watch she realized that TJ had gotten there in twelve minutes. He must have been speeding. Recognizing the helmet in his hands, she knew why he had gotten there so quickly. TJ had a love affair with bikes. He had a need for speed. Any opportunity that he had to ride one of his favorite bikes, he would use.

Opening the door, for a moment Erica could only stare at TJ. In his rush to get to her house quickly, he had thrown on an old pair of jeans that seemed as if they were molded to his skin. The jeans showed every sinewy muscle in his thighs and in his legs.

As her eyes travelled upwards, towards his chest, she forgot to breathe as the hair on his chest peaked above his open collared polo shirt. It was all she could do not to run her hands through it. Remembering the reason for his visit, she ushered him inside, swallowing repeatedly in order to satisfy her throat which had suddenly become very parched.

When TJ didn't move, she gazed questioningly at him over her shoulder to see what was wrong.

TJ, as he stood in the doorway was doing some gazing of his own. He didn't know whether to laugh or cry. Erica was slowly killing him. It would seem that another cold, very cold shower would be in store for him when he returned home.

Just looking at how beautiful Erica was in the pink, very transparent, silk bathrobe that hid little from his view, had him aroused to a fever pitch. How he wished that their relationship was different because at that very moment, he felt like kissing her in all the tantalizing places that the robe revealed to him.

Once he kissed those places he would then kiss the lips that she was sucking on worriedly until neither one of them would be able to breathe. Careful not to grasp her head, he would then make his way to her hair.

With her long, shoulder length hair piled high on top of her head, by a single Swarovski hair clip, all he could think about was pulling the crystal clip from her hair as it cascaded down his arms. As her hair fell into place down the middle of her back, he would run his fingers through it, inhaling its wonderful scent as he lost himself in its essence.

TJ, as if in a trance, walked through the door and closed it quietly behind him, shaking his head to clear his vision before he acted out the fantasy that had just run through his mind. He didn't want to scare her away again but he couldn't seem to steer his steps away from her.

It was as if there was a magnetic force in the air that compelled him to walk towards Erica and gather her in his arms. Unaware that she stood rooted to the spot, Erica began to gnaw at her bottom lip as she watched TJ come towards her.

"Please stop me if you don't want this," TJ whispered as his lips lowered to tease and taste hers. Keeping his arms on her waist, his lips fastened on hers for a searing, provocative kiss that lasted until air was the only thing that broke their mouths apart.

When the heat of his hands scorched their way through her clothes, it was only then that Erica realized that she didn't have anything on underneath her bathrobe. Her brain told her to move but the sensations that he was evoking, kept her still within his arms.

Finally TJ's brain began to function again as Erica, whimpering in ecstasy, moved closer to his body, wrapping her arms around his neck. His body hungered for more of her touch but he had to distance himself from her, otherwise the bedroom would be the only place that they would see for several days. He knew she wasn't ready for that step yet.

Breaking the kiss, TJ stated, "Sweetheart, as much as I want you, I don't think we're ready yet for this next step that's going to happen if you remain in my arms, dressed in this provocative bathrobe. I think that for my sanity you might need to change clothes otherwise the only talking we'll do will be in the bedroom."

Screaming, "Oh no," Erica rushed from the room and ran upstairs to her bedroom. She had forgotten that she didn't have anything on. It had registered at some point when his hands touched her waist but she was so caught up with the feelings that were washing over her that she didn't care.

Walking back downstairs, Erica blushed when she saw TJ reclining on the sofa with his feet stretched out in front with his eyes closed. How she wanted to go over and straddle him and kiss him senseless. Where were these thoughts coming from, she wondered? It was as if overnight, she had turned in to a wanton woman that was craving the touch from her man.

Okay maybe this was the real her but couldn't she control it?

Sensing her presence, TJ opened his eyes. Smiling at her, he rose as he reached out his hand to her across the sofa. Instinctively she put her hand in his as he led her to the sofa to sit down.

"Thank you for allowing me to come over. Can we talk about what happened this afternoon?" TJ asked when they were both comfortable on the couch.

"TJ, I'm sorry for freaking out this afternoon when you kissed me. I know that you would never hurt me, but I'm not quite sure how to explain how I felt."

"Can you tell me at what point you began to feel uncomfortable? When we kissed, it was surreal and I felt that you were with me right from the beginning, then all hell broke loose. I sincerely apologize again for moving too fast. It was never my intention to hurt you."

"It wasn't you. It's me. I loved it when we kissed. Unfortunately when you attempted to deepen the kiss and your hands came up and grasped my head, it brought back painful memories of when I was tied up and Tim held my face and forced his kisses on me."

"Oh darling, I'm so, so sorry. Please forgive me." TJ said softly as he looked at Erica, whose eyes remained downcast.

She found it hard to talk to TJ about what happened.

"Do you want to tell me what happened?"

"No. I've tried to put that behind me." Sighing to himself, TJ decided not to push her. When she was comfortable with him, maybe one day she would share that catastrophic sequence of events.

"Erica, look at me." Taking his finger, he gently touched her chin to lift her head so that she was looking directly into his eyes.

"At any time that you feel uncomfortable with what we're doing, just stop me. A simple stop will work. Even if you have to cry because of the memories; that's all you will ever have to say. Promise me that you won't run away again."

Tears crested in Erica's eyes and spilled forth. He was too good to be true. What did she do to deserve this?

"I'll try not to run away again."

"No baby, you have to do better than that. If we're going to be in a relationship, we have to have honesty between us. That is, if a relationship is what you want from me."

"Yes TJ, I do want a relationship with you but I'm not sure I can promise what you're asking. I still have nightmares from the incident."

"Baby, we can get through this but I have to know when I inadvertently do something that you don't like. Tell me then and we can deal with it. Don't let it fester. I can't promise that I'll always understand but I would never hurt you."

"Okay. I need to know what the parameters of our relationship are. What's permitted and what isn't? Why were you hugging that woman this afternoon? I wasn't close enough to see who she was but it hurt me none the less. What happened with Mia and is she out of the picture?"

This was where things would get a little tricky. He had just told Erica that there needed to be honesty between them yet he was getting ready to tell her a semi-truth. When they were married, maybe then he would tell her the truth. "Erica, do you trust me?"

"Yes, I think so."

"If you saw us, why didn't you stop and come over? I would have introduced you to Shauna and Carl, my cousins who have moved back here from New Jersey. Don't you remember the twins that came every summer when you were little?"

"Only a little. Remember I was always at various camps during the time that they were here."

"Erica, please know that if I'm in a relationship, that person has my full attention. I will be faithful and expect the same in return. Mia was not the woman for me. She realized it and so did I. We're good friends and nothing more."

He hoped that Erica would be able to laugh once she found out who Mia was. He didn't want to tell her now because it would break the fragile, tenuous bond that they had built this evening. Boy, would he have hell to pay when she did find out. He would just have to cross that bridge when it came.

"Is there any ground rules you want to stipulate?"

"I basically want the same things that you want; fidelity, honesty and trust." Glancing away from him, she asked the only other question that was important to her: What about making love?"

"When we make love, it will be up to you. When you're ready for that step, we'll take it together."

"What if I'm never ready for that step?" Erica questioned, afraid that the past memories would keep her from creating and experiencing the greatest love of all.

"Darling, don't think like that. Come here." TJ motioned for Erica to sit on his lap. "Feel what you do to me. Remember how you responded when you opened the door. You have too much passion and fire inside of you not to release it. It's just a matter of feeling loved and your partner being willing enough to try whatever makes you feel comfortable. I'm patient. Hell, I've waited all of these years, a few more won't kill me," he muttered.

Hitting him with a pillow, the tension that she was feeling melted. Looking at her watch, she realized the amount of time that had passed since they began talking. It was three o'clock in the morning. They needed to get some sleep.

"TJ, since it's late and we both have to work tomorrow morning, will you stay with me? I mean, please don't drive at this time of night. What I mean is..."

Putting his fingertips to her lips he quietly interrupted her. "Yes, I'll stay Erica. I know this isn't an invitation into your bedroom. If you'll allow me to sleep in the guess room, I'll be fine and leave in the morning. Oh and by the way, don't ever wear that robe again unless you mean business."

Blowing out a deep breath, she smiled. Standing on tiptoe, her lips unerringly found his in a sizzling kiss that left her hot and throbbing for more. Saying goodnight, she went to her bedroom to catch a few hours of sleep.

Chapter Fifteen

The following day, Max was flying home from France. He mission had ended and he was due for some rest and relaxation. This last mission had been tough for his team. Frank and Alexis, his partners at the Bureau, were recuperating from some minor injuries that they had suffered in a shootout.

His first stop would be at Sole Impressions, so that he could catch TJ and Erica up to speed on some commitments he had received while he was there regarding prospective buyers. His cover for most of his missions was that of a well respected businessman whose personal care company sold products worldwide. He was also anxious to know if they had resolved their differences. Maybe love could be attained for them since his heart was still broken and he longed for Chelsea. No matter how many women he dated, she was always at the forefront of his mind.

He often wondered if she ever thought about him; if her current life was good and if what her relationship was with her baby's daddy. These thoughts drove him to contact her since he couldn't shake her from his mind.

In the past, when those thoughts arose, something was usually wrong. Having to depend on his instincts had saved his life as well as the lives of his team members many times. Pulling his cellular phone from the case on his hip he dialed her number.

Waiting on her to answer the telephone, he thought back to the events that had led him to this point...

After his sister's surgery, Max had been sent on another special mission when he returned to base that extended his service time an additional year in the military. Because of the secrecy of the mission, he couldn't contact his family nor could he contact Chelsea.

Without having any type of communication from Max, no postcard, no letter, no telephone calls, over the next four months; Chelsea determined that Max couldn't handle the fact that she was carrying Alex's baby.

Desperate times calls for desperate measures. After several more months without any word from Max, Chelsea was about to give up but felt as if she had to make one last ditch effort to contact him. He would have been out of the military by then, yet he hadn't come to see her nor had he contacted her. She even went so far as to contact his unit and the Red Cross to see if she could at least get an address to send him a letter. They were of no help. Although she didn't want to, she even contacted his parents but they couldn't shed any light on the situation either.

They hadn't heard from him within the last six months so unfortunately they didn't have any idea where he was. His mother however did steadfastly maintain that when he was out, he was coming for her so she shouldn't lose hope.

Easier said than done.

By this time, Alex had matured enough to realize that whether or not he liked it, he had a child on the way that he needed to support. He made measures to win back Chelsea's trust and the love that she had once offered him even though it was second best. At first, she didn't want anything to do with him but eventually realized that for the baby's sake they need to at least be civil. Therefore she relented during the Christmas holiday to see Alex.

They worked on developing a civil relationship so that when the baby arrived, his visitation could occur seamlessly without stress.

One day when Alex was at Chelsea's house, dropping off some things for the baby, the telephone rang. Since she was being sick in the bathroom, Alex took it upon himself to answer the telephone.

"Hello."

"Who are you and why are you answering Chelsea's phone?" Max demanded feeling a sense of dread spike down his spine. Having been imprisoned for the last twelve months, he wasn't in the mood for chit chat.

"Chelsea is busy at the moment. Do you wish to leave a message?"

"Yes, could you tell her that Max is calling? I'll wait for her to come to the phone."

"I'm sorry but my W-I-F-E can't come to the phone right now. She's too busy being sick right now from the pregnancy of our first child."

"I'm sorry, could you repeat that?"

"What part didn't you understand? The part about Chelsea being sick or the part about her being my wife?"

"I'm sorry to disturb you then. Perhaps instead of answering the telephone, you should be in there helping her while she's sick. Tell Chelsea that I hope she feels better and that I hope she has exactly what she wants." Slamming down the telephone, Max angrily muttered a string of expletives and proceeded to the nearest bar to buy a drink. Life sucked. Yet again, Alex had his girl.

This time there was no turning back. They were married. To Max marriage was sacred; it was irrevocable.

He might have stood a chance if he wasn't in the military and was being sent to every third world country for months on end. Feeling heartbroken, Max immediately made a decision that would change his life. The last time that he was in town to visit Chelsea, with what he thought was only six more months in the military; he had been offered a position with the FBI. He had delayed giving them an answer until his military duty was completed. Now that the love of his life had married another man, he didn't see any reason not to join. He needed something that would keep his mind off the hurt, anger and desolation that he felt upon losing her love yet again. He consequently threw himself into his work in an effort to forget everything about his previous life.

Walking into the living room Chelsea asked Alex, "I though that I heard the telephone. Who was it? I didn't see the message light flickering on the answering machine. Did you answer my phone?"

"Yes, I answered it. It was just a telemarketer." Alex said with a straight face. Finally he was able to get satisfaction! Max would believe him simply because he had answered Chelsea's phone. He wouldn't have any reason to doubt him and Chelsea would be none the wiser. They could go ahead and get married without any interference from Max. He had planned on asking her that evening.

"Alex, you know better than to answer my phone. You do not live here. In the future, please remember that."

"Chelsea, I thought that maybe it was one of your sister's calling to check up on you," he lied. "There's something that I want to ask you."

Getting down on one knee, Alex looked at Chelsea and asked, "Will you marry me and give our baby my last name?"

"I'll have to think about it. You know that getting married is not high on my list of priorities right now. Can I let you know after I pray about it?"

Although Alex didn't like her answer, he planned to put enough pressure on her to make her consent. It was just a matter of time before she realized that Max wasn't coming back.

Instead of praying like she should in order to get guidance from the Lord, she tried to solve matters on her own. Chelsea decided that if she couldn't be happy, then she would make sure that her baby grew up in a loving environment with two parents.

She decided to marry Alex.

The following months were hard both physically and mentally for Chelsea. She was still grieving the loss of her love for Max and she continued to have difficulty with her pregnancy. Because the baby was so large on her small frame, she was constantly in pain with no end in sight until the delivery of her child, which brought another set of issues.

When her baby Taylor was born, she stopped breathing. Although they were able to revive her, she had to be kept in the hospital for several days to confirm that everything was all right. It was determined that she had a heart murmur which would require extensive tests to be performed periodically throughout her life. Chelsea was glad that she had a good job with adequate insurance.

While she was raising their child, it became evident that Alex was not ready for marriage; that he wasn't mature enough to handle a wife and a child and often resented the fact that they existed. Chelsea felt that she was doing everything by herself. He often stayed out late at night and when he came home he was often belligerent about where he had been. Then add to that the problems with his family and how they treated her and you had one heck of a mess. She might as well had been a single parent for all the help Alex gave.

Chelsea knew that she was partly to blame for their circumstances. She never got over her love for Max. She tried to hide it but it was always there in her heart. When she suggested counseling, he adamantly refused to go. Without counseling, their problems continued to fester and grow. Consequently their marriage fell apart after only a year and a half.

Chelsea filed for divorce and Alex didn't contest it. She petitioned for full custody of their child Taylor, with visitation rights for Alex. She didn't fully expect him to come and see her, when he didn't want anything to do with her while he lived in the same house, but one could always hope.

Max tapped his hand impatiently on the steering wheel of his Lexus 470 SUV. *Why didn't she answer*, he wondered. He had received confirmation that her divorce papers had been filed which lead him to end his business in France earlier than planned.

He had to see her to confirm that she was free.

Having filed for a divorce, several weeks prior, the day that Alex was served with papers, he came over to Chelsea's house in a rage. He knew that they were having problems, but he never suspected that she would file for a divorce. Their separation was only supposed to be for a couple of months. Ultimately he knew that his jealousy of Max, kept him from showing her any of the love that he once felt for her. Although his comments had kept Max away for a year and a half, he kept looking over his shoulder everyday, expecting the truth to surface about the phone call that he had intercepted.

When he returned to their house, Alex used his key to get in. Chelsea didn't have a chance yet to change the locks. She didn't feel that she needed to do that since they both knew their marriage would never work.

It was shocking to see Alex acting so hostile and antagonistic towards her. Sure they had disagreements during their marriage but never had they escalated into a full blown fight. Luckily Taylor was spending the night with her sister.

"Alex, I think that you should leave and come back to retrieve your clothes when you're in a better mood."

"Why did you have to file for a divorce Chelsea?" Alex asked in a hostile voice.

"Alex, let's not start this. We both know it isn't going to work. You got what you wanted; you're finally free, so don't complain. Maybe you'll find someone that can love you like you deserve to be loved."

"I tried to love you but you wouldn't let me. There was always Max. He was in our house each and everyday. Especially in our bedroom, he was there. You never let go of him."

Menacingly he advanced towards Chelsea, ready to do her bodily harm with the rage that was boiling inside of him. "Do you remember the day that you got violently sick and had to go to the Emergency Room? Remember the call that came when you were in the bathroom and you got mad because I answered it? Well it was Max. He was back and wanted to see you. I'm glad that I told him we were already married. That was before I had even asked you, and he believed me." Laughingly he went on to explain the conversation that he intercepted as he circled Chelsea, who was inching back towards the sofa table, ready to grab the lamp if he came any closer.

"What do you mean he called? Why didn't you tell me? You mean that for the last two years, while I've been mourning the loss of his love, he really didn't leave of his own accord that you forced him to think that we were already married? How could you? Were you that afraid of some competition?"

"I only fight battles I know that I can win," he yelled steadily advancing on her.

The ringing of the telephone stopped Alex in his path, but only momentarily. Watching him warily, Chelsea reaching quickly to her waist to unhook her cellular phone flicked it open and answered. With trepidation she spoke huskily into the receiver, "Hello."

"Hello Chelsea, this is Max. Are you all right?" He asked as if he spoke with her everyday. As if it hadn't been over a year and a half since she had last spoken to him.

"No Max, I'm not okay. Alex is here and we're having a bit of an altercation about you. Momentarily distracted at the glimpse of fear in Alex's eyes, she paused in answering him.

The pause must have been enough to scare Max because he gave her instructions of what to do next.

"I'm about ten minutes away. Do you think that he will harm you? Can you make it outside? Where's Taylor? If you can go into the kitchen, get a butcher knife and fend him off if you have too. Be careful! I don't want you to hurt yourself. Better yet, where's Mr. RightNow? I'm calling the police as we speak.

They are on their way! Give him the phone! Throw the phone to him. Don't let him get too close to you."

Stepping his foot on the gas, Max efficiently and expertly sped towards Chelsea's house. Although she was married to another man it didn't stop him from keeping tabs on her. He wanted to know at the first opportunity if she ever filed for divorce, because then he would go after her and make her his.

With the modified Bluetooth attached to his ear, he was able to contact the police while waiting for Alex to take the phone that Chelsea had given him.

Speaking with more bravado than he felt, Alex picked up the phone that Chelsea had thrown on the couch. "Do you think that you can stop me? Not this time, Max. You're to far away," he laughingly replied! Do you want to know what I've gone through these past two years, trying to love someone that only married me because she was having my baby and the person that she loved beyond reason was gone from her life based on a lie?"

Max let Alex rant and rave, giving himself and the police time to approach the house stealthily. As they were circling the wraparound porch, Max could see Chelsea through the window. She appeared to be okay. She didn't have a gun pointed at her nor a knife. Alex must have thought that he could overpower her. With deadly intent, Max asked, "Alex what lie are you talking about?"

"Do you remember the last time that you called and I answered the telephone? How I told you that Chelsea was my wife and you believed me? Right after I hung up, Chelsea tore into me because I answered her phone. Well little did you know that she was patiently waiting for you to come back; that if she had received that call, our marriage would never have taken place. That's right. I lied. I hadn't even asked her at that time to marry me," he bragged, oblivious to the danger that he was in.

With steely determination, Max kicked down the front door and advanced on Alex before he knew what hit him. Beating him to a pulp was the least of his worries. He beat him for the old and the new; for the hurt, the anger and the pain that he had felt for the last two years while his woman was married to another man. He beat him for all the anguish that Chelsea must have suffered at his hands. He continued to beat him for being a lousy father to Taylor who didn't ask to be brought into the world.

Finally, the police, thinking that Alex had suffered enough, pulled Max away. There would be a ton of paperwork to complete based on this incident. They might as well get it over with. Since Chelsea had felt threatened, Alex was taken downtown to the police station but was released because Chelsea decided not to press charges since he hadn't physically hurt her and because he was still Taylor's father. He was coward; otherwise he would have hurt her long before now. Plus, with Max living in the same city, it would be hard for him to run or hide from his wrath. Max and Chelsea had to go to the police station for questioning as standard procedure.

Riding in Max's Lexus 470 SUV from the police station, Chelsea had all kinds of questions. How did Max know that she was in trouble? Why was he back? Why had he contacted her after two years? Was there any truth to what Alex said that he had tried to contact her only to be intercepted by Alex? How did he feel about her, knowing that she was the cause of all of his pain and suffering? Did his return, mean that he still loved her?

She didn't know which question to ask first. Silence filled the space as each one dealt with all of the emotions from that day.

Max drove silently to Chelsea's house. While at the police station, he had contacted the local Lowes to come and outfit the hole that he had created when he broke down the door with a new one. Hopefully they were finished by now.

He was holding himself in check. His emotions were still at a fever pitch. Beating Alex was not enough. He had wanted to kill him. Never before, even in his line of work, had he wanted to kill someone in cold blood. Luckily the police had allowed him to work off some of his anger and had stepped in to pull him off when it was obvious that his anger wasn't going away any time soon.

Finally Chelsea couldn't take any more of the silence. She needed answers. Turning towards Max, she looked at him in a different light. Gone were some of the softer edges that used to be there in his persona. Instead he emanated a hard edge that was comforting as well as sexy. He was still protective of her and for that she was glad. He was and had always been, her hero.

Pulling into Chelsea's driveway, Max turned off his SUV and turned in his seat towards Chelsea. "Do you want to talk now, or wait until tomorrow when you're feeling better?"

He was giving her a way out if she was uncomfortable talking about what occurred.

"I'd rather go ahead and talk tonight if that's all right with you."

Getting out of the SUV, Max walked around to the passenger's side, to open the door for Chelsea. Reaching inside the confines of the SUV, Max unfastened Chelsea's seatbelt. Her lips parted in surprise when Max reached down to encircle her waist to hoist her from the SUV. Clutching his shoulders, Max brought her completely flush against his body, as he slid her down so that her feet would connect to the pavement. His body burned for her touch. He had been scared earlier that he might not arrive in time to stop Alex from hurting her.

Reaching up, Chelsea pressed a blazing kiss to Max's lips. "Thank you."

Hugging her tightly, Max released the breath that he had been holding. His heart was finally starting to settle down.

Walking together towards the house, he was glad to know that the home improvement store had installed the new door without any problems. Reaching into the mailbox on the front porch, he retrieved the new key.

Inserting the key into the lock, he went in the house first to make sure that nothing was amiss. Finding that everything was okay, he motioned for Chelsea to come in.

Checking on Taylor was Chelsea's first priority. Finding that Jackie had everything under control and that Taylor was well taken care of, she hung up the phone.

Deciding to get to the heart of the matter, Chelsea started verbalizing all the thought that were running through her mind. "Max, how did you know where I lived? How did you know that I was in trouble? Why did you come back? Was it true what Alex said about intercepting your call?"

Choosing to answer the most difficult question first, Max replied, "Yes Chelsea, I contacted you as soon as I was free to do so, once my top secret mission was completed. Alex answered the phone and told me in no uncertain terms that you were his wife."

"Why did you believe him?" She demanded.

"Why wouldn't I believe him? It had been over twelve months since I had contacted you. My guess was that you had moved on otherwise why would he be answering your phone? It nearly destroyed me when he said that you were married. When I searched for any records that could prove what he said, it only confirmed what I had been told."

"Max, you don't know how sorry I am that I didn't get that call. It would have changed my life. I would have waited for you. I assumed that since you hadn't communicated with me nor called, that you couldn't handle the fact that I was carrying Alex's baby. Since I couldn't have the man that I loved, I was willing to provide the best family life that I could for Taylor. For that I apologize. Can you forgive me?"

"Sweetheart, that's the past. I forgave you a long time ago. The question is; can you forgive me for believing a lie that was told to keep me away from you? I should have known better. He was my competition. I shouldn't have trusted anything that he had to say."

"It's enough to know that you cared enough to call me once you were free. How did you know where I lived and what caused you to call me today? Can I get you anything to eat or drink?" She inquired as she fixed herself some hot cider.

"What's on the menu? Do you really want the truth? I'm not so sure that you will like the answer."

"Haven't we always been honest with each other?"

"I had tabs put on you. I wanted to know the minute that your marriage fell apart so that I could be next in line," he said simply.

Smiling, Chelsea asked, "You were that sure that my marriage wouldn't work? How come you knew that and I didn't?"

"How could it when you loved me so completely?"

"Good point. What about the reason that you knew that I was in trouble?"

"Baby, whenever you hurt, I hurt. I felt your pain deep in my heart. My instincts were crying that something wasn't right. Those same instincts have kept myself and my team members alive on more than one occasion, so I've learned to trust them and act on them."

Leaning forward, Chelsea kissed Max again on the lips. "Thank you from the bottom of my heart. I wasn't sure what Alex was going to do."

"Don't thank me; thank God that I was able to reach you in time."

"We'll tackle the keeping tabs on me at a later date. Since you got here so fast, were you planning on coming to see me today?"

"Yes. I wanted to see where your relationship with Alex stood. What do you plan on doing now?"

"I've filed for divorce and it should be finalized within the next seven months."

"I know, my resources told me that the papers had been filed. Is there any chance that the two of you will get back together, even after today?"

"Not a chance in hell. Even before today, things have been over for quite some time. Alex was correct. I never got over you. He could never measure up. Hopefully in time, he'll find someone that can love him for who he could be if he ever grows up."

"Sweetheart, I've had the same problem. After all that I've been through, in every woman I saw you. No one was ever good enough. Isn't it time that we stop fooling ourselves and find out if the love still exists beyond the passion?"

"Can you do that without holding any animosity against me from the past and the hurt that I've caused?"

"Yes, otherwise I wouldn't have been keeping up with your life and I certainly wouldn't be here right now, if I didn't still love you."

"Then yes, Max, I want to explore whatever is left of our feelings."

"Chelsea, can we agree on how our relationship will be handled until your divorce is finalized?"

"What do you mean Max?"

"Given everything that's happened, I'm a little cautious. I don't want to be hurt again. I won't be satisfied until your divorce is final. We can date and get to know each other until then."

Laughing at Max, Chelsea demanded, "So, no making love; is that what you mean?"

"I think that since we've been away from each other for awhile, that we need to use this time to get to know each other again."

"How long do you think that will last?" Chelsea asked, thinking that a miracle would have to take place, since the chemistry between them had always registered off the Richter Scale.

"I don't know. We've been here for all of what, two hours, and it's all I can do not to ravish you. Maybe I'll be so busy at work and on frequent trips that the time will go by quickly."

"One can always hope. It's good to have you back. I've missed you."

Kissing her passionately and ardently on the lips, Max whispered, "I love you still" then "I'll be in touch" as he left her house while he still had the willpower.

Over the next several months, they communicated by phone and email if Max had to go away on business. Whenever he was in town, they went on dates as part of their getting to know you again phase.

Chapter Sixteen

Erica woke up the next day feeling sleepy but at peace. After sitting down to a gourmet breakfast, TJ with a long, lingering kiss filled with promise, left to go home to shower before he made his way to the office. They had a conference scheduled with Max at eleven to discuss the new sponsorship opportunity with the NHRA, the National Hot Rod Association, that TJ was instrumental in setting up. They were thinking about becoming a sponsor for one of the female drivers.

Getting out of the shower, Erica decided to dress to suit her happy mood. She pulled out an outfit that Pauletta had designed. It was a pair of black, wide legged mélange trousers made with acetate and viscose that complemented her figure, giving her a long silhouette. To make her outfit pop, she paired the trousers with an orange wrap shirt with kimono sleeves and her favorite Donald Pilner sling back wedge shoes. Grabbing her Donald Pilner pocketbook she was ready for anything.

At least that's what she thought until she got to work and walked into the conference about the NHRA sponsorship.

Excited to meet an actual female driver for the NHRA circuit, Erica was stunned when Mia, TJ's ex-girlfriend, walked into the room. Erica wondered what in the world was going on. How could TJ be so disrespectful to think that he could have a relationship with her while their company sponsored his ex-girlfriend's racing car?

To caught up in her own thoughts, she missed TJ's introduction of the driver as none other than his cousin, Shauna Miaonette Carver. Seething in her chair, Erica looked at her brother, to see what he thought about the entire episode. He knew how she felt about TJ.

Max, who knew the driver's identity thought nothing of the introduction and therefore was listening intently to TJ's presentation. Since TJ and Erica were now dating, he thought that they had resolved all of their past issues so the sponsorship shouldn't have been a problem. Consequently he missed the nonverbal inquiry that Erica threw his way. Instead he focused on the projected cost of the sponsorship and the benefits they would receive from the increased exposure.

Mia, as she preferred to be called, surveyed the room, seeking the reaction to the proposed sponsorship. Everyone but Erica was excited about the prospect. Laughing to herself, she thought it was funny that TJ had gone to such lengths to get the attention of the woman who had stolen his heart at an early age by using her, his cousin, as his girlfriend.

Picking up on the icy, unfriendly vibe that was coming from Erica, Mia was surprised that she was still being so hostile towards her, since they had gotten on so well during their childhood. Granted it had been awhile since they had seen each other but she didn't deserve the murderous looks she was being thrown unless…

Nah, she thought to herself, TJ wouldn't be so stupid. Looking at the hurt expression in Erica's eyes as she watched TJ during the presentation and the way that her eyes were welling up, Mia put two and two together that Erica was suffering from a grave misconception.

Abruptly things came to a head during the presentation, when Erica got up and stormed out of the conference room on the verge of tears because she couldn't vent her frustration. Usually if her feelings were hurt and she was really mad and couldn't vent her frustration, she would end up crying. It was one of the habits that had stuck with her from childhood that usually she was able to control. Immediately Mia left the room to straighten out the mess that her cousin had initiated.

Concerned, TJ stopped talking in the middle of his sentence as he watched Erica run out of the room. Feeling that something was wrong, he made a move to go after her.

He got as far as the door before Max stopped him.

"Everyone break for lunch. We'll resume at two o'clock. TJ, can I talk to you for a minute?"

"Would you tell me what in Hades is going on? Why did Erica look so surprised when Mia in came today?"

"I don't know. That's what I was going to find out before you stopped me," he said exasperatedly as he opened the door. "Erica has run from me one time already and I was stopped by Mrs. Maness, when she got scared of the intimacy between us. I promised myself that I wouldn't let her do that again, without following her. You'll just have to wait, Max until I make sure that she's okay."

TJ raced down the corridor to her office but she wasn't there. He searched all over the Executive Wing, but couldn't find her before deducing that she was probably in the bathroom, down the corridor from the conference room.

Erica ran down the corridor to the nearest bathroom to gather her composure and to put a cold compress on her puffy eyes. She couldn't believe that her love for TJ could cause her so much pain.

That's where Mia found her several minutes later.

Walking into the bathroom, Mia bent low to check to see how many people were in the restroom and to see if Erica was inside. Finding only one set of legs she returned to the door to lock it. She didn't want anyone to interrupt their conversation. Leaning against the sink, Mia waited until Erica came out of the bathroom.

As Erica unlocked the bathroom stall door, she was startled to find Mia leaning against the granite countertop. Averting her eyes before she resorted to calling her names and scratching her eyes out, she washed her hands and dried them on the Egyptian Cotton towels. Turning to face her, she stared into the face of the woman who was offering her a genuinely friendly smile.

Trying to be as cordial as possible even though she wanted to hit the woman, Erica took the time to really assess her competition. She was beautiful, with long, flowing, coal black hair that hung to the middle of her back. Her eyes were a smoky gray that reminded one of a cat. If her eyes were green, they would remind her of TJ. He had the prettiest eyes on a man that she had ever seen.

Noticing that the light bulb moment was about to arrive, Mia held out her hand in a friendly greeting. "Erica, it's me, little Shauna Miaonette Carver, TJ's cousin, just in case you spaced out while he was giving his presentation. My friends call me Mia. I know that it's been awhile since you've seen me, but we used to be friends. I hope that after we beat TJ down, we can regain the friendship that we had growing up when my twin brother and I visited during the summers."

Looking at Mia like she was crazy, Erica murmured, "Shauna and her twin brother" then screamed, "Shay-Shay", before laughing and crying hysterically as she threw her arms around Mia's neck.

"Ahhh, I see you remember now. How could you forget what I looked like? It's only been a few years. I haven't changed that drastically, have I?" Mia asked with her hands on her hips, as she handed Erica another towel.

"Do you realize the pain and suffering you and your cousin put me through, thinking that he was deeply involved with another woman? That I had lost the opportunity to regain the love that I once threw away? Why didn't I realize the resemblance before? What's different? You still look just like Mrs. James."

"It could be my hair. In between races it's hard to visit my regular stylist so I grew it long so that I didn't have to do too much with it. Plus a helmet wreaks havoc with a hairdo. Erica didn't TJ tell you I was in town? I spoke with him yesterday, when he was on his way to your house to apologize and he said that he explained to you that we were back. If I'm not mistaken, he spent the night at your place because he didn't come back home. We're staying with him while they complete a few more changes to the house."

"Um, yes TJ did explain that his cousins were here, but he called you Shauna. I only remembered Shay-Shay from our childhood. He failed to explain that you and Shauna were one and the same. For the past several months, I've wanted to kick your butt for taking my man at HangOut Night because I was too scared to participate." Thinking back to that time, Erica pulled the letter that she kept from Mia from her purse.

"You sent this to me didn't you?"

"Yes. I figured that you needed some help. Both of you were tip toeing around each other. Always staring at each other but unwilling to take the next step. I thought that I was pretty clear what needed to happen in order to recapture TJ's heart. He would never tell me the story about what happened. All he would say was that he needed my help in order to light a fire under you so that he could reclaim his princess. If you don't mind my asking, what happened between the two of you?"

"It's a long story. If you really want to hear it, let's go to lunch and I'll tell you."

"That's a deal. What are you going to do about TJ? You know that he's my favorite cousin. When no one else wanted to see me drag race, TJ was the one that would get everyone in the car and just drive to the races. It would be too late for anyone to refuse by then, because they would already be at the track. He holds a special place in my heart. How much do you love my cousin?"

"He's my best friend, my knight in shining armor and my hero. He's everything to me. Once I tell you about our past, you'll understand what happened after your family moved North. However, he's going to pay for this little charade, at least for a little while, until he makes this up to me."

"Will this scheme have a happy ending?"

"That depends on TJ." At Mia's look of horror, Erica burst out laughing. "Yes, barring death, it will definitely have a happy ending."

Backtracking to the conference room, TJ stopped by the bathroom. Knocking on the door, he told the occupants that they needed to leave because he needed to speak with Erica.

Hearing his voice from outside the door, Erica replied, "TJ, go away. I'm really not in the mood to talk to you civilly right now."

"Sweetheart, please let me explain…"

"No TJ, you had all of last night to explain when you spent the night at my house. Why didn't you then?"

"Because I didn't want to lose you. I knew that if I explained my scheme, you would say to hell with me; that you were too old to play games. Then all the ground that we had gained would be lost. I couldn't risk going back to "best friend". I wanted more," he replied desperately, no longer caring that he was baring his soul. He felt as if once again, Erica was slipping through his fingers.

"Please Erica, let's talk about this."

Unlocking the bathroom door, Erica attempted to brush past TJ. Expecting her dismissal, TJ was quick to grab her hand as he swung her around to face him. The momentum of the swing slammed her body into his, making the impact, a shock of pure pleasure as their bodies collided.

Erica's startled eyes flew to TJ's, whose eyes had darkened with desire as her body of its own accord, had sensuously rubbed against his. Bending his head, he quickly captured her mouth with his, licking and sucking, exploring all of the crevices of her mouth until she frantically pulled away.

With her chest heaving and a sob in her voice, she whispered, "TJ, I can't handle that right now. Just let me be," before walking away rapidly to the elevator to exit the building.

Hitting his head against the wall repeatedly, TJ muttered to himself, "Why can't she just accept my love and let me help her heal? Okay so I made a miscalculation. The scheme accomplished more than I had anticipated. What do I do now?"

Straightening up from the wall, TJ walked back to the conference room to face Max.

Looking at TJ's tight expression, he knew that things didn't go well. He had received a text from Erica from the car that she was all right; that she finally remembered Shay-Shay and that she was going to make TJ pay for his scheme for a couple of weeks. The least he could do was to give him hope, because he was going to need it.

"Let's start from the beginning TJ. Surely you told Erica the reasoning behind Mia showing up at HangOut Night and who she really was? Have you straightened out all your past issues? What just happened here today?"

"I told her who Mia was when they first moved back here when Carl and Mia met me at the gym. Erica happened to be driving by the gym to find me after she freaked out when I kissed her and she saw me give Mia a hug as soon as she got out of the car. Unfortunately, we didn't see her. After going over to auntie's house, I went by Erica's house to apologize for letting my desires rush her. She didn't answer any of my calls so I went home. Finally about twelve o'clock, I guess she had calmed down enough to return my call. I went over for a face-to-face conversation and we worked everything out. I thought that I had explained everything enough but it seemed that I didn't.

"Did Erica see the person up close that you were hugging if she was driving in her car and probably crying seeing you with another woman?"

"Probably not because there were other things on her mind that day. She only said that she glanced at her. Did I explain why Mia was participating in HangOut Night? No. I thought that after I told her who Mia was, that she was my cousin Shauna, she would remember her from our childhood. Trust me Max, Erica and I already had this conversation yesterday about Carl and Mia before we digressed into some other issues. Obviously she didn't connect the two."

"TJ, I'm only going to say this once. Don't hurt my sister again! Figure out a way to make your relationship work. Handle your business. If I know Erica, she's not going to forgive you anytime soon. Plan on groveling and begging for the next couple of months. You know how long she can hold a grudge. If you want her back, I would suggest you get ready to be a participant in HangOut Night. I'm sure she's going to try to get you back for what you did."

"Yeah I know but this time its not some insignificant matter. It's my life, my best friend, my love, my future and my destiny. If she tries, I'll be ready for her."

"By the way, you mentioned that she freaked out when you kissed her. Do you think she's ready for you?"

"No, I don't think so. I'm willing to be as patient as she needs me to be. She initiated the last kiss but when I tried to deepen it she literally bolted. Given time though, she'll come around, I hope. Since we've dissected my love life, how's yours?"

"It's looking better. Chelsea's divorce is almost final. Then that means there will not be any obstacles between us. I finally will be able to claim her as my wife. I can't wait. Unfortunately I'll be going to Japan within the next two days for about four weeks so I won't be here, when it's finally official. Once I get back though, get ready for a wedding!"

Chapter Seventeen

Two weeks later, Chelsea got the call, all mothers dreaded. The daycare called and told her that Taylor had fallen and cut herself pretty deeply and was bleeding profusely. Taylor just happened to be a bleeder like Chelsea. The ambulance was en route to rush her to the hospital. Chelsea had someone from the office rush her to the hospital because she was afraid that if she drove, she would have an accident.

"How bad is she?" Chelsea asked, as she ran through the doors of the emergency room straight to the nurse's station. The nurse immediately told her that the doctor would be the only one able to give specific information about Taylor.

"Ma'am, the doctor should be with you shortly. He's still attending to her right now."

"She's still bleeding," said the daycare director, Mrs. Tensley as she arose from the couch to meet Chelsea halfway across the room.

"Can I see her? When is the doctor coming back out?" Chelsea asked in a whisper, fearing the worst. She started to nervously pace the floor in the emergency waiting room.

"No, they are still trying to stop the bleeding. She's lost a lot of blood. The doctor that examined her said that she might have to have a blood transfusion. I'm so sorry that this happened.

One minute all the children were playing nicely in the playground area then all of a sudden, one of the children cried out that Taylor had fallen on a stump in the ground and had hurt herself. When we went to check on her, blood was everywhere. There was a raised nail in the stump that she fell on. We cleaned it at the center as best as we could, but we could not stop the bleeding. That's when we contacted you." Mrs. Tensley replied as she tried to explain the horrible events that occurred. She was so agitated that her words were coming out in great heaving gasps.

Fearful that the woman was going to have a heart attack, Chelsea put her hand on the woman's back in an attempt to soothe her. "Mrs. Tensley, I know that accident's happen. You've done a good job with Taylor so I know how meticulous you are."

At that moment, the doctor emerged from the Emergency Triage area. "Is there anyone here yet from the family?"

"Yes, I'm her mother. How is she? Will she be all right?" Chelsea asked tremulously.

"I've got some bad news for you. Her injury is very serious. Because she has lost a lot of blood, she possibly will need a transfusion and because of the raised nail the possibility of an infection is probable. Is there anyone in the family that has the same blood type? What about you or your husband? Unfortunately, at this time, we are running low on our rare blood supply," the doctor said apologetically.

"I do, but due to a viral infection from Operation Desert Storm, I can't give blood, however, her father Alex does." Chelsea secretly wondered if Alex would even show up if she contacted him.

"Call him, we need him here ASAP," said the doctor imperatively.

"He lives in Tennessee. I don't know how soon he could come," said Chelsea with a new type of worry in her heart.

"He has to be here within the next twenty four hours otherwise she's not going to make it. Excuse me, while I go back to check on her. Right now she's stable but I can't say for how long." The doctor left the waiting room.

Oh my God, O my God! I can't lose her now. Chelsea thought to herself.

"Chelsea, Chelsea, what can we do to help?" asked her sisters as they came running through the emergency room doors. It seemed as if the entire emergency room was filled with Chelsea's family and friends. Everyone started talking at once until Chelsea screamed for them to HUSH!

"Look, someone call Alex, he has to get here within the next twenty four hours to donate blood otherwise, Taylor's not going to make it."

Chelsea's sister Anita ran outside to use her cellular phone to try to reach Alex at home and at work. No luck, which meant that he was out in the field working. Alex was a pharmaceutical salesperson for a large corporation. Anita rushed back into the emergency room with the news that she was unable to reach Alex.

"Call his job and have them give you a list of the numbers for all the businesses that's on his route for today. They should be able to pinpoint his whereabouts. If not call all of them and leave a message." Chelsea sat down on the chair and began to pray.

"Done. I'm on it," Anita replied as she once again left the emergency room.

Brian, Chelsea's best friend and Taylor's godfather came over to comfort her.

"Brian, come over here please." Chelsea asked as she led him to the farthest corner of the room, away from prying ears. "Can you contact Max and let him know? I'm sure he would want to know." She pulled out a pad from her voluminous pocketbook to write down Max's telephone number.

"Okay Chelsea. Anything you want me to tell him?" Brian asked taking the slip of paper from her and sticking it into his pocket.

"Tell him to be ready to donate some blood if needed." Chelsea whispered.

"Chelsea, is there something you're not telling me? Is Max the father, and if so, why did you get married to Alex and let him think that Taylor was his?" Brian asked as he put his arm around her shoulder to comfort her.

"Brian, when I went to the doctor I was already pregnant or so I thought. The doctor told me that I was having a miscarriage. She said that I was in the last stages of the miscarriage because I was spotting and had been bleeding heavily. Unfortunately you remember the trauma that Alex caused asking me to get an abortion and the resulting pain that I experienced after that."

"When Alex asked for an abortion and I told him that I was keeping my baby, we argued, and he walked out. He up and left me remember? Well, I didn't believe that doctor so I went for a second opinion. The next doctor took two blood samples during different weeks to see if I was pregnant. One test result came back negative. That's when I knew that I really did have a miscarriage.

Well the next week, Max came back to town and time stood still. I was glad that Alex was gone. In my heart I knew that I had never stopped loving Max. Therefore when he came to visit, we sought refuge in each other's arms. It was as if we had never been apart. Anyway, I kept having cramps and light spotting. We had used condoms that night but one had a tear in it, we found out later the next morning. I went to the doctor and the pregnancy tests came back positive this time. I was barely four weeks pregnant. At that point, I didn't know what to believe. I thought that the tests were just wrong and the baby was really Alex's."

"Then what makes you so unsure now?"

"Well, Momma has asked me on several occasions if Taylor was Max's child. I always said no because that's what I believed. Now, I'm not so sure. My baby needs blood from her father and right now I can't say one hundred percent who that is. What if Max can't be reached? What if he doesn't get this message? What if Alex doesn't get the message? Who will I find to give blood?" Chelsea asked, working herself into a frenzy.

Brian pulled Chelsea close. "Don't worry. We'll find both of them. If I have to smack both of them and put them in a chair to take their blood, I will. Taylor will be fine. Don't worry." Brian left the emergency room to call Max.

As he dialed Max's cellular telephone number, he got a recording. He left a message, praying that Max would get the message in time. "Max, this is Brian, Chelsea's best friend and

Taylor's godfather. I'm not sure if you remember me or not from a cookout you attended awhile back. Chelsea needs you. Taylor was in an accident. She's not doing to well. The next twenty-four hours are critical. Please page me a.s.a.p. We're at the Moses Cone Hospital."

Meanwhile Max was soon on his way back to his hotel after several long meetings with a major buyer for some of Sole Impressions fragrances, in Japan. He had a funny feeling that something was wrong. Max couldn't put his finger on the problem that would cause the sinking feeling in the pit of his stomach.

He reached into his suit jacket to retrieve his cellular phone and contacted his mother and sister to check to see if anything was wrong or if someone was hurt. They both were surprised to hear from him, but they assured him that indeed, everyone was okay. He hung up the phone feeling sick to his stomach. As he pulled into the hotel's parking lot, Max felt for his pager on his hip. It wasn't there. He must have left it in the hotel room. That would explain why it didn't go off.

Max was one that always relied on his hunches. If he felt this way, then something was definitely wrong. Once in his hotel room, Max checked his voice mail at work. Still nothing. He then called his answering machine at home and got Brian's message.

"Oh my God. I'm not even sure if there's a plane at this hour going back to the States." He stated aloud as he grabbed his suit coat that he had just discarded on the bed and dialed the concierge to get him a taxi to the airport.

As the taxi came to a halt, Max quickly handed the driver a bill and told him to keep the change as he hurriedly exited the taxi and ran to the airline counter. "I need to book a flight on the Concord back to the United States to North Carolina on the East Coast, immediately."

"Sir, this ticket is going to be very expensive," replied the airline ticket counter person, looking suspiciously at Max.

"I don't care how much it costs! Do it now! My child is critically ill and not expected to make it within the next twenty-four hours. She needs some blood, so cut the red tape and book the flight now to leave in the next thirty minutes. If I need to purchase all the seats on the entire flight, just do it! My daughter doesn't have time to spare!" Max then handed her his Citibank Ultima Card. This card allowed him to purchase anything, even a jet, anytime, anywhere and was only offered to customers by invitation.

Once the ticket clerk, punched in his card number, a flashing message was displayed. It read that the owner, Maxmillian Teal, had unlimited credit and was able to purchase anything and that in the event of a medical emergency, the airlines, in cooperation with the French Government, would extend to him a flight on the Concord, back to the States from wherever in the world he happened to be, without question, at any time, or place.

Immediately, the clerk apologized profusely and made the necessary arrangements for the flight. "Sir, the flight should be ready within the hour. Please accept my apology."

Max sat on the plane, he reflected how ironic it was that he referred to Taylor as his child. He grabbed his cellular phone once he was in the air to try to contact Chelsea. He only had Brian's cellular number. Chelsea was opposed to using her cellular phone.

"Hello, this is Max. Can I please speak to Chelsea?" He strove to be as calm as he possibly could given the situation. His manners seemed to have left him at the moment. He shook himself as he tried to get his emotions under control.

"You can't, she's in the room with Taylor and the doctor right now. However, whenever they finish, I'll give her the phone to call you right back, okay?" Brian compromised.

"This is Brian, right?" asked Max.

"Yes."

"Thanks for calling me. Do you know what happened? How's Chelsea holding up?"

"Not good. She thinks that she's about to lose the only thing that she has left. She lost you, or so she thinks. She couldn't stay married to Alex. Taylor is all she has left. Save her if you can. The details of the accident are vague. Chelsea was too distraught to tell us." Brian could feel the emotion in Max's voice as he asked about Chelsea and Taylor.

"How does Chelsea think that I can help Taylor?"

"I really don't think that I'm the one to tell you why. Chelsea should talk to you. Suffice to say that Taylor needs a blood transfusion immediately. Why don't you wait for the details until you arrive? How much longer will you be in the air? Why don't you take a short nap? I know that you are exhausted, or you will be before the night is over."

"Approximately another two hours. You're right. In this state, I won't be much help to Chelsea. Please let her know that I will be there in two hours to help in any way that she needs me too." Max clicked off the phone and settled back to get at least thirty to forty five minutes of sleep.

At that point, Alex rushed into the emergency waiting room. "Brian, how is Taylor?" He asked as he walked toward the family that was in waiting room.

"Not to good. She's in critical condition. Chelsea is in her room with her. Why don't you go on down there," said Brian with as much sympathy as he could muster for Alex. He could not stand the man after the way he treated Chelsea but at least he came.

Alex walked into Taylor's room. He stared at all the monitors surrounding the room. Tears started to run down his face. He realized that life was too short to hold a grudge. Life was too precious to waste. Alex looked towards the sky to make a plea to the Lord. *God, please let Taylor and Chelsea forgive me. Please spare her Lord. Let her live. Let me get the chance to show her how much I care.* He reached over to touch Chelsea, whose head was bent over Taylor's hand. "Chelsea, Chelsea."

"Thank God you're here Alex. I'm not sure what happened. The daycare told me but the details are hazy. She needs blood. She has a rare blood type and she's a bleeder like me. Hopefully, you are a match. What's your blood type?" Chelsea asked as she gave him a brief hug for showing up. She never could remember what type of blood everyone had. Since Alex hardly ever got sick, that small detail from the time that they got their marriage license escaped her.

"O positive. When do I need to give the blood? Where are the doctor's? Please forgive me for all that I've put you through. How can I make it up to you? I want both of you in my life. I was stupid. Can you forgive me? Alex asked with tears streaming down his face.

"Alex, I told you that I forgave you a long time ago. I was just disappointed and hurt. Just help me to help Taylor. All is forgiven. But what did you say your blood type was?" Chelsea asked desperately hoping that she had not heard correctly.

"O positive. Why?"

"It's not a match for Taylor. I'm a match but ever since I got back from Saudi Arabia in Operation Desert Storm, and had that viral infection, I can not give her the blood she needs." The ramification of him not being a match eluded Alex at that moment however it didn't elude Chelsea. *Oh God, what have I done?*

"Who can help her?"

"I don't know. They are broadcasting on television right now to find a donor. Let's hope someone will call in the next twenty-four hours and come in and donate clean blood," replied Chelsea wearily.

"Just pray that they will. Will you be all right? I need to go and pray." Alex left the room in search of a chapel. It didn't dawn on him that he should have stayed to offer his support to Chelsea.

A few hours later Max walked into the hospital. He stopped at the emergency room's information desk to ask which room Taylor was in. The attendant told him that she had been transferred to Room 2002. He rushed to the room that Taylor was in. As he was about to open the door he noticed Alex. Max turned away towards the waiting room. He didn't think that he could be civil to him as much as he had hurt Chelsea. He noticed that the family was there. Everyone spoke but Chelsea's mother came up to him and hugged him.

"Thank God that you made it Max. Please help Taylor. She needs some rare blood. Chelsea and Alex are in her room right now. I don't think that he can give her the blood that she needs. I think that only you can. Please help. I know you care about her as if she were your own," pleaded Mrs. Bailey.

"What do you mean I'm the only one with the right blood? You don't even know what type of blood I have. However you are right in one regard. I do love Taylor as if she were my own. If I can give my life for her and Chelsea, I would. What can I do? My blood type is AB negative."

"Great! It's a match. Go get Chelsea." Mrs. Bailey urged Max towards Taylor's room.

At that moment, Chelsea walked out of Taylor's room and saw Max. She immediately went into Max's open arms. Max took her in his arms and started to kiss the tears away. "Sweetheart, I came as soon as I could. I was in Japan and caught the Concord back to the States. It was the quickest route I could take to make sure that I would get here in time. What can I do to help? Lean on me Chelsea. Let me ease some of your pain. Talk to me, cry if you need too. I'm here for you," murmured Max as he held her tightly to his heart.

Chelsea looked into Max's eyes and read the love there. She just wasn't sure how he was going to take her next news.

"Max, there is something I have to tell you." Chelsea released her arms from around Max's neck so that she could grab his hands. She led them to a separate corner of the room so that she could tell him the rest of her suspicions. "Only Taylor's father is a true match to donate blood. Alex is here. He's with Taylor now but his blood type doesn't match."

"What are you telling me?" asked Max whose ears did not hesitate to pick up on the meaning behind Chelsea's words.

"It appears that the doctor's didn't make a mistake after all when they told me I was going through a miscarriage back in October. Six weeks before, the doctor confirmed that I was pregnant. At that point I started spotting. They said that I had a miscarriage approximately two weeks later. It appears that when you came back, I immediately became pregnant again. Instead of being two months like the doctor told me I was less than four weeks."

"I don't know how it happened that I became pregnant so quickly. What's even more amazing is that we used condoms. I pray that you will forgive me. I thought that I was one hundred percent positive that Alex was the father. Now I know he's not. Regardless of how you feel about me, please save Taylor." Chelsea pleaded in a weary voice. She was too emotionally distraught to keep looking in Max's eyes. She didn't want to see the condemnation that she was sure would be in them. All she could do was pray for forgiveness. In time, Max would forgive her, she hoped.

Max dropped his hands from around Chelsea. He started to pace the floor. He was getting more worried by the second. "You mean to tell me that I'm her father?"

"Yes."

"So where does Alex fit in? He's here also. What does he want? You haven't even asked me what my blood type is. Don't you want to know?"

Chelsea's head was bent so that she missed the huge smile that Max had on his face. Max looked up towards the ceiling and thanked God for the wonderful gift Chelsea had given him. Please help her to pull through, was his silent prayer. Max put his finger under Chelsea's chin.

"Look at me, Chelsea. For a while I have wondered whose child she truly was. The timing was so coincidental. I always accepted the fact that she was Alex's child. I had every intention of adopting her if we ever got married. I loved her as if she were my very own. Now that I know she is, I hope that Alex will not have any objections to letting me adopt her. I love you Chelsea. Nothing can keep us apart. Life is too precious. Let me share your life. Let me bring sunshine into all the dark recesses of your mind. Let me be the one to hold you in your sleep, to grow old with you, to share life's ups and downs."

Max bent down on one knee and pulled out the blue Tiffany box that he carried with him at all times. He had loved Chelsea for so long that he didn't know when the opportunity would present itself for him to declare his love again. "Chelsea, will you marry me and be my soul mate forever, as long as we're on this earth and beyond?"

"Yes!" Chelsea replied happily through her tears.

"Baby, I believe you're supposed to look at the ring before you answer." As she opened the box, she gasped in surprise. The ring was gorgeous. It was a three-carat, marquis diamond ring with two rows of six diamonds and six sapphires, channel set on each side of the ring.

"Good, now kiss me. Boy, am I tired. Jet lag is something else. Chelsea, does anyone else know I'm Taylor's father?"

"No, only Brian."

"Okay, let's keep this between us then. Alex has had enough. I don't think that he would be able to take this on top of everything else. Let him continue to believe that Taylor is his. She can have two fathers. I won't mind if he comes by to visit because I'll get to see her all the time. I can see her grow up. He can't. Don't take that away from him. Just let him believe that I was the one to donate the blood to keep her alive. However, she has to be adopted by me and carry my name. Even if it's a hyphenated name. Agreed?"

"Agreed! You're wonderful."

"Yeah, I surprise myself sometime. Let's go get the doctor so that he can take my blood and save Taylor. I'll see you after this is over"...

Chapter Eighteen

Love was in the air since Max and Chelsea had made their engagement official and the news about his adoption of Taylor was finalized. Another HangOut Night had been planned for the following Friday, this time at Ryan's Retreat, the coffeehouse owned by Chelsea's sister, Ryan, who was having her grand opening and was donating the proceeds from this event to several local charities. Plus since HangOut Night for this evening only, was open to the public, the event, which was sponsored by the regular guys, was guaranteed to be a huge success. They had wanted a change of setting where they could woo the ladies with a live jazz band and show off their culinary skills.

That Friday night, at Ryan's Retreat, the men had a packed house. A plethora of men and women came out to enjoy the Cooking Competition, the Bachelor Auction, the Dating Game and the Pocketbook Swap. Erica, Mia, Chelsea, Sasha and Yvonne were on hand to help in any way that was needed. Mia had even convinced Erica that the best way to get revenge on TJ was to participate as a contestant for HangOut Night. That would force

TJ to bring his A game to go out on a date with her to make up for the drama that he had caused.

The first game for charity would be the Pocketbook Swap. Each woman was asked to bring a gently used pocketbook, wrapped in wrapping paper or a decorative bag to the HangOut Night. The pocketbooks would then be placed under a tree with a number on each one.

For each pocketbook that was submitted, the women would be given a ticket with a number on it. The first ticket would then be announced. The person with the first ticket would then be given the pocketbook with the corresponding number to unwrap. If they liked the pocketbook then they could keep it and donate five dollars to charity. If they didn't like the pocketbook, then they would have to donate twenty dollars to charity.

The person with the second number would then receive their pocketbook and upon unwrapping it, if they didn't like the pocketbook, they could take person number one's gift to keep, and donate their five dollars to charity. If they didn't like their pocketbook then they would have to donate twenty dollars to charity. This sequence would continue until the last pocketbook was given out. Therefore the person with the last ticket could have their choice of any of pocketbooks that were opened during the game and keep it.

What made the game fun was that new pocketbooks were mixed in with the gently used ones so women were laughing and arguing with each other for the distinctive bags. Some of the bags were from Marc Cross, Dooney & Burke, Gucci, Chanel, Prada and Dolce & Gabanna. It was hilarious. Erica ended up walking away with one of her favorite Prada bags since she had the last number.

The next event was the Bachelor Auction. Several of the nation's top bachelors had flown in to participate in the auction to help support the fight against cancer thanks to several favors that were owed to Max and TJ. Max even convinced Frank and Solomon, his partners from the military to participate.

When the bidding started, several basketball and football players were auctioning themselves for everything under the sun;

from dinner dates, to a night on the town, dancing under the stars, season tickets and a shopping spree. The bidding almost started a riot. Since the gifts were so valuable, a bidding war commenced between two women for the season tickets for the Dallas Cowboys. Everyone thought that the two would come to blows over the tickets. After about twenty minutes of bidding, when the price had escalated to ten thousand dollars, the judge called the bidding a tie. Each person was given season tickets, which made the two women very happy.

The highlight of the evening though was the twenty five people that opted to participate in the Dating Game. Due to the large number of people willing to participate, Max, TJ, David and Malcolm, who were Chelsea's brothers, and Frank and Solomon, decided to have five individual games where each of them would play host.

As the MC, Max laid out the ground rules, "We want to welcome you to the first, public HangOut Night Gathering. During this portion of the evening there will be twenty five people participating in our version of the Dating Game. In order to participate in this event you have to be single, unmarried and unattached; meaning no girlfriend or boyfriend, no baby mama drama, and you have to be financially solvent. These individuals have been investigated and meet all of the requirements."

"Each game will have five participants. We will ask a series of questions that you should answer as candidly as possible so that the contestant will be able to gage whether or not you're a potential match for them. Additionally, you may have to perform a task that's required from one of the questions."

"There will be a different host for each of the five games. We ask that you answer the questions as cleanly as possible and be respectful of the ladies that are here. If you choose not to act accordingly, you will be escorted out of the building. Please keep in mind that the lady or gentleman has the final choice in deciding who they select. If there are no further questions, then let's begin."

It was agreed that TJ would be the first host so that when Erica was one of the contestants, he would be free to participate.

TJ selected the contestant that would be asking the questions by pulling a name from the box that Mia held.

"The first contestant this evening is Pauletta. Please take your position behind the curtain on the stage, Pauletta."

With a squeal of delight, Pauletta, wearing one of her own designs; a red halter top that had a draped plunging back, over black, high-waisted, wide leg pants, which accentuated her slim figure, stepped onto the stage. A roar could be heard from the crowd. Things were off to an auspicious start.

"If the following gentlemen, Thomas Simms, Caleb Maine, George Holiday, Sebastian Cannery, and Miles Montgomery, who were chosen randomly could use the steps to the left to take their seats on the stage, we can begin."

A couple of ohs and ahhs could be heard from the audience as the ladies looked at the gorgeous, handsomely dressed gentlemen that took their places on the stage.

Holding out five cards, Pauletta selected one for her first question.

"Thomas, please describe the perfect morning date."

"Any date that I would be blessed enough to spend with you would be the perfect morning date," said Thomas glibly.

"Caleb, same question."

"The perfect morning date Pauletta, would start with a telephone call the night before, to confirm our date and to figure out if you had any food allergies that I should be aware of. Once that was taken care of, I would stop by your house the day of the date to pick you up early that morning. As we are walking to the car, I would open the door for you and get you settled. We would then drive to the beach and watch the sunrise. As we are watching the sun rise, I would serve you breakfast that I had previously packed in a basket that was stored in the back seat. Since I don't know you that well, the breakfast would be an assortment of a variety of foods that I'm sure you would enjoy. Over breakfast, we would get to know each other. The date would end with a walk on the beach. As we headed back to your house, as I walked you to the door, if we both enjoyed ourselves, I would ask to take you out again."

"Honey, if you don't pick him, then I'll take him," yelled someone from the audience.

"Thank you Caleb, that sounds like a wonderful experience. When do we leave?" Again laughter could be heard from the audience.

"George, if you had fifty dollars to purchase a gift that we both would enjoy, what would it be?

"If I had only fifty dollars to purchase a gift, I would treat you and me to a manicure and pedicure session at a local spa. That way, you would be relaxed as you get to know me and would not feel any type of pressure as the date progressed."

"I love relaxing."

"Sebastian, if we were dating and I had been out of town for two weeks, when my plane landed at eight o'clock in the evening, what would you have planned for me?"

"Pauletta, first I would pick you up from the airport in a limousine and then since you're probably tired, I would take you home where dinner would be delivered of some of your favorite foods, timed just right so that it would be nice and hot when you got home. While you were eating, I would run a hot bubble bath for you filled with luxurious bath salts, with candles lit around the bathroom for a soothing soak. Once you're finished with your bath, I would ask if you wanted a massage. If you did, then I would give you one and afterwards I would tuck you into bed and then say goodnight so that you could recuperate from your trip."

"Miles, what is your favorite fantasy?"

"My favorite fantasy is to spend five days on an island with ten of the most beautiful women in the world, from different countries to wait on me. Some would test my endurance athletically, climbing mountains, parasailing, things I haven't had the opportunity to do; others would challenge me mentally, while the rest would challenge me physically."

"Miles, is that a king mentality that I hear?"

"No, just a man enjoying everything that life has to offer."

"Pauletta, based on the answers given, who will you choose to take you out on your date?"

"TJ, this was a very hard decision. Some of the answers were very good. I choose Caleb because the picture that he painted with words for a morning date was beautiful. He showed that he was thoughtful by asking if I had any food allergies, which I do, as well as confirming our date the night before. He then talked about getting to know me, not assuming that we would hit it off. Lastly, he would ask for another date if it seemed that we both enjoyed ourselves. Again, not taking anything for granted, but making sure that if the chemistry was there that there wouldn't be any wondering on either of our parts."

Caleb, at that moment, came around the screen and held out his hand to Pauletta to help her rise from the chair. She almost swooned in the process because Caleb seemed at first glance to be everything that she looked for in a man. He seemed to be sincere, was six feet three, maybe four inches; was dressed divinely, like he was made for the suit, and not the suit made for him. Additionally, he was very muscular, like he worked out on a frequent basis. Being conscious of her health was important to her so she respected a man that could workout but not take it to the extreme.

As his hand enclosed over Pauletta's, Caleb felt a tingling in the pit of his stomach, as heat curled its way up his spine. Leaning over slightly, he pressed a short, fleeting kiss to Pauletta's cheek. It felt to her as if the wind were brushing against her skin; encircling her, bending and twisting, leaving her breathless and wanting.

"Ladies and gentlemen, let's hear it for our first couple." Applause could be heard as well as some of the haters. TJ stepped off the stage as he handed the mike to David.

Sasha carried the box to the stage so that David could pick the next contestant. This time it was a female who was chosen. "Erica, it's your turn. Please have a seat and will Sammy Nichols, Joshua Silverton, Derrick Jones, Carl Alexander, and Matthew Peters also take your seats."

Before the men took their seats, TJ pulled Carl to the side to remind him what was at stake. He had to use the answers that they had rehearsed earlier. TJ knew that in order to make amends for his previous scheme at HangOut Night, he had to utilize everything in his arsenal to deflate Erica's anger with the things that she loved the most in order to secure a date with her.

It had been three weeks since the Sponsorship Conference, and Erica still wasn't speaking to him. She had managed to avoid talking to him for the last three weeks. If there was something she needed at work, Pauletta or another employee would deliver it. If a deadline was due, either it got pushed back or she completed her portion of the project, signed off on it and had it delivered to him.

He was actually starting to have a little fun, trying to outwit her. At the most inopportune times, he would show up wherever she was to let her know he was on to what she was doing. Going to extraordinary lengths to see if he could catch her, was fun. To see her scramble to avoid him was priceless. Tonight wasn't any different. Carl would just have to be his decoy. No one else was going to date her, of that he was certain.

"Erica, the first question, please."

"Matthew, if money was not an object, meaning if you had an infinite amount of it, and I asked you to prepare dinner for me, what would you prepare?"

"I would buy dinner from the most expensive restaurant in the city and have it delivered to your house. I would pull out all the stops for you; candles, champagne, the best china with waiters to be at your beck and call for the entire evening."

"Carl, how would your answer be different?"

"Erica, first I would use whatever contacts were available to me to reach your best friend, to get your likes and dislikes, and any known food allergies. Then I would get your mother's telephone number, with your permission of course, so that I could convince her to let me fly her in so that she could teach me how to prepare two or three of your favorite meals. After I had mastered the meals under the tutelage of your mother, I would purchase a dozen roses or orchids to present to you at dinner, which would be spread out in the park on a blanket with soft music, playing in the background."

"I like that Carl. Any man that's willing to do all of that get's points in my book."

"Derrick, explain the perfect evening date."

"The perfect evening date would be a candlelit dinner in an intimate restaurant that you've never been to before that offered dancing and live music, where we could sit back, relax and enjoy one another in comfort."

"Derrick, that sounds romantic."

"Joshua, I like to watch Dancing with the Stars. Which dance, the samba, the quickstep, the tango, the salsa, rumba or the waltz, would you teach me and why?"

"Erica, I'm sorry to admit that I can't do any of those dances, but we could go Fred Murray's studio and learn the salsa together. That way we can teach other how to have fun, how to make a dance sexy while at the same time dancing uninhibitedly, letting our passions flow in the process. It would resemble the dance on Take the Lead, where the professional comes to the classroom to teach the students what dancing could be like."

"Good answer; loved the move."

"Sammy, if you were given a choice to receive a gift, a S500 Mercedes, a Lexus 470 SUV, a Rolls Royce, a million dollar home, a prominent franchise opportunity or a book full of unlimited love coupons, which one would you choose."

"That's a hard decision. I guess I would pick the one that would provide long term wealth. I would pick the prominent franchise opportunity so that I could provide you with the finer things in life. It would be something that we could build on together and provide a legacy for future generations."

"Carl, if you had to recreate one night or one moment in your life, what would it be?"

"If I had known you in a past life, it would be the Senior Prom. It would have been a magical evening where we would be caught up in the rapture of each other, dancing and holding each other close. I would have the pleasure of holding you in my arms without feeling guilty about our age difference, since I'm slightly older than you. That ceased to matter because I was totally captivated by your astonishing beauty. I knew that you felt it too, because your body trembled as I held you close. We laughed, we talked, we had so much fun that I didn't want the night to end, but of course, you had a curfew. As I kissed you gently on your lips at the door, my future, my destiny flashed through my mind. That evening will always remain in my mind because you chose to share it with me."

"Did you come to my Prom?" Laughter could be heard around the room.

"Joshua, I love to sing. Write a song for me or sing a song that best describes how you feel about me if we had been dating for awhile."

"If we've been dating for a while, the song that would best describe us would be…."

Joshua then picked up the mike and started to sing, "*Spend My Life With You*, by Eric Benet, in a velvet smooth, crooning voice that had the crowd singing along with him at the chorus.

"Matthew, same question."

"Erica, I would choose, *Still In Love* by Brian McKnight." Not to be outdone, Matthew pulled the mike and went out into the audience to serenade another female.

"Sammy, same question."

"It would have to be "Kem's, *Heaven*." Going to the piano in the corner, he started to play the song while singing and sounding just like the record.

"Derrick, what song would you choose?"

"The songs that would best describe our relationship would be, Boyz II Men *Your Love, This is My Heart and I'll Make Love To You*. Singing acapella, Derrick sung a medley of the three songs.

"Okay Carl, what do you have for me? Joshua, Matthew, Sammy and Derrick have serenaded me and others," she laughed, "with beautiful songs. What song would you sing?"

TJ who was sitting by backstage grabbed a mike as Carl grabbed the guitar that was leaning on a stand. After Carl played the first few bars, TJ started to sing the hauntingly beautiful song that he had written for Erica right after her horrific incident.

My Love

Your pain and suffering
I want to make them mine.
Trust in God and
All things will heal in time.
Your dreams, your goals, your fears,
Let me wipe away all your tears.
You are not alone in your pain,
Lean on me; let me ease your strain.

You take my breath away, please stay,
Listen to my heart, I pray.
For I love you, from now until eternity,
You are my life, my love, my destiny.

When times are hard and you can't cry anymore
Know that God will restore
All that was lost, it will be given back to you,
Your faith will make it come true.
Believe in our love; bring back your smile,
This too shall pass, in yet a little while.
Whatever life throws your way,
Together, we can face it, each and every day.

You take my breath away, please stay,
Listen to my heart, I pray.
For I love you, from now until eternity,
You are my life, my love, my destiny.

Carl, or rather TJ, who was singing at the back of the stage, drew a standing ovation. Applause could be heard all around the room.

After wiping her eyes, Erica asked the audience to give the participants a round of applause for singing so beautifully.

"Erica, which gentleman and crooner will be chosen for your date?"

"I choose Carl. May I ask if he wrote that song? It simply touched my heart."

Coming around the screen, Carl bent low over Erica's hand and kissed it. With TJ glaring from backstage, he thought it best to stick to the original plan before his cousin committed murder. His.

"Yes, that song was written for someone just like you. Whenever we go out on our date, I'll let you hear the rest."

Smiling, David congratulated the couple.

As Carl helped Erica from the stage, down the steps to an empty table, they made plans for their actual date to occur the following Saturday.

Tim, who had sent one of his basketball buddies to participate in the HangOut Night, stepped back into the picture when they inform him that Erica was a contestant. He then tracked down the limousine company that was scheduled to pick Erica and Carl up for their date from a flyer that the vendor had passed out. All of the vendors that participated in HangOut Night had a booth and were on hand to offer additional services if necessary.

Getting the limousine driver to contact him once he had dropped off the contestants at their destination was a piece of cake. Most drivers jumped at the opportunity to serve professional players, anticipating a good tip and the possibility of becoming their regular driver, especially if they frequented the city a lot. In his case, since he was from the area, the driver knew that he would get a lot of business.

Chapter Nineteen

Erica awoke Saturday morning with a feeling of euphoria. She was sure that TJ was behind the events that occurred at HangOut Night. The song that Carl had sung so beautifully, were the exact words that TJ had spoken to her time and time again, after her surgery, to help her heal. He must have given the words to Carl to put it to music.

She wondered if he was responsible for Carl participating in the event. Would TJ show up on the date, she wondered? Picking up the telephone, she thought about calling Mia, to get her take on things but decided not to. She wanted whatever TJ had come up with to be a surprise. If the surprise was a good one, it would definitely lessen the time he would have to spend asking for forgiveness. Deciding that she would be prepared for anything, Erica took her time getting ready and picked out an outfit that was sure to raise TJ's blood pressure.

It was another one of Pauletta's designs; a vivid pink, v-neck, knot front, bell shaped sleeve dress which showed off her gorgeous legs. Slipping on a pair of three inch stilettos, she was ready for her dinner date.

Looking at her watch, she realized that Carl would be there at any minute. Her conscience, who had been unreasonably quiet for too long asked, *"What if TJ isn't behind this? What will you do then?"*

The doorbell rang as she was walking downstairs.

Right on time, she thought, at least he had good manners. If TJ didn't show up then she would make the best of the date without leading Carl on. There was only one man for her, even though she was still presently mad at him.

Opening the door, "Hello Carl, won't you come in?" Erica asked with a voice filled with warmth. Looking at the limousine at the curb, she smiled. She liked the fact that he did things in style.

Bringing his arm from around his back, he produced a bouquet filled with roses and orchids and presented them to Erica. Bending her head to sniff the flowers, she smiled with joy.

Grabbing a camera out of his pocket, Carl asked, "Do you mind if I take a picture of you with the flowers? I want to have a little memento to remember this date by.

Never one to shy away from the camera, Erica eagerly agreed. Carl smiled because Erica was appreciative of the little things in life. He could understand why his cousin was so in love with her. He often wondered if there was a woman out there for him that would make him go to extreme lengths to win her love.

Enough of the pensive thoughts; it was time to head to the restaurant.

Locking the door behind her, Carl led Erica down the driveway to the limousine that was waiting. Trying to look through the tinted windows, Erica speculated whether or not TJ would be in the car waiting for her.

As the chauffer opened the doors, she was disappointed to find that the car was empty. Sitting back against the luxurious seating, she tried to attentively listen to Carl as he kept up a steady stream of conversation. Trying to snap out of her disappointment, she vowed that she would put TJ out of her mind and just enjoy the moment. Driving through the city, in less than thirty minutes, the limousine pulled up in front of Carrabbas, one of her favorite restaurants.

The driver, once he parked, used his cellular phone to text Tim the destination for the date, then exited the car to open the door for his passengers. Carl searched the parking lot before entering the building to see if TJ had arrived. Not seeing the familiar black, 745I BMW, he urged Erica inside. Maybe traffic had detained him.

After supplying the hostess with their last name, they were immediately whisked away to a private dining room that was adjacent to a stone paved courtyard. The room was decorated like a lover's paradise. There were a plethora of candles lit all around the room. Roses and orchids filled vases in every corner of the room with their tantalizing fragrance. Two flutes had even been placed on the table near the china place settings. Someone had gone all out for this evening. Gazing around the room in awe, Erica noticed that there were French doors that led to a private courtyard. With light jazz music playing in the background from the speakers in the ceiling and from speakers in the archway of the courtyard, a couple could easily feel like they were in a world straight from their dreams.

A dancer at heart, Erica stepped out into the courtyard and performed a series of dance moves to the music, before returning to the table to take her seat. Carl could only smile at Erica. She was enjoying herself. After they had gotten into the limousine, he thought that he had lost her for a while. Assuming that she was looking for TJ, she looked so forlorn and sad that he almost told her of TJ's plans.

"Excuse me Carl, but I love music and I love to dance. I hope that I didn't embarrass you. This is a very nice room. I've been here many times, but I've never seen this room decorated like this before."

"No apologies needed Erica. This date is all about you enjoying yourself. If you'll excuse me, I'm going to the gentleman's room. I'll be right back."

As soon as Carl walked out of the private dining room, Tim silently walked into the room from the courtyard. The French doors had remained cracked in order to fill the breeze that was blowing. With her back turned, Eric didn't hear Tim come into the room until he spoke.

"Hello Erica, I see that we meet again."

"What the hell are you doing here?"

"Funny you should ask. I'm waiting for your man to show up. Where is he? Where is TJ?"

"I don't know what you're talking about. TJ and I are not an item. I'm here with someone else and he'll be back shortly so I would advise you to leave. He doesn't take to kindly to someone talking to his woman."

"He's not going to be back for a while, Erica. He's been unavoidably detained right now as we speak. Tim answered with a smirk. He had covered all of the bases this time. He had a foolproof plan.

Reaching down to slip off her stilettos, she grabbed one in her hand, ready to strike at a moment's notice if Tim came any closer. Unobtrusively, she used her big toe on the other leg, to slide the other strap down from around her ankles. With both shoes off, she was prepared to run if Carl or help, didn't arrive. With the same hand under the table, she felt blindly into her pocketbook to turn on her cellular phone.

"Record. What do you mean, Tim," Erica asked? By speaking the word record, their entire conversation was being taped, thanks to one of Max's inventions.

"Let's just say that he might be feeling a little pain, right about now. I would advise you that when TJ walks in that you tell him you're not interested in him and that you and I are back together."

"Why would I do that? Didn't I tell you that TJ is not my date?"

"You might as well save your breath. Don't you realize that TJ is behind this entire charade? I've had people watching you Erica. He still loves you. What do you think all that crap was about on HangOut Night for the Dating Game?"

At her gasp of surprise, Tim decided to push the issue. "Didn't you see him backstage, singing that song to you?"

"How would you know? You weren't there. Even if it's true, he's not coming tonight."

"How about we wait and see? If you attempt to leave, I will punish you. So sit back and relax. Once he arrives, you'll never see him again if you refuse to cooperate. I'll kill him for sure this time. I won't miss like I did in the forest."

With fear in her eyes, Erica paled beneath her makeup. She jumped up and attempted to run to the door but Tim was quicker. He grabbed her from behind and slapped her across her cheek. Stunned from the unexpected blow, she fell back against the table, knocking her chair over.

That was how TJ found them when he opened the outer door to the private dining room. TJ, resplendent in a lightweight, linen Ralph Lauren suit, walked in with a bouquet of a dozen roses. Seeing Erica's eyes filled with fear and her cowering position against the table as if she had been thrown there, TJ went ballistic. All the hurt, the anger and the pain that both of them had suffered came to the forefront. He ran into the room and threw a roundhouse kick at Tim's midsection then followed up with a series of boxing jabs and uppercuts. Screaming for Erica to run, he punched Tim straight in the face, breaking his nose.

Before TJ could land another punch, Tim's friends, who were on standby outside, just beyond the courtyard, rushed to his rescue. They proceeded to throw a few punches of their own. A good martial arts expert, TJ quickly dealt them blows that knocked them to the ground. All of the fight went out of him however, when Tim grabbed Erica as she was attempting to stab him with the heel of her shoe.

He had a gun pressed against her neck, yet she was coming to his defense.

With his movements abruptly checked, TJ with his hands raised high, backed off of the men. "Please don't hurt her. If it's me you want, here I am. Let her go. Baby, why didn't you run?" TJ asked aggravatedly.

"Because I refuse to leave you. If you go down, then we both go down together."

"Aw, this is touching. Erica, we are going to leave now, before management comes with the police. If you want to see TJ alive, you have one hour and thirty minutes to show up at the designated address on this piece of paper without any federal agents, the police, or your brother Max. Once you arrive at that location, you will then be given instructions of what will be needed to gain TJ's freedom." Tim smiled as he prepared to leave the room, wiping the blood from his nose so that he would not draw undue attention to himself. He knew, that based on her actions today, Erica would show up at the address without calling anyone. It was obvious that she loved TJ if she was willing to take a bullet for him. What sane person would try to stab someone when they had a gun to their neck?

"Remember Erica, no cops. Show up alone or else. You now have only one hour to arrive at the location because of the little stunt that you just pulled."

"Erica, my love, don't do it! Go get help. I can handle this. I love you too much for you to risk your life for me."

"I'm not just going to stand by and let him kill the man I love. I'll do anything he wants if it means keeping you alive." Looking at Tim, she asked, "Where do I need to go? What's the address?"

Pulling a piece of paper from his pocket, Tim leaned on the table to write the address. He then motioned for his boys to finish what they had started. He then walked calmly through the door after removing his shirt, which was soaked with blood and disposed of it in a nearby trashcan. While he was in the bathroom, he also stopped the flow of blood from his nose.

Some of the patrons went berserk, seeing a famous, professional basketball player in the restaurant. Many of them stopped and asked for autographs. Tim spent the next fifteen minutes signing autographs, which provided him a good alibi.

Tim's thugs shoved TJ through the French doors, with a gun pressed into his back, into a waiting car. Carl burst into the empty dining room, just as they were hustling TJ around the corner of the courtyard.

He was too late.   Erica was gone and TJ was being kidnapped.

Pulling his revolver from his leg holster, he quickly ran outside, firing shots at the car that the thugs were getting into. Taking cover behind several columns, he kept firing until they were out of sight.

Someone would pay for kidnapping his cousin and for the welcome party that he had received in the bathroom.   Spinning around, he raced back to see if there were any clues that would point him in the right direction.   Flipping out his cellular phone he hit the speed dial number for Max.

Immediately Max came on the line.   "Max."

"Max, this is Carl. I need you to come to Carrabbas immediately! The HangOut Night date for Erica and TJ went terribly wrong. Erica's missing and some guys took TJ away in a car. I'm still at the restaurant, trying to find a clue as to where they went. I left the room, just like we had planned so that TJ could surprise her. Unfortunately, a little surprise was waiting for me in the bathroom.   There were four men that tried to take me out. After I managed to subdue them I ran back into the private dining room; Erica was gone, there was blood on the floor and there were two men leading TJ away with a gun to his back. I raced after them, shooting at them, but to no avail." Carl was a detective with the New York Police Department who was relocating to the South with his parents, so he was licensed to carry a weapon.

"I'm on my way." Disconnecting the call, Max then called Frank and Todd, his partners at the agency for backup. If both Erica and TJ were missing, there was only one person that hated them that much to pull a stunt like this. Getting into his car, he called Trevor, another agency team member to put a trace on Tim, Erica's high school boyfriend, to find his whereabouts.

The stakes had just gotten higher. They had to find them soon, before a desperate man went over the edge.

After arriving at Carrabbas, Frank and Todd proceeded to investigate the dining room for clues as to what occurred. The police who had been called by management were questioning the staff that was working the night shift. No one seemed to have any idea of what took place until the commotion had escalated to a shooting match outside. Max asked that the policemen investigate the limousine driver and all the remaining patrons to see if they remembered anything.

Carl and Max then joined Frank and Todd in the private dining room. "What do we have here?"

Frank responded, "It appears there was a scuffle. Several chairs were knocked over which indicates that someone who was previously standing, was knocked backwards against the table."

Todd then interjected, "There's quite a bit of blood here also, so someone's hurt."

A flash of pain entered Max's eyes as he remembered the last time he had to deal with Tim, and Erica's life had hung precariously on the line while she was in surgery.

"Can you test the blood to see who it belongs too? We need to verify that it's not Erica's, or it could be more of an immediate situation of life or death."

Todd nodded his head as he drew his equipment to him to test the blood.

Investigating the courtyard revealed little except for the profusion of bullets that littered the stone. Since blood wasn't found on the path in the courtyard to the parking lot and curb, TJ, who was last seen being propelled through that path, at least wasn't bleeding.

Once the results were tested, Todd was happy to tell Max that the blood belonged to Tim, not to Erica. The question now was where to start looking for them.

Chapter Twenty

As the police continued to investigate the premises, one of the officers went into the restroom and uncovered a bloody shirt. He placed the shirt in a plastic bag to take it to the crime lab to check for identification.

Max, Frank, Carl and Todd were retracing the events that occurred in the room. Taking the fingerprints off the various surfaces in the room, they were able to pinpoint the positions of each person.

The busboy came into the room to clear the table of the flowers vases, the champagne flutes and the bouquet of roses and orchids. Once he had cleared the dinnerware from the table, he reached over to grab the linen napkins when he noticed the telephone.

"Sir, I think this might be of some use to you." Handing the phone to Max he discreetly left the room.

Examining the telephone, Max noticed that the record button was still on. Pushing the left arrow key on the side of the phone, he was able to rewind the microchip that was an integral part of the telephone. Calling Frank, Carl and Todd to his side, he then pressed the right arrow or forward key. They listened intently to the conversation that Erica had recorded.

Searching frantically around the room, they looked for the piece of paper that would lead them to the address where Erica was supposed to meet Tim. After hunting for the paper for ten minutes, they surmised that the paper was no where to be found. Gazing out the French doors, and estimating the slight breeze that was blowing, Frank deduced that the paper could have flown out the door.

Splitting up, Carl and Frank dashed to the courtyard to look for the piece of paper that could be lying about in the shrubbery or on the ground. Todd stayed back to try an experiment on the linen tablecloth. Sometimes if one pressed down hard enough, you could read the indentations of the written letters or numbers from the cloth under a microscope or magnifying glass.

Pulling a pencil from his pocket, Tim ran the pencil back and forth along the tablecloth, stopping in sections to see if any letters or numerals stood out or appeared to be raised. Progressively he worked his way across the entire table then stopped when he came to a section where the champagne flute had rested. Since the busboy had removed all the dinnerware, there was just the circumference of the circle that marked where the flute once stood.

It seemed as if someone had started writing down the address on the tablecloth but ran out of ink. They ended up only writing down the street numerals and the first two letters of the street address. Using the pencil method, Todd ran the pencil back and forth in a sweeping motion to decipher the writing. He was finally able to determine that the numbers were 810 Da...

Max, who had been looking around the room for a clue, felt like he had missed something. Pacing back and forth, he suddenly stopped as he felt something gritty on the carpet. Bending down he examined the carpet and touched the grainy, brown granules. It reminded him of sand. What would sand be doing in here unless someone's shoes had recently been in the sand?

Todd got up from the table and walked over to where Max was inspecting the carpet. "I think this is the beginning of the address."

Pulling out his phone, Max called Trevor, who was working on tracing Tim through any means possible; mortgages, credit cards, spending patterns within the last six months and any real estate holdings that he might have.

"Trev, this is Max. Can you run a search in the city for an address that matches 810 Da? Todd found this written on the tablecloth. It appears that someone had started writing but their pin went out or either they changed their mind, because the rest of the information is blackened out."

"Max, I'm running it now, checking all available cities within a fifty mile radius. It looks like the address belongs to an old abandoned house on Darwin Street about fifteen miles from where you are near Randolph County. There's also an address that matches this near the suburbs of Raleigh."

"Thanks Trev. Can you send the maps to Frank, Todd and myself? Also, can you tell me how long it would take to get to the beach from the address in Raleigh or if there's a house somewhere nearby that has a grotto style pool with a natural "beach style" entry, meaning a sandy beach leading up to the pool in their backyard?"

"The maps are on the way. The grotto pool may take awhile. I'll let you know what I come up with."

Hanging up the phone he relayed the information to the men. Sending the police to the address on Darwin Street seemed like the smartest route while they focused on the address in Raleigh. One, it was closer to the airport in case Tim needed a quick getaway. Two, it was a bigger city that he could get lost in. Being that close to Duke and Carolina, famous athletes were around all the time sponsoring different programs so it wouldn't be unusual to see a professional basketball player at this time of the year.

As they got on the road to drive to the airport to catch a private flight to Raleigh, the policemen that were in the Darwin Street neighborhood called to tell them that the house was vacant.

Erica was almost in Raleigh when she discovered that she knew where she was headed. Tim's family had purchased another residence in Raleigh when Tim received a scholarship to Duke. He didn't want to live in Durham so he opted to commute each day. Pulling off the road into a gas station, she reached down into her purse, to pull out her phone to call Max. When she couldn't find it, she shook her head in disbelief. She had left it as a clue back at the restaurant.

Well she couldn't go into the gas station to make a call. What now? God, why does this keep happening to me, she wondered? Have I done something wrong? Why is this man, the bane of my existence?

"Okay, take a deep breath," her conscience urged. What doesn't kill you will make you stronger. If you and TJ can pull through this, nothing can stop you. The devil has peaked into your future and knows that God has something great in store for you! Stay strong, stay focused. You can overcome anything because God has overcome the world."

Leaning her head over the steering wheel, she said a silent prayer for TJ's safety and for guidance. Just then a man tapped on her window, asking if she was okay. Not knowing what to think, if it was a setup or if the man was legit, she rolled her window down a couple of inches to respond, "It seems I'm lost and I forgot my telephone." An eighteen wheeler roared into the parking lot, blocking her car from any other onlookers.

"Ma'am, your car is equipped with a telephone in the floor console. If you just push the button that opens the lid for the storage box you'll have access to the phone. Then you'll be able to reach your brother very quickly."

Erica looked at the console but didn't see anything different. When she turned back to ask the man a question, no one was there. Even the eighteen wheeler truck had vanished or pulled out of the gas station. Not knowing where the man went to that quickly, she thought that maybe God had sent divine intervention. She looked back at the console then pressed the base of the console and the lid slid open. Inside there was a telephone. Bending over, she quickly punched in Max's number.

Where was Erica, Tim wondered? Surely she was going to show up. Turning on his Blackberry, he called Big Man, one of his homeboys that was supposed to follow her to make sure that she didn't alert the cops or contact anyone that could come to her rescue.

"Yeah?"

"Where are you and where is my girl?"

"She just pulled into a gas station. From what I can see, she's leaning over the steering wheel like she's passed out or something. I need to check this out." Big Man started to get out of the car when he saw a stranger approach Erica's vehicle. Deciding to remain where he was until he could figure out if the man was a cop or not, Big watched the byplay between the two.

As he was watching the byplay between Erica and the stranger, with binoculars, off to the side of the gas station, near the back, an eighteen wheeler pulled into the gas station, blocking his view.

"Wait a minute Tim, I can't see what's she's doing. An eighteen wheeler just pulled into the parking lot. Before the eighteen wheeler pulled in a man had gone up to her car. I'm going to investigate."

Max answered Erica's call on the first ring. Looking at the caller id, he noticed that she was using the car's cellular phone. He wondered how she figured that out since he just had it installed.

Picking up the phone he demanded, "Erica, Erica, where are you?"

"Max, I can't talk long. Listen, I'm in Raleigh going to the house address that Tim gave. It's the house his parents purchased when he went to Duke."

"Erica, tell me where you're at! Wait for us. We're almost at the airport."

"I can't Max. Tim said that he would kill TJ if I didn't show up alone. I love him Max. I have to do everything within my power to help him. What if it was Chelsea Max? What would you do?"

"Move heaven and earth to rescue her. Sis, we're landing at the airport now. It should take us fifteen minutes to reach the house. I've already contacted the police to watch the house but not to go in until we arrive. Whatever you do, don't go into the room alone with Tim. You know what he's capable of. Try not to talk about TJ. That will only make him mad. Mad people will do unpredictable things."

"Max, there's this man coming over that looks like one of the thugs that carted off TJ. I need to hang-up." Quickly she disconnected the call and closed the storage box before straightening in her seat. Reaching over to the glove compartment, she withdrew a compact disk to act as if she was changing it.

Big Man walked up to the car and tapped on her window. Fearfully she rolled down the window again a few inches. "Tim wants to talk to you on the phone," the man suggested.

"Erica, Erica, what are you up to?"

"Tim, I'm in Raleigh as you asked but I needed gas so I stopped at a gas station."

"Who were you talking too?"

Pretending   innocence,   she   asked,   "What   person?"

"Erica, I've had you followed so don't play dumb."

"Oh, you mean the guy that came to the window? He was asking if I was alright. I was leaning over the steering wheel saying a prayer."

"Don't you know by now that God can't help you?" Tim laughed.

"He helped me before and He'll help me again. My God is able to deliver me from the hands of my enemies."

"Well, we'll just see about that won't we? You have ten minutes to get here before I start dismembering TJ's body parts.

Frustrated beyond measure, Erica asked, "What do you want from me Tim?"

"To sleep with you, of course. Haven't you been able to figure that out? You are the one that got away. I can't that. It damages my reputation."

Too angry to talk, Erica thrust the phone back at Big Man and drove off.

Scrambling back to his vehicle, Big Man whirled out of the gas station parking lot in an attempt to catch up with Erica. A policeman who was in the neighborhood when Max called the police station immediately drove to that area for a stakeout. Upon seeing the interaction with the car that matched the license plates of the vehicle in question, he sprung into action. Big Man was pulled over for suspicion of drunken driving for the way that he had careened out of the gas station. After taking the sobriety test, he was only given a ticket for reckless driving.

Erica was free to drive the rest of the distance alone.

While talking to Erica, Tim had made his way to the basement where TJ was hanging from a rope that was attached to an exercise pole that was suspended from the ceiling by sturdy cables. The pole was about five and a half feet long and was suspended in the middle of the room towards the back. If one could swing on the rope, they could gain momentum from hitting the wall to propel themselves across the room.

When Tim was going to college, his parents had added a workout room for him and his teammates in the basement so that they could stay in top physical shape. Tim used the exercise pole for chin-ups to develop his upper body strength.

Figuring that Erica should be there within minutes, he told his friends to go join the others upstairs to watch for any unexpected visitors. He didn't want any other witnesses to watch while he got his groove on with Erica. The only person that would have that privilege would be TJ and he would be helpless to prevent the outcome. What a sweet revenge since he had been thwarted previously!

Chapter Twenty-One

TJ warily watched as Tim approached him. Expecting to receive a blow to the stomach, he prepared his mind for yet another hit. Thank God for boxing sessions where he was required to take hits to the abdomen, for extended amounts of time! When the blow didn't occur, he felt relieved. He had to conserve his energy for when Erica arrived and he had to break free from the rope that he was suspended on. It would take what was left of his strength to get down.

Hearing a car pull up into the driveway, Tim reversed his direction and headed back upstairs.

The doorbell rung. That had to be Erica, thought TJ. Time to play hero again.

Kicking his legs outwards, he swayed his lower body, back and forward to develop a pumping motion. His goal was to use his strength to swing his legs up and over the bar in a criss-cross fashion where he would then use his hands that were tied together by the rope to "walk" the bar until it ended. He didn't have much time until Tim brought her back down to the basement. TJ assumed that Tim was going to try to accost her in his presence.

With an increased surge of adrenaline flowing through his veins, TJ was able to get his legs up to the bar on the first try. Now the hard part was to gain the needed momentum to force his hands and legs to operate in sync to edge down the bar five feet until he could jump off. Arching his back, and propelling himself forward, he was able to inch his hands down the bar. Next he pulled his legs forward. This two step motion was sufficient to move his body to the end of the bar.

TJ decided that since he was so high in the air, if he had his legs parallel, he could then do a somersault off the bar, which would prevent him from breaking any bones. Bending his right leg to his chest, he was able to move it alongside of the other leg. At the end of the bar, he let his hands fall free, letting them drop in mid-air. Hanging literally by his legs, he swung back and forth as if preparing for a dismount. Doing a one and a half somersault, he was able to land on his feet, on the floor, unscathed. He thanked God for each and every karate lesson that he had ever taken.

Catching a movement out of the corner of his eye, near the only two windows in the basement, TJ moved to investigate. The two windows were located in a small room primarily used for card games.

Moving stealthily towards the two windows, TJ cautiously glanced outside. Seeing movement in the yard, with miniscule flashes of white light, that resembled lighting strikes, snaking through the surroundings, TJ knew that Max and his team had arrived to rescue them. Lifting the window every so slowly, praying that it wouldn't creak, TJ let out a nightingale birdcall. As kids, the entire neighborhood, including the girls, used to play spy games all the time so this behavior was second nature to him. An owl hoot was the answering response.

It was now up to him to rescue his princess. Edging back towards the stairway, he positioned himself to ambush anyone that came down before they got into the open expanse of the basement.

Several pairs of footsteps could be heard coming down the uncarpeted basement stairs. Advancing into the room, Tim shoved Erica forward, holding her in front of him, as a barrier. He was wary because things were going a little too smoothly. Just for protection, he kept the gun poised in the air, ready for action. He moved toward the interior of the small room, and checked inside.

Only a cricket's chirping sound could be heard in the stillness of the room, twittering its own special song in a steady, continual rhythm that lasted for one minute.

Erica, who was silently praying that TJ was still alive, tilted her head from side to side in a rocking gesture, when she heard the familiar sound. When the sound was repeated, she knew that the sound she heard was TJ's attempt to let her know that he was nearby.

Oblivious to the nonverbal communication that was being sent, Tim continued to the part of the basement that he had setup as a bedroom. It was part of the open expanse of the room, but was partitioned off by a wall.

Now to surprise Erica with the horrific sight of TJ being suspended from a nine foot ceiling, all banged up and bruised from the beatings his boys had given him.

The cricket's chirping sound could be heard again, this time is a short, staccato echo. Anyone hearing the sound would not know the direction the sound was emitted from.

Tim, upon hearing the sound, drew the gun that he had poised in the air, closer to Erica's body. Then he propelled them around the corner into the open expanse of the room.

After walking no more than five steps, Erica slumped to the ground in a proposed "faint". She lay prone on the floor, unmoving. Wondering what could have caused her to faint; Tim looked at the place where TJ should have been hanging. The bar was empty. Looking back at the floor, it was too late to notice that Erica had rolled to the other side of the room, because TJ chose that moment to attack Tim. The element of surprise worked in his favor.

TJ then knocked Tim's arm upward that held the gun as he grabbed his wrist and all in one motion, broke Tim's arm; as the gun fired into the ceiling. Grimacing in pain from the broken arm, Tim dropped the weapon. Getting to a fighting stance, Tim attempted to charge TJ. Using his body as a dangerous weapon, TJ kicked Tim in the mid-section, followed by several hits to the upper body and the head, knocking him unconscious.

Rushing to Erica's side, he hugged her fiercely as his mouth closed passionately upon hers in a searing kiss.

That's when Max and his team stormed the house and the surrounding acreage, using every available weapon possible to take out the thirty or so men that were on the grounds and that were in various parts of the house. Max and Carl, made their way to the basement to rescue TJ and Erica, always alert to any movement that would indicate that someone else poised a threat.

Heavy gunfire was exchanged as the policemen and the FBI agents were able to quickly bring the situation under control. Without Tim to give them direction, once the gunfire started and people started dropping like flies, the rest of the men gave up.

Downstairs though, things were a different story. Tim, who had been knocked unconscious, slowly regained his senses, and was moving towards the weapon that he had dropped when Max and Carl came to the basement. Seeing Erica in TJ's arms, Tim picked up the gun and before he could get a shot off, Carl and Max took aim with shots of their own; hitting Tim in the shoulder and in the hand that held the gun. Luckily for him they decided not to kill him although he deserved it.

Hopefully, with Tim behind bars, that would be the last time he would interfere with their lives. There wasn't a judge in the nation that would let him get out of this.

Picking Erica up in his arms, TJ walked outside to the awaiting car that would take them to the police station for a brief statement. Since the hour was so late, the police chief advised them that their statement could be taken in their city on the following day.

For safety reasons, before they flew back to Greensboro, Max took TJ to the Emergency Room for an examination to identify the damage that Tim's men did to his body. While at the hospital, Max checked in with Chelsea to let her know that he was okay and that TJ and Erica were also okay. He knew that she would not be able to sleep until she had word that the rescue was successful.

After the examination was complete, it was discovered that TJ had a couple of broken ribs that they were able to tape up, but otherwise was given a clean bill of health. They prescribed some pain medication for the soreness but was released.

To tired and two sore to drive for an hour to two hours to return home, TJ and Erica decided to stay in Raleigh overnight. Max and everyone else, drove to the airport to catch their return flight where the pilot was on standby.

Checking into the Embassy Suites hotel, TJ asked for two rooms as he was reaching into his pocket to retrieve his money clip. Shaking her head, Erica turned to the reservation clerk and corrected TJ, asking for a suite instead.

Looking TJ squarely in the eye, she whispered, "We only need one room. When I wake up, I need to know that you're there with me, alive and safe from harm."

"Are you sure?" TJ asked, not wanting to put any pressure on Erica. She had been through enough. Leaning over, he lightly brushed his lips across hers, grimacing slightly from the pain in his ribs.

"Yes, I'm sure."

Taking the elevator up to their suite, they rode in silence; both content to just hold each other, realizing that things could have turned out differently.

Sliding the card through the card reader, TJ opened the door to the suite. Proceeding Erica into the room to make sure that everything was okay, he then stepped aside so that she could enter.

"Is the room okay for you?" TJ asked.

"It's perfect."

"Sweetheart, do you want to order something to eat since our dinner was interrupted?"

"Yes, I'm hungry. TJ, how did you happen to be at the restaurant and who is Carl to you? You always seem to be at the right place at the right time. You've become my knight in shining armor." Erica stated as she walked into the bedroom to pull back the covers on the bed after she inspected the cleanliness of the sheets.

"You might not think that after I tell you who Carl is."

"What do you mean?"

"Carl is Mia's twin brother; my first cousin. Since I blew things with you over the way I handled HangOut Night when I used Mia to pretend to be my girlfriend, I had to do something pretty drastic to make you talk to me. You've been avoiding me for several weeks now, yet you risked your life for me. We'll get to that later."

Erica sat down on the bed, cross legged, Indian style, staring at TJ with rapt attention.

Seeing that he had her full attention, he sat down on the bed, resting against the headboard. Needing to feel her touch, he pulled Erica to sit between his legs and recline on his chest.

"Carl agreed that he would help me win you back. Max told me that you would seek revenge using the same method that I had used to make me jealous or to make me realize my love for you. So I was prepared. If you decided to participate in HangOut Night, I knew that you would recognize my voice so I had Carl to participate, using the answers that I had already prepared. When it was time to show up for the date, Carl would come and get you, then take you to the restaurant. I would show up as your date, begging forgiveness."

TJ stopped talking as Erica started laughing.

"What's so funny?"

"The only reason I was a contestant for HangOut Night was to make you realize what you were missing. I wanted you to see how it felt, loving someone yet finding them unreachable when they went out with someone else, even though that was my fault. I was so scared to participate that night that you were a contestant. So we both had the same idea. I'm just sorry that you had to suffer yet again for me. By the way, were the answers that you gave from your heart?"

"Of course. I was trying to win your love so I had to pull out all the stops."

"Who was singing the song and who wrote it? It was so beautiful. Was that you?"

"Yes. The song was written right after the first incident with Tim. It was all the things I wanted to say to you but couldn't. You weren't ready then."

Undeniably drawn to touch is body, Erica turned on her knees, in between TJ's legs and put her arms around his waist as her lips devoured his mouth with reckless abandon.

Breaking the kiss to breathe, TJ said, "Sweetheart, why don't you let me run you a bubble bath so that you can relax while I get everything ready for our late night dinner? I'm sure that you want to cleanse yourself of the entire incident that occurred this evening; then we can continue where we left off."

"I'd rather just stay here in your arms, but you do have a point."

"Just stay right here and look over the menu and I'll fix the bath for you."

TJ was determined that the dinner that he had planned earlier that evening would still occur. After running Erica's bath, he went back into the living room. Picking up the telephone he called room service and ordered their dinner and a fruit tray of strawberries, pineapples, grapes and chocolate fondue, along with some sparkling cider, since neither one of them drank alcoholic beverages.

Next he telephoned the Concierge to order four dozen roses to be delivered with the room service since in all likelihood, the orchids probably were not available, given such short notice. Asking the Concierge if there was a lingerie store on the premises, the Concierge regrettably said no there wasn't, but his daughter was a designer and that she could bring him some of her designs over immediately to choose from.

TJ asked the Concierge to contact his daughter and if it wasn't to late, he would like to see several outfits, plus two matching robes and that he would need them immediately because his fiancée didn't have time to pack any luggage and he wanted these items for her after she finished soaking in the tub, which should take about an hour.

Deciding to forgo his shower until after Erica went to sleep, TJ waited for his gifts and the food to arrive. He walked to the door to tell Erica that he was going down to talk to the Concierge for a few minutes but would be right back. After hearing her response, he headed out the door.

After reviewing the few items that the Concierge's daughter, Toni had brought, TJ was astonished at the intricate designs and at the transparency of the material that would delight any man's fantasy. Questioning Toni further, TJ asked if she had exhibited any of her designs for Fashion Week or if she had an entire collection ready to show.

Toni, being the honest woman that she was, answered truthfully thinking that possibly if his fiancée liked the designs, she could get more exposure. "Sir, I have a small collection but I haven't exhibited anywhere but local events."

"So can I assume that you don't have a sponsor?"

"No sir, I don't have a sponsor. I design and sew my own clothes."

Reaching into his pocket, he withdrew a business card an told her that if she brought her collection to Sole Impressions, the company that he was part owner of, and if his fiancée and future sister-in-law approved of the collection, then they would be able to work out a deal. He selected four of the designs that she had brought with her; two gowns and two robes. Paying cash for the purchases that he had withdrawn from the teller machine, he thanked her for taking the time to come over at such a late hour.

Profusely offering him thanks, Toni quickly gave him a hug then stepped back, offering her hand in a business like gesture. TJ laughed as he shook her hand then shook the Concierge's hand. With a reminder for her to show up the following Thursday to Sole Impressions, TJ left to head back to his suite.

He prayed for strength because the designs were provocative to the extreme. Sensual, sexy and daring were the words that came to mind, yet the clothes were not trashy. They were made from some of the finest silk with great attention to detail. Any woman would love to wear the clothes.

Now the only thing he had to do was make it through the night without making love to Erica. Although a couple of his ribs were broken, he wouldn't let that stop him if the timing was better. He had waited this long for her and he would continue to wait until their wedding night. He just prayed that it would be soon. He hadn't made love to another woman since he had taken Erica to her Senior Prom and that was over five years ago. Even though he had dated numerous women while he waited for her to come of age, none had tempted him to settle for second best.

TJ opened the door to the suite and hastily placed his gift on the bed so that when Erica dried off, she could slip into one of the gowns and a robe. Going to the bathroom door, he knocked.

"Come in."

Steeling himself for what he might find, he entered the bathroom cautiously. Erica was really working on undermining his self control. As many times as he had pictured her naked in his mind, the last thing he needed in order to keep his promise was to see her naked or submerged in bubbles.

Fortunately, Erica wasn't in the tub any longer. She was sitting on the chair in front of the mirror trying to decide what she was going to put on while she ate dinner. Lounging in the robe that was too big and too heavy for her, she felt like shedding the robe and pulling the sheet around her body. She felt that she was ready to make love to TJ but she was shy. She didn't want him to think that she was a hussy, flaunting herself in front of him, but she didn't have anything else to put on.

"Sweetheart, come on and eat. The food just arrived."

"I don't know if I can," whispered Erica.

Concerned, TJ squatted down in front of her. "What's wrong baby?"

"I don't have anything else to wear. I can't walk around like this. I look like a frump. I don't want you to think that I'm throwing myself at you. I mean, I am but…Well I feel rather…"

TJ put his fingertips to her lips to stop her from babbling. "Shhh."

Raw emotion flashed in his eyes as he pulled her towards him. Mindless passion swept through them as his lips branded her with his possession. Sensuous chills raced down her spine and all over her body as she welcomed and answered his invasion.

"Sweetheart, I don't know how much more I can take. If we don't stop now, I'm not sure that I'll be able too."

"Honey, I not sure that I want you to stop."

"When you're sure, I'll be waiting for you, but until then, let's just enjoy the moment. I don't want to spoil your surprise." Leading her out of the bathroom, TJ left Erica to unwrap the gifts that he had purchased, while he checked on dinner.

Squealing with delight, Erica could only stare at the exquisite gifts that TJ had thoughtfully provided for her to sleep in. Discarding the robe, she tenderly placed the gown over her head and let it cascade to the floor. It was made of pure silk, with a long slit in one leg, coupled with a shear bodice that dropped in a v-neck pattern to the waist. The bodice was so transparent that it looked as if she was naked. The outfit was enough to spark a flame that only hours or days of intense loving could eradicate. The matching robe had a similar design and was just as provocative on its own.

Rushing through to the living room, Erica started to throw herself at TJ then remembered that he had a couple of broken ribs. Standing in front of TJ, she smiled as she modeled the clothes for him. "How do I look," she asked?

"Like heaven. Like my favorite fantasy come to life. Everything that I have ever dreamed of and then some," TJ said in an unsteady voice. He knew that the designs were beautifully made but he couldn't have fathomed how great they would look on her. It was as if they were created just for Erica.

Wanting desperately to hold her, he gathered her to him, blindly taking her lips in remembered pleasure. Arching her body closer to his, he drank in her beauty as a maelstrom of emotion swamped them both taking them almost to the point of no return.

The changing of the compact disk that was playing music softly in the background was the only thing that forced them back to reality.

With his head leaning on her forehead, he tried to still the erratic beating of his heart. He struggled for control. With her breasts heaving, Erica wisely took her seat and began serving the food. Finally mastering his emotions, TJ joined her.

"Honey, where did you get this delicate, no, make that exquisite, garment from? I love it!"

"Believe it or not, the Concierge helped. I knew that you would be uncomfortable without something to wear and his daughter brought over a few of her designs. I told her to bring her collection to the office next Thursday for you and Chelsea to preview. If you like it then I want to sponsor her collection. If the rest of the garments look this good on you then I'll personally buy the entire collection."

Sitting in his lap, she hugged him as she ran her hands up and down his chest. "You spoil me. I love you. When you're feeling better, maybe I can then show you what you mean to me." Getting up she sat back down in her chair and resumed eating.

"Baby, you can't make a statement like that and then continue to eat."

"You're the one that claiming I'm not ready. I just beg to differ."

"Erica, you've had a long, frightening day and I don't want to take advantage of you. It's almost dawn. Let's just get some sleep. I promise that soon, we'll both explore each other to our heart's content."

"I'm going to hold you to that too."

Rising from the chair, she held out her hand to TJ who brought it too his lips. "Why don't you take the bedroom and I'll sleep out here on the pullout sofa."

"I have a better idea. Why don't we both share the bed? I promise not to make your ribs feel any worse but I don't think that I will be able to sleep unless you're with me."

They went to bed and TJ held Erica in his arms for the remainder of the night. At first he couldn't sleep but as her body settled comfortably against his, he finally drifted off.

Chapter Twenty-Two

The following day after submitting their statement to the police, they drove back to Greensboro. Erica dropped TJ off at his house, since she had driven to Raleigh the day before. He had suggested that she take a couple of days off to relax and regroup.

Assuring TJ that she was fine, Erica headed home. As she finished showering she heard the doorbell. Grabbing a pair of sweatpants from the drawer, and a tank top, she quickly thrust them on as she headed down the stairs to see who would be ringing her doorbell that early in the morning.

Staring through the peephole, she was surprised to see her parents who should have been at work that morning. Throwing the door open, Erica rushed to hug them.

With tears streaming down their faces, Erica's mother and father cried openly, thanking God that He had sparred their child yet again from the hands of the enemy. Pulling them inside the house, Erica teased them about having nine lives and having her own personal knight in shining armor that was able to rescue her time and time again.

Wanting to hear more of the story, Erica cooked them breakfast. Even though they heard the story from Max the previous night, they were willing to listen to it again from their daughter's perspective.

Mr. and Mrs. Teal upon seeing the love in their daughter's eyes as she described how TJ had been abducted then subsequently freed himself in order to rescue her, they smiled with joy. It was finally time for their princess to let go and love the man who had held her heart since she was a teenager. They couldn't have chosen a better man for her. He had proven just how much he loved their daughter by rescuing her not once, but three different times.

Getting up from the table, her parents said goodbye, stating that they wanted to thank TJ personally for all that he had done to make sure that she was safe and unharmed. Mr. Teal of course had something else on his mind. He wanted to tell TJ that he had their blessing to go ahead and marry Erica and that the age stipulation was irrelevant at this point. Therefore after pulling out of the driveway, they headed over to Sole Impressions.

Erica went back upstairs to change into her office clothes, deciding that the best way to forget about what happened was to work. She didn't arrive at the office until around twelve o'clock.

TJ was just finishing a conference call with one of their buyers for the latest perfume that they were going to release when Mrs. Maness buzzed him that the Teals requested thirty minutes of his time.

Letting her know that they could interrupt them at any time, he stood to his feet and walked to open the door. As they walked in, he shook Mr. Teal's hand and leaned over to kiss Mrs. Teal on the cheek. Seating them in the two cub chairs, he returned to his desk.

Looking worriedly from one to the other, he asked, "Is there something wrong with Erica?"

That one statement gave them the opening they needed.

"Son, words cannot express our gratitude for all that you've done and continue to do for our princess. Your love for her shows brightly in all that you do. We would like to thank you from the bottom of our hearts for rescuing her."

"Sir, I would like to spend the rest of my life loving and taking care of her. If I could have your blessing, I plan to propose to her very soon. I assume if you deem me worthy that we'll have a long engagement sir, to hold fast to the promise I made that I not marry her until she turned twenty-five."

Standing, Mr. Teal, extended his hand to TJ. "TJ for all that you've risked, consider the age stipulation null and void. We could not have picked a better man to become my son-in-law. Welcome to the family!"

Mrs. Teal, stood also as she hugged TJ, with tears in her eyes. "TJ, let me warn you that while I think she's healed from the first horrific incident, be patient with her. Loving her might not be easy but it will be well worth it in the long run."

Kissing his cheek, she made her exit to go visit her son to see what was taking him so long to marry Chelsea. Just then a thought hit her. Turning around, she told her husband to find Max; that she would catch up with him shortly.

Walking back into TJ's office, Mrs. Teal interrupted him as he stared out the window. Rising from his seat as she walked through his door, he met her halfway into the room.

"Was there something else, Mrs. Teal?"

"Yes, as a matter of fact there is. You realize that Max and Chelsea's wedding will be in two weeks, right?"

"Yes, ma'am."

Being a take charge type of person, Mrs. Teal wasn't afraid to ask for what she wanted. "How soon do you want to marry Erica?"

"I would marry her today if she would let me. I've wanted to marry her for quite some time now. I actually asked your husband the night of her Senior Prom for her hand in marriage but he made me promise not to declare myself until she turned twenty five."

"So that's what was taking you so long. How do you feel about double weddings?"

Erica pulled into the parking lot and headed to her office. Seeing TJ's car already there, once she got to her office she called to ask if she could see him for a minute.

"TJ, are you busy?"

"Never to busy for you sweetheart. Do you want me to come to your office?"

"No, I'll come to yours."

Walking by Mrs. Maness' desk, Erica knocked, then proceeded into TJ's office. TJ stood up from his desk to meet Erica halfway across the room. Grabbing her waist, he pulled her to him for a searing kiss.

"I thought that you were going to stay home for a couple of days."

"Well, I was but you were not there so I decided to come in and tackle some work. Also I forgot to tell you thank you for rescuing me. I kinda had other things on my mind," she murmured.

"Baby, you thanked me in ways that I consider priceless. You trusted me enough to spend the night with you without taking advantage of you. That's the first move you've made to spend some time with me alone, in a bedroom. For that I thank you."

TJ bent his head again to kiss her sweet, luscious lips. His body had been burning for her touch since he had awoken with a fierce erection after having lain awake half the night with her body snuggled so close to his that it actually seemed like it was a part of him. Cold showers were becoming a part of life for him. Seemingly with a mind of their own, his lips and his hands roamed over her body. Caught up in the pleasure that his kiss invoked, Erica started to explore TJ's body as he was exploring hers.

Pleasure swept through her as his hands fastened beneath her hips before he lifted her to his height to deepen their kiss. Her legs wrapped themselves around his waist as he backed up against the wall, their lips never leaving each other. Each was consumed by the fire that was threatening to spiral out of control.

Only the ringing of the telephone brought them back to earth. Slowing, ever so slowly, they came back down to earth. TJ was the first to recover.

"Can you get away for the weekend?"

"What do you have in mind?"

"I wanted us to spend some time together."

"Honey, this weekend is the Bachelor and Bachelorette parties for Max and Chelsea. Unfortunately since we're both in the wedding, we can't miss it."

"What about a date this evening? I know things are going to get a little crazy for us between now and next week."

"I'm all yours for the next two days. Do you think you can handle that?" She laughingly asked as she backed towards the door.

"If that's the case then block out your schedule for the rest of today and tomorrow and go home and pack a bag for an overnight stay. We're going away until Thursday morning."

"Are you serious?" Erica looked at TJ as if he had lost his mind.

"Where are we going? What do I pack? Give me details."

"Pack something for sunny weather and be ready in three hours." Unerringly his mouth found hers once again just before he ushered her out of the room.

Punching in Max's extension, he waited for Max's secretary to answer. His answer determined what would happen next.

"Maxmillian."

"Max, do you have a moment?"

"Sure TJ. What's up? I see that both you and Erica made it in today. Why? I thought you were going to take a little R and R."

"That's why I'm calling. Erica thought that by working she could forget the past but I want to take her somewhere and make her relax. I can't do that without your help. Can I come to your office on my way out?"

"Okay." Max disconnected the call as he smiled. He was willing to bet that his sister and his best friend had ironed out all their differences and was now headed towards holy matrimony. Love was definitely in the air.

As TJ walked into his office, Max could see that TJ was now at peace with the love he had felt for Erica since they were teenagers.

Giving him the brother's handshake, he asked, "Now that you've rescued her three times, when are you going to make her yours for ever?"

"Tomorrow. I know that your wedding to Chelsea is next week, but I can't wait any longer to make Erica my wife. Would you be opposed to flying to the beach to share in our nuptials?"

"Not at all. I have an even better idea though. Why don't we have a double wedding? All of my family will be here and most of your family will also be here because they are all good friends. If you hadn't talked some sense to me to try and straighten things out with Chelsea, we wouldn't be getting married. Plus you're my best friend and you have loved Erica for a long time. Why do you think I pressured her into accepting the job here? Why do you think she finally accepted it? Both reasons were because of you. I wanted her close so that your relationship could develop naturally."

"Are you sure Chelsea won't mind?"

"No. She even suggested it last night after we returned home and you and Erica chose to stay in Raleigh. You know how close they've been since Erica had her surgery."

"If she's okay with it then I accept your offer. I've got to go and get a ring before I head over to Erica's. Thanks!"

Pulling his cellular phone from his hip as he left Max's office, he dialed his mother, told her to hold on, then dialed Erica's mother, clicking the button on the phone for three way calling. "Everything is set. We're leaving in a few hours and won't return until Thursday morning. The two of you can do your thing. Just remember what Erica likes and I'll be happy with whatever you choose."

Epilogue

TJ barely made it on time, within the specified three hours to pickup Erica for their trip. After stopping to pick up the ring that he had on standby at the jewelers, TJ pulled up in Erica's driveway with only ten minutes to spare.

Ushering her into the car, after her luggage was stored in the trunk, they made their way to the airport. Asking questions all along the way, TJ smiled when he refused to tell Erica where they were going except that she would love it.

Arriving at the airport with one hour to spare, TJ and Erica settled on a quick snack. All the while she kept trying to figure out where they were going but TJ simply smiled and showed her photographs of other destinations.

When their flight number was called, TJ led Erica to the gate so that they could board the plane to Vegas. His plan was for them to get married in Vegas and then have a mini honeymoon at Lake Tahoe until next week when he would take Erica on a two week trip to Aruba.

As they boarded the flight and the plane took off, the pilot told them the arrival time of their destination. Distracting Erica when the pilot was speaking wasn't a problem since they enjoyed kissing each other and tended to forget their surroundings.

Since the flight would be approximately five hours, Erica decided to go to sleep. While she was asleep, TJ marveled over the events that he had been able to organize on such short notice.

He had given instructions to Toni for the wedding dresses; one that he would need the next day and a formal one for the following week. He gave her the address of the hotel that they would be staying in while they were in Vegas. She told him that she already had a dress waiting for him and would fax it if that was his choice; otherwise she could fax it to his fiancée's best friend for approval. Instructions were also given to Pauletta to bring Erica pieces from her collection of casual wear.

Sitting in the car in Erica's driveway he had contacted Sasha and asked her opinion. "Sasha, this is TJ. I need a favor. I'm sure Erica has brought you up to speed on what happened yesterday. I plan on marrying her tomorrow in Vegas and then Max has agreed to a double wedding next week. Can you look at the dress that this designer has made to see if Erica would approve of it for tomorrow's nuptials? It's a surprise for her."

After Sasha ohhhh and ahhhh over the dress, TJ assumed that it was perfect for what he had in mind. Thanking her, he hung up and called Toni back with a definite yes for the dress. She advised him that the dress would be waiting for him when they checked in. When he asked her how she was able to have a wedding dress ready she replied, "Whenever a man wants to make you happy that early in the morning after what you went through, he's a keeper."

TJ settled back in his first class seat and took a nap with Erica until the plane landed.

Once the plane landed, it wasn't hard to figure out where they were. TJ had explained that he wanted her to concentrate on having fun for the next several days which was why he had brought her to Vegas. Erica was excited. She had always wanted to come to Vegas to catch a show, see the Cirque du Soleil, and to see all the bright lights.

TJ had surprised her again. It was as if he had remembered every dream that she had ever shared with him and he was making them all come true. Taking the shuttle to the Venetian hotel, they were able to immediately check in. Eager to explore the hotel, they put their luggage in the room and went exploring.

The hotel offered everything that reminded one of Venice, Italy. It had gourmet food, five star restaurants, like Emeril Lagasse, or Wolfgang Puck, to name a few; canals, gondolas and performers that would sing as they strolled. The best part was the five hundred square foot Grand Canal Shoppes, which could be seen as one drifted down the canal on the gondolas. It was the perfect way to view the shops that were available before actually stopping to shop.

Deciding to have dinner at Emeril's, they went back to the hotel to shower and to change clothes. Erica couldn't stop talking about how much fun they had shopping. TJ stored their purchases and brought out the gift that had been delivered in their absence.

"Sweetheart, I know that you purchased a lot of things today, but this dress was delivered this afternoon and when I saw it, I instantly thought of you. Could you wear it for me tonight?"

Unwrapping the gift, she was rendered speechless as she looked at the dress that seemed to be a vision of nothing but white silk. Jumping up she disrobed and slid the dress on without a thought. It was a perfect fit and felt fantastic on her skin. Nothing beat wearing silk.

Waiting for TJ to finish showering, she smiled to herself. This had to be one of the most perfect evenings she had ever experienced. It would be better if it ended with them making love. Once he saw her in this gown, she didn't know if they would make it out of the room. She wouldn't mind at all.

When TJ came out of the bathroom, he did a double take. The dress was innocent yet provocative. It was breathtaking. If the church wasn't already booked they wouldn't be going anywhere but to bed. Releasing the breath that he had instinctively held, he whistled.

"Sweetheart, you look gorgeous. I wish we could stay in tonight but I've got another surprise planned for you."

"Will it be as nice a surprise as the one I've got for you when we return?"

"Behave." Looking at his watch, he noticed that they needed to leave to make it to the dinner then to the church on time.

"We've got to go." Swiftly kissing her with the pent up emotion that he was feeling, he regrettably released her.

Over dinner, they discussed everything under the sun; their family, where the company was going, and what they wanted for the future. When dessert came, several of the strolling performers came to serenade them as they partook of their dessert. In the middle of her chocolate mousse was a jeweler's box.

With a squeal of, "Oh my God," Erica started to cry as the waiter pulled the box from the mousse and handed it to TJ.

Taking the box and bending on one knee, he looked at Erica with love shining from his eyes.

"Erica, my love, my life, my everything. You are my fantasy come true. Being married to you, waking up in your arms each day, seeing my child grow within you and growing old together is what I live for. Will you marry me and let me love you for all eternity?"

Taking several deep breaths, Erica replied, "TJ you're my knight in shining armor, my best friend; the one that has held my heart for years. You loved me when I didn't love myself. I treasure the love that you've given me and yes, I want to spend eternity loving you."

Cheers, whistles and congratulations could be heard throughout the restaurant. Smiling at everyone, they quickly made their exit. Getting into the horse-drawn carriage that was waiting outside of the restaurant, they rode down the street for about two miles, then back to the hotel.

Turning to Erica as they were riding, TJ asked, "Will you marry me tonight and make me the happiest man on earth?"

Without hesitating, she nodded yes; amazed at what TJ was able to plan and pull off in such a short time. He was wonderful.

Assisting her from the carriage, they walked hand in hand to one of the wedding chapels. Opening the door, they were greeted by family members and friends. With tears of joy streaming down her face, she hugged TJ fiercely and kissed him with passion and power.

Chelsea, Sasha, Yvonne and the bride and groom's mother, whisked Erica away to change dresses and to repair her makeup.

Thirty minutes later they reassembled for their wedding. It was as exquisite as the man she was marrying. Their bishop had even flown to Vegas to officiate for the wedding.

The chapel was breathtakingly beautiful with old world charm. The custom created bouquet of cala lilies, roses and orchids were astonishing. That theme was carried out in the two lavish floral arrangements that flanked the alter. Every chair was adorned with a silk chair cover in the hues from her bouquet. The aisle runner was littered with rose petals and the three candelabras were another magnificent floral arrangement. The entire room was filled with candles making the wedding intimate and romantic.

In the background, music could be heard playing from the guitar, the violin and the flute. Yvonne stepped up to the mike to sing a song she had created just for the bride and groom. A dry eye could not be found anywhere in the chapel as they exchanged their written vows. Soon they were pronounced husband and wife.

After the reception was over, Erica and TJ said goodbye to their family and friends and headed to their Venetian Prima Suite. They could barely control the desire that had been mounting all day. It was now at a fever pitch. As they made it through the doors, a need so fierce struck both of them into a frenzy of need. Their mouths fused together, in a scorching kiss that left Erica's knees trembling.

Making their way to the bedroom, they discarded their clothes as they walked and kissed and hungered for each other's touch. Too impatient to slow down, they tumbled naked onto the bed. TJ caressed Erica's body from head to toe, kissing all the places that his hands touched; getting her ready for his possession.

Whimpering in ecstasy, Erica moaned TJ's name as sensations began to overwhelm her. Easing into her moist heat, he waited for the pain to subside. Within minutes, she was moving her body in a rhythm as old as time. She met him stroke for stroke. Intensifying the building need by fastening his hands beneath her hips, he surged deeper into her.

She welcomed his invasion, drawing him further into her satin heat, as he brought them to the pinnacle of pleasure only to retreat and build the spiraling need over and over again. Racing towards completion, too caught up in the rapture, she screamed his name as she clenched around him. Exploding together they hurtled over the abyss as tremors shook their body in a magnificent orgasm.

Never had he experienced anything so intense, so satisfying. Looking down into Erica's eyes, he smiled, "I love you, my heart. Words can't explain how you've made me feel."

Reaching up to cup his cheek and bring his head down for another kiss, she replied, "My love, I love you more. Do you think that we can do that again? It was wonderful."

"No, you were wonderful. I'm glad I waited for you."

TJ and Erica didn't leave their suite until it was time to head back to Max and Chelsea's wedding, the following week.

Finally, the knight in shining armor had captured his queen.

Discover exciting and intriguing romantic sagas where the hero/heroine through faith, overcomes adversity while producing a legacy for future generations.

Don't miss another saga in The Romance Chronicles...

Hasten To Me
Adrienne Woods

A Bailey Novel...

Escaping from an abusive husband wasn't easy but Jackie Bailey was determined to start her life over. But when nursing her sister back to health after an accident leads her to a doctor who claims love at first sight, will she trust her vision of them married with children? Or will she run away from her destiny because her visions let her down in the past?

Available October 2008 from Pass It On Publishing!

Pass It On
Publishing

Discover exciting and intriguing romantic sagas where the hero/heroine through faith, overcomes adversity while producing a legacy for future generations.

Don't miss another saga in The Romance Chronicles...

Love's Purpose

Adrienne Woods

The flame is burning low in Sebastian and Dominique's marriage. Dominique's career as a boutique owner and jewelry designer has sky-rocketed. Sebastian, while supportive of his wife's endeavors, feels left out. He misses the love and camaraderie that they used to share. No longer able to spend quality time together, Sebastian devises a scheme that would put the sparkle, the passion and the sensuality back into their marriage by sending his wife on a scavenger hunt for his heart.

Available December 2008 from Pass It On Publishing!

Pass It On
Publishing

Discover exciting and intriguing romantic sagas where the hero/heroine through faith, overcomes adversity while producing a legacy for future generations.

Don't miss another saga in The Romance Chronicles...

<u>Lay it on the Line</u>
Adrienne Woods

A Bailey Novel

Although David and Tamera have been dating exclusively for the past seven years, Tamera's clock is ticking and she wants to know where their relationship is headed. David has a ten year plan of accomplishments that he would like to achieve before settling down and doesn't understand what all the fuss is about. Tamera believes that he has commitment issues and delivers an ultimatum.

Available February 2009 from Pass It On Publishing!

Pass It On
Publishing

Discover exciting and intriguing romantic sagas where the hero/heroine through faith, overcomes adversity while producing a legacy for future generations.

Don't miss another saga in The Romance Chronicles...

Delayed but not Denied

Adrienne Woods

After struggling as an entrepreneur, Dustin's charter boat business finally takes off. With his wife Janice by his side, all his dreams have finally come true. Returning from a long trip geared towards expanding the business, Dustin is stunned to learn that his wife has left him for another man. After she leaves, he also discovers that his business is all but destroyed, and that he is penniless. Left to pick up the pieces, with faith and determination, his dream that had been delayed, through the will of God, was not denied!

Available May 2009 from Pass It On Publishing!

Pass It On
Publishing